IN LOVE WITH THE PREACHER'S DAUGHTER

"My father ruined us!" she said, her voice shaking. "He ruined our good name, and he preached with such authority about orality and community, and the strength of our Amish faith . . ." Her lips turned downward. "And now he's coming back, and I'm no longer the preacher's daughter, I'm . . . *his* daughter."

"And you love him," Solomon murmured.

"I love him, and I hate him, and I want him to be safe, but I want him to stay away, and—I'm now the daughter of a criminal!"

"You're Lizzie Yoder," he said, and he tugged her closer, feeling the swish of her skirt against his pants. She had an unnoticed tendril of hair loose again. "You're not just someone's daughter, you're a woman in your own right."

"Everyone is someone's child," she said. "Everyone."

And while Solomon had to agree with her logic, it wasn't her argument that had his attention. He wanted to soothe her, to protect her, to take this burden from her, but he couldn't. He tucked the tendril of hair behind her ear, and her free hand fluttered up to touch it.

"Then be your mother's daughter," he said. "You have more than one parent."

Elizabeth blinked up at him, her hand frozen at her face, as if the thought were a new one, and he reached out and ran his thumb down her soft cheek. He didn't know why he was doing this—it was going too far, again, and he knew it. But she didn't pull away as he traced his thumb along her jawline and brushed it across her lips. . . .

Books by Patricia Johns

THE BISHOP'S DAUGHTER

THURSDAY'S BRIDE

JEB'S WIFE

THE PREACHER'S SON

THE PREACHER'S DAUGHTER

Published by Kensington Publishing Corp.

The
Preacher's
Daughter

PATRICIA
JOHNS

ZEBRA BOOKS
KENSINGTON PUBLISHING CORP.
www.kensingtonbooks.com

ZEBRA BOOKS are published by

Kensington Publishing Corp.
119 West 40th Street
New York, NY 10018

First Printing: June 2021
ISBN-13: 978-1-4201-5237-1
ISBN-10: 1-4201-5237-8

ISBN-13: 978-1-4201-5240-1 (eBook)
ISBN-10: 1-4201-5240-8 (eBook)

10 9 8 7 6 5 4 3 2 1

Printed in the United States of America

Chapter One

Solomon Lantz had been given a plastic bag containing his personal belongings on his way out of Forest State Correctional Institution: a pair of jeans, some scuffed-up running shoes, a white T-shirt, a comb, some ChapStick, a pair of suspenders because he never was able to get used to wearing *Englisher* belts, and his wallet with exactly $107 in cash. He was surprised to get the money back at all but was grateful all the same—it was going to pay his cab fare the rest of the way home. The prison had provided a bus ticket to Bountiful, Pennsylvania, and he was on his own after that.

His palms were sweaty and his stomach roiled from the movement of the taxicab. Outside the window, July sunlight warmed the rolling, green fields of ripening oats. He knew the area well—he used to walk down this road to get to school every day when he was a kid. They were close . . .

The car slowed as it moved around a buggy, and Solomon dropped his gaze and sat back. He'd meet people soon enough—after he'd seen his *mamm* again.

Solomon hadn't seen his *mamm* since her last visit to

the prison six months earlier. Mamm, sitting there with a yellowed telephone receiver in one hand, contrasting with her crisp, white *kapp*, and her teary eyes fixed on him through that thick, prison glass. . . . She'd been like the first crocus in spring—the first bud on a naked, gnarled tree. But she'd had some choice words for him, the worst of which were, "What would your *daet* think if he'd lived to see you like this? You'd have broken his heart! He wanted more for you—*I* wanted more for you. You could be working a good job, finding a wife . . . You could be starting your life properly, but instead you're in a jail cell, and you have no one to blame but yourself. You knew better, Solomon! I taught you better than this! And me coming here to visit isn't any help at all. I'm only making it easier for you. So I'm not coming back. You can face your consequences alone."

Tears had welled in Solomon's eyes when his *mamm* hung up that dingy phone and walked stoically away, her gray shawl pulled close around her and her black shoes squeaking against the polished linoleum floor. He sat there by the glass, his breath stuck in his throat, waiting for her to turn—waiting for her to look back. . . .

"Are you Amish?" the cab driver asked, pulling him out of his own thoughts. The driver glanced at him in the rearview mirror, and Solomon self-consciously pulled his hand through his short-cropped hair. He didn't think he looked Amish anymore, but he'd been told more than once he still sounded Amish. He talked more slowly, and his words still had that Dutch roundness to them.

"I used to be," Solomon said.

"Yeah? Are you one of those . . . what do you call them . . . those Amish runaways?" the driver asked.

"Not really. It's been too long to call me that. I'm just coming for a visit," Solomon said.

A surprise visit. His *mamm* had no idea he'd been let out early. He wouldn't let the prison officials notify anyone on his behalf. He wanted to come home on his own terms—and didn't want to give his *mamm* a chance to not come pick him up. That would have hurt too much. So he'd decided to come to her instead, and she'd be forced to look him in the face.

"So what do you like better, regular life or Amish life?" the driver asked.

Solomon shut his eyes for a moment, looking for patience. "I don't know."

He didn't care. His mind was already moving toward thoughts of home cooking—his *mamm*'s brown buttered noodles, and her blueberry crisp, and those little sugar cookies she made when the weather cooled off. . . .

"Seems like a lot of work to be Amish," the driver said. "A lot of extra work for nothing if you ask me. Like, why take a horse and buggy when you can just drive somewhere and be comfortable, you know? I don't have to feed and groom this car. And why make farming that much harder than it has to be? I don't get it."

"Your car doesn't breed and give you a free replacement either," Solomon said.

"What?" The driver looked back in the mirror at him, then a grin split his face. "Ha! Yeah, you're right there. Okay, you got me . . ."

As if it was a joke. Solomon stifled his annoyance— he'd had plenty of experience doing that over the last thirteen months in prison. He was out on good behavior. His full sentence had been two years, and he'd spent half his time in jail hiding behind his big, hardcover Bible. But fighting couldn't be avoided, even with a Bible in his hands, and he'd learned pretty quickly to start working out in the gym and learn how to defend himself.

Solomon saw his *mamm*'s drive coming up. The same old green mailbox sat out front, and behind it, wild raspberries grew up out of the underbrush.

"Right there, on the left," Solomon said.

The cab slowed and turned onto the drive. The two-story house sat on a slight hill, a clothesline stretched from the side porch, out over a length of verdant grass and out to a pole at the edge of a vast garden. The clothesline was decked in fluttering kitchen towels, and as the cab came to a stop, Solomon's breath was stuck in his throat.

"That'll be thirty-four dollars," the cab driver said.

Solomon counted out the cash and handed it over, then grabbed his bag and got out. The cab driver gave him a salute and started to pull out when Solomon saw his *mammi* at the side door. She shielded her eyes with one hand. Bridget Lantz was a short, plump woman with iron-gray hair and a pair of thick glasses she kept pushing up on her nose.

"Sol?" she called, bewildered. "Is that you?"

"Yah, it's me. Hi, Mammi," he said.

His grandmother came carefully down the stairs and then hurried across the rocky ground toward him. He bent down to give her a hug, and she clamped her arms around his neck and rocked him back and forth with a strength that surprised him.

"Are you really here?" she said, pulling back and looking at him tearily.

"Yah, I'm here," he said.

She pulled him back down into another fierce hug, then released him.

"You look like a fool dressed like that," she said, gesturing to his clothes.

Solomon couldn't help but laugh at that. "I guess it all depends on who you're talking to."

"So . . ." She put her hands on her hips. "Are you here to stay?"

"I—" Solomon licked his lips. "I was hoping to see Mamm."

His gaze moved toward the house again, and this time he saw movement at the door. But it wasn't his mother's familiar shape—this was a different woman. She was slim, with brown hair pulled back under her *kapp*, and wary eyes fixed on him. Was that Lizzie Yoder?

"Where's Mamm?" he asked.

"Your sister, Waneta, just had the triplets," Mammi said. "Your mother went to help with them. Actually, your *mamm* left the beginning of March to help out while she was on bed rest. One of the little mites isn't doing as well, and he's been in the hospital. It's to do with his lungs. They weren't developed enough. So your *mamm* is helping your sister keep things afloat, what with the babies at home and the other little one in the hospital and all the travel in between . . ." Mammi's voice faded, and she reached out and touched his hand. "I'm sorry. I know you must be missing your *mamm*."

"Waneta's okay, though?" he asked.

"Yah. She's healing up really well. And the baby in the hospital is almost ready to go home, your *mamm* said in her last letter."

"I'd wanted to surprise her," he said, trying to sound cheerier than he felt.

"Yah . . . well . . ."

"I missed you, too, Mammi," he said, closing his hand around hers. "And I'm starving."

"I imagine you would be!" Mammi said, and a smile broke over her face. "Come inside. Elizabeth made pie this morning—cherry. Oh, I should mention—Elizabeth Yoder is staying with me until your *mamm* comes back."

Solomon looked up again. So that was Lizzie Yoder— all grown up now. She wasn't the same teenager he remembered, always so prim and proper. Her *daet* was a popular preacher, and she'd always been proud of that, but trying to hide her pride because it wasn't properly Amish. But looking at her standing in the doorway, her dark gaze locked on him with a wary look, reminding him of how English he looked right now. She'd be judging that. He looked down at his blue jeans, feeling uncomfortable.

"Come on," Mammi said. "Let's get you inside and fed."

Solomon followed his grandmother toward the house, and Lizzie disappeared inside.

"When is Mamm coming back?" Solomon asked, and his grandmother slowed her steps.

"As soon as your sister can handle things on her own," Mammi replied. "Soon. You can write to her and tell her you're back."

Did he want to do that? An image rose in his mind of his mother's back as she walked away from him. If her own son's desperation hadn't changed her mind, another letter wouldn't either. Maybe even surprising her wouldn't make a difference.

"I'm not really good with letters," he said.

"Your mother will be glad to see you, Sol," Mammi said softly.

But he wasn't sure about that. He'd already disappointed his *mamm* almost beyond repair.

"Maybe I'll just wait and see what happens when she gets back," he said.

Mammi looked up at him sadly. "She loves you."

And he knew that his *mamm* did, but sometimes love was tough. Sometimes love imposed its own shunning. She'd wanted him to come home and be properly Amish again—and he was home now, wasn't he? He might never be properly Amish, but maybe she'd be able to see that he was trying to mend his ways.

Solomon followed his grandmother into the house and sat down at the table, where a pie was cooling. Mammi fetched him a plate and a fork, then cut him the first piece. His stomach rumbled as he took a large bite, followed by a second in quick succession.

"You're out of prison, then?" Elizabeth said.

"Yah."

"Hmm." She didn't say anything else and turned away. He was getting a lot of that lately—people turning their backs on him. But this wasn't just any woman—he'd known her rather well back when they were teenagers, and he wasn't about to be pushed around by her, too.

"Lizzie Yoder," he said with a small smile. "It's been a while."

She looked back at him over her shoulder. "Yah. A long while."

"Have people been talking about me?" he asked. He could only imagine what the gossip about him had been like. He left home at seventeen and went English, then got caught up with the wrong people. They'd been doing some petty theft, and Solomon tried to keep clear of that part of things, until one day they jumped in the car and told him to drive. Legally speaking, that was accessory to a crime.

"People always talk, and you gave them plenty to discuss." She met his gaze easily. "You're home now? Ready to reform?"

"I'm visiting," he said. "So you don't have to worry about me upending everything. I won't be here long."

He caught his grandmother's gaze locked on him, and he read the disappointment there. She pushed up her glasses on her nose again.

"For as long as you're here, you'll have a bedroom and a grandmother," Mammi said quietly. "This is your home, Sol. It always was and it always will be."

That was what he'd needed his *mamm* to say—to reassure him that he was hers, no matter what, even if he'd let them all down. That was what he'd come back to hear . . . and while he loved his grandmother deeply, it was his mother who'd turned her back.

"Thanks, Mammi," he said. "Do you mind if I take another piece?"

Mammi cut another ample piece of pie and dished it onto his plate. At the very least, while he was here with Mammi, he'd eat.

Elizabeth stood by the counter and watched as Solomon took another big bite of cherry pie. His gaze flickered in her direction as he chewed. He looked different now—almost English. His hair was cut short and he looked bigger than regular Amish men looked. That was the kind of muscle that came from a gym, not farmwork. That was the kind of muscle that was for appearances, vanity, and she wasn't supposed to be appreciating it . . . But she couldn't help but notice the bulk of his biceps as he lifted another bite to his lips.

"I'm surprised you came home," Elizabeth said. It sounded blunt, but she really was surprised. He'd left their community years before he got into trouble.

Solomon's chewing slowed. "Why?"

"It's been . . . five years? I thought you'd have gone back to your English life. I thought you . . . liked it there."

She'd heard a few rumors—some of the local young people had seen Solomon a few times over the years. They always said the same thing—he liked living English. He could do as he liked. There were no elders or bishop to curtail his activities. He'd been a rebel, and they'd all simply accepted that fact.

"There wasn't much to go back to," Solomon said, and he dropped his gaze and scraped his fork across the plate, picking up the last of the cherry filling. "I got caught up with the wrong people. It's fun while it's fun, but when things go wrong, they don't exactly wait for you. A couple of them are in prison, still."

Mention of prison brought up goose bumps on her arms and she looked away.

"I'm starting over," he added. "Putting all that behind me."

"Oh . . ." She wasn't sure what to say to that.

"You believe that?" he asked.

"I don't know what to believe," she said with a faint shrug. "So you're going to be Amish again?"

"Maybe not," he replied. "I don't think the Amish community here in Bountiful is going to accept me—"

"You don't know that, Sol," Bridget broke in.

"Mammi," Solomon said, and his gaze softened as he looked over at his grandmother. "I'm not holding my breath, okay? Besides, I'm not sure I make much of an Amish man anymore."

Elizabeth had to agree there—he didn't. The Amish community protected their way of life, and Solomon had not only gone English, he'd gone criminal.

Yet she had her own family taint in that respect, too. Her father was in jail for fraud, and she'd believed so earnestly in his innocence for far too long. Now, she knew the truth about her *daet*—he'd defrauded members of their community purposefully. He'd known what he was doing, and it was fueled by his own sense of vengeance because the community hadn't helped her *mamm* get the medical interventions necessary to save her life.

And here was another man fresh from prison.

"If you're turning your life around, and giving your heart back to Gott, then you need to come back to our community," Bridget said. "That is how you make it right—you come home."

"There was a Catholic priest who'd come do a worship service at the prison," Solomon said. "It was different. They . . . they have something called a rosary? And they dress differently, too. Anyway, he was a really wise man—humble, kind, strong—and he talked to any of us convicts who wanted to discuss faith with him. And he suggested that I should turn my life around and become Catholic."

The room was silent for a moment. Catholic. He might as well suggest becoming a fence post. Amish didn't become Catholic! They did become Mennonite sometimes, though . . .

"Oh, Sol!" Bridget shot him an annoyed look. "Very funny."

"There was a Baptist minister who'd visit, too," he added. "No Mennonite minister, but I mean, that's always an option for us Amish, isn't it?"

Solomon shot Elizabeth a wry smile and winked. She could see the humor in his gaze, but she didn't find it amusing. Bridget didn't seem to either, because the old woman's cheeks flushed and she shook her head in annoyance.

"You're not funny," Elizabeth said.

"I am a little bit," he replied. "But my point is, there are a good many ways to turn a life around. And I left our Amish life because I was frustrated with all the restrictions. Well, I can see the point of them now, but that doesn't mean there aren't other ways of living that could help me do better, too. There are other people who believe in Gott who order their lives to live better."

"You're just trying to argue now," Bridget said. "You've come back. That's the right thing to do, and there isn't anything else to say on the matter."

"I don't want to argue," Solomon said, and he sobered.

"Good. Then no more mention of that," Bridget said.

"I'm just happy to see you, Mammi," he said, and Elizabeth could see Bridget relax. Solomon always had been charming.

Elizabeth went to the counter and pulled down some bread. Solomon looked hungry in the way he was scraping that plate, and she slathered a thick slice of white bread with sweet Amish peanut butter, then brought it to the table.

"Oh . . . thank you." Solomon accepted the plate and gave her a grateful smile.

"When did you last eat?" Elizabeth asked. "Really?"

"Yesterday," he replied.

"Yesterday!" Mammi pushed herself to her feet. "I'm going to whip up a proper meal now, Sol. My goodness . . ."

Solomon took a bite of bread, followed by a second bite before he'd swallowed.

"They don't feed you there?" Elizabeth asked. In prison was what she meant, but she didn't want to say it.

"I was nervous," he said, swallowing. "Excited. I was getting out. I couldn't choke anything down."

She nodded. "I can understand that."

"How's your family?" Solomon asked, taking another bite, and then speaking past the food. "I haven't kept up with anyone lately."

So he didn't know about her father either . . . the one person in this community who didn't know the worst about her family. Was it wrong of her to want to keep it a secret?

"Elijah got married to Bethany Glick," she said.

"Bethany Glick . . . wasn't Micah courting her?" he asked. "Someone told me that a long time ago."

"Things change," Elizabeth replied. So many things had changed, including who she felt she was . . . including her confidence in the woman her father had raised her to be. "Micah actually went English a few months back."

"Really?" Solomon sobered. "I didn't know that."

"So did my sister," she added.

Solomon eyed her, and he looked genuinely shocked. "Lovina went English?"

"Yah."

"She was younger than us, so maybe I didn't know her well, but . . . your family always seemed like the last ones to have *kinner* jump the fence," he said. He paused for a moment. "Did Micah and Lovina leave together? Like, were they in a relationship or something?"

"No, they went separately," she replied. "And we haven't heard from Lovina since, so . . ."

"I'm sorry I joked about it," he said quietly. "I thought I was the only one."

"Far from it," she said, then sighed. "But if you came back, maybe they will, too, right?"

Solomon didn't answer, and she searched his face for some hope that his return might mean something about the others. But Solomon's situation was so much worse than anyone else's. If Lovina went English and things went moderately well for her, she might not return. She might have no reason to . . .

"She hasn't written?" Solomon asked.

"No—not beyond what she wrote in the note when she left us."

"That's not a good sign . . ." he said. "No one has looked for her?"

"Where would we look?" she asked. "I talked to the *Englisher* police and they took down the information, but when an Amish person leaves, the police just think it's another runaway not wanting to live Amish anymore. And maybe they sympathize with it."

Solomon nodded. "Yah. They don't understand out there. They think that Amish teens deserve more than our communities offer. They think it's awful we stop schooling at eighth grade."

Elizabeth dropped her gaze. "They think a lot of things."

Solomon finished his bread, then pushed back his chair. "Mammi, can I help you with the outdoor chores?"

"Yah." Bridget beamed over at him. "You'll be the man here, Solomon. I'd much appreciate it if you stepped in."

Solomon's gaze rested on Elizabeth for a moment, and a smile tickled one corner of his lips.

"It's nice to see you again, too, Lizzie," he said softly.

Before she could answer him, he headed for the door, and she watched him leave—looking so very English going out to do an Amish man's duty.

"Elizabeth?" Bridget called.

Elizabeth startled and turned toward the old woman, hoping that the heat in her face wasn't visible. Bridget clasped her hands in front of her apron, and she looked slightly sheepish, her glasses slipping down her nose. She took them off and put them on the counter.

"I knew he was coming," Bridget said, and she licked her lips. "I knew it months ago."

"You knew?" she said.

"He wrote that he might get out early on good behavior. I didn't know when or anything, but I knew it might be a possibility. But my daughter would never have let me see the letter if I'd handed it over to her, and she'd likely burn it and not answer, so I—" Bridget licked her lips again. "I opened it and I answered it myself. He said in the letter that he might be able to get out early and I said he should come home."

Elizabeth nodded. "I understand . . ."

"When my daughter went to help Waneta, I asked for you to come stay with me because—" Bridget picked at her white apron. "I asked for you because I thought you of all people might understand Sol a little better. If he were to come back when Anke was away, that is. It was just a . . . guess."

"You thought I'd be more sympathetic to him because of my *daet*," Elizabeth surmised.

"Yah, because of him," Bridget agreed. "You know that someone can go wrong but still be a part of the family. And you know that someone can make a mistake and still need love."

Perhaps Bridget had given Elizabeth a little more credit for her forgiving heart than she really deserved. Her feelings toward her father right now were complicated at best.

"My *daet* isn't returning," Elizabeth said.

"Don't be so sure about that," the old woman replied.

"What do you want from me, then?" Elizabeth asked. "Is Solomon being home a secret or something?"

"No, not a secret," Bridget replied. "People will find out soon enough. But now that he's back, he's right about having a hard time settling in. People won't just forget what he did, and they won't just trust him after he's been in prison. It'll be hard for him—anywhere he went, it would be hard. I just hoped that maybe you could help him feel . . . welcome."

So Bridget's request that Elizabeth come stay with her while her daughter was away had been more than simple kindness to one of the grown Yoder *kinner*, reeling after their father's incarceration. This had been more calculated.

Bridget reached for her glasses on the counter and put them back on her face.

"How would I make him welcome?" Elizabeth asked. "This is your home, Bridget. I'm only helping you out."

"Be kind to him," Bridget said softly. "Don't treat him like he's different. Let him just be Amish, a regular man. Let him feel what it would be like to step back into this life. I think it would mean the world to him to have one person besides myself who sees him as he really is."

"You think I'll be able to?" Elizabeth asked hesitantly. "My *daet*'s sins don't make me sympathetic to people who break the law, you know."

"I think if you looked deep enough, and you gave him a chance, you'd see the boy I see," Bridget said, and her eyes misted. "I think you would."

Bridget was asking for more than help around her house; she was asking for more than companionship. Bridget wanted someone to help her bring her grandson back to the community, and that was a very big request.

"What if he doesn't want to be my friend?" Elizabeth asked.

"He does." Bridget smiled, and her eyes twinkled with sudden mirth. "Trust me, my dear. He does."

Elizabeth went to the window and looked outside. Solomon had the door to the stables open wide, and he came outside with a pitchfork in one hand and looked around himself as if trying to find something. His gaze moved past the house, and then he glanced back when he saw her in the window.

Gone was the look of flirtatious teasing, and in its place, she saw such deep sadness that it made her breath catch in her throat. He wasn't the confident *Englisher* after all. He was scared . . . Solomon gave her a nod and then headed over to the buggy shelter and disappeared under it.

"Yah," Elizabeth said, turning back into the kitchen. "I'll try, at least."

Bridget smiled. "Thank you, Lizzie."

It was the first time Bridget had called her by her childhood nickname, and the old woman moved back toward the stove.

"Let's get dinner started," Bridget said. "We have a man to feed now."

Chapter Two

That night, Elizabeth lay in bed listening to the sounds of the house. There were the usual creaks and groans that came with an old house, and the distant bark of some dogs that surfed a faint breeze through Elizabeth's opened bedroom window. Her blanket was folded back so that only a cool sheet covered her nightgown, one leg thrust out to catch some of that breeze.

Bridget seemed to be restless, getting up to use the washroom several times, her slippered feet shuffling along the floor. This time, Elizabeth heard the old woman's footsteps stop in front of her grandson's door and tap softly.

"Are you comfortable, Sol?" Bridget asked quietly.

"Yah, Mammi." Sol's voice was deep, and it traveled better than his grandmother's.

"Do you need another blanket?"

There was the creak of a door opening. "No, Mammi. It's July."

"Sol, you know I want you to stay, don't you?"

"Of course."

"And your *mamm* will come around. She loves you. You don't understand a mother's love, Sol—"

"Mammi, it's fine."

"Do you want me to write to her? I'm sure she'd . . . come back. . . ."

Was Bridget sure, though? Even Elizabeth knew how angry Anke was at her son for his mistakes. She didn't hide it in social gatherings—Elizabeth had heard her complain about his poor choices numerous times during quilting circles. Right now, Anke was needed where she was with her premature grandbabies. Would she return for her prodigal son who wasn't promising to stay?

"Mammi," Solomon had said quietly. "Don't write to her. I don't want you to. It's fine."

"Okay . . ." Bridget said. "If you need anything, you tell me."

"Good night, Mammi."

Her footsteps passed toward her bedroom again, and Elizabeth held her breath. Solomon's door clicked shut, and Elizabeth rolled over to her side, sleep elusive. If Anke didn't come back quickly, she might not see Solomon at all. He sounded like a man passing through . . .

Elizabeth heard the squeak of springs as Solomon rolled over in the bedroom next to hers. After a few minutes, there was some soft snoring, too. She must have fallen asleep shortly after because she was startled awake in the middle of the night when the moon was full and all was silent and still. What had woken her?

She lay there for a moment, listening to the stillness, her heart pounding.

"No!" It was that muffled kind of shout—Sol was talking

in his sleep. That must have been what woke her up. There was silence again, the bed springs creaked. She heard an audible sigh.

Nightmares.

She shivered, despite the hot night, and as she tried to go back to sleep, she silently said a prayer for Solomon, that Gott would give him a peaceful rest and chase out whatever darkness seemed to be haunting him.

The next morning, Elizabeth got up at her usual time. Solomon's door was shut, and when Elizabeth went downstairs to start the fire in the stove, Bridget was already in the kitchen and had started kindling a fire.

"He's sleeping still," Bridget said. "Let's let him rest. He must be exhausted. Besides, it would feel wonderful to be in a real bed again, I'm sure."

Elizabeth's mind went back to that shout in the night, and a shiver went down her spine. Was this Gott answering her prayer, giving the man some rest?

Solomon slept in until well past eight, and he seemed embarrassed when he came downstairs. He'd washed up and combed his hair already. He wore the same clothes from yesterday, but he'd shaved, and that musky, masculine scent of shaving cream followed him. Bridget had gone next door to the *Englisher* neighbors yesterday and come back with a small bag of men's toiletries. The Livingstons were good friends of hers.

"You should have woken me up, Mammi," Solomon said.

"It's fine," the old woman replied with a smile. "I kept your breakfast warm."

There was love in that breakfast.

Solomon ate quickly, and Elizabeth noticed how his

eyes moved around the kitchen warily as he chewed—almost like he was scared still. Was that habit now? When he finished, he brought his plate to the counter and went out to do the chores. He was still out when Bridget's two friends, Edith Stuckey and Lydia Helmuth, arrived for a visit. Bridget didn't need Elizabeth underfoot while she chatted with her friends, so Elizabeth left the older women to talk in peace and headed outside with plastic tubs to harvest some vegetables for the roadside produce stand that Bridget planned to open on the following day.

Elizabeth knelt in the garden, picking cucumbers off the vine and depositing them into a plastic tub. The vegetables prickled against her hands and she stopped to rub her palms together. It was a bright morning, the warmth of the day already seeping into the air. The sun warmed her back and shoulders, the dirt cold against her knees and hands as she worked her way down the row.

The cucumbers were good this year—well formed and big. Some curled off in strange directions, and those wouldn't sell as easily, so the family would likely eat most of those. Elizabeth knew a recipe for a good cucumber salad. There would also be bread-and-butter pickles and sliced cucumber added to sandwiches. Bridget had already sent Elizabeth over to their *Englisher* neighbors with other produce—lettuce, zucchini, some potatoes. They were decent people who'd accepted the food with enthusiasm and always said, "If Bridget needs anything at all, you remind her that we're here. If she wants to go into town or run an errand—anything."

The cucumbers would be used up one way or another. But her mind wasn't really on the cucumber crop as she tossed another pair of the vegetables into the tub.

Elizabeth looked toward the stable and the buggy barn. The horses were outside, grazing, their glossy brown coats shivering in pleasure in the warm morning sunlight. The stable door opened and Solomon appeared in the doorway. She looked away hurriedly, turning back to the cucumber vines, moving broad, prickly leaves aside to reveal another three hidden vegetables. She picked them and they thunked into the tub.

"Hi, Lizzie."

Elizabeth looked up and squinted through the sunlight to see Solomon approach the edge of the garden. The sun shone from behind him, marking his strong, broad-shouldered silhouette. He pulled off a pair of work gloves and slapped them against his jeans.

"You need Amish clothes," Elizabeth said.

"Yah." He looked down at his own *Englisher* clothing and shrugged. "I'll get to it."

"It was nice not to have to do the stables," she said. Very nice. That had been one of her jobs because Bridget couldn't possibly lift bales of hay or shovel out stalls at her age.

"You and Mammi have been alone for a while?" Solomon asked.

"A few weeks," she said.

He rubbed a thumb over his palm. "It feels strange to be back. Like a dream, almost. Like I'm going to wake up."

"Should I pinch you?" she asked, the humor coming out before she could think better of it.

"No." He chuckled, and he put his attention into rubbing that spot on his palm again.

He was different than the Solomon Lantz of her youth,

but she could still see the boy deep down under the layers of muscle.

"Did you dream of home?" she asked. "When you were . . . away?"

"In prison, you mean," he said. He caught her eye. "You don't want to say it, do you?"

Her cheeks heated. No, she didn't want to say it. Prison and crime were things that she and her brother avoided talking about at all costs. It hit too close to home for their family, and they had their father's shame to shed.

"Yah, I did dream of home," he said when she didn't answer. "Everyone does in that place. They talk about it a lot—what they'll do when they get out. Most of them have food they want to eat, or wives or girlfriends they want to see again. I had a cellmate, and he wasn't ever getting out. He'd done some bad stuff, and a parole hearing came up once while I was there, and he got denied. He didn't expect anything different—it wasn't the first time. Anyway, even he talked about this little town he lived in when he was a kid. I think he made up most of it, truthfully. But he'd ask me about where I'd go back to, and I told him about the Amish life."

"You told him where to find you?" she asked, squinting.

"I'm not stupid," he replied with a bitter laugh. "I never used names of places. I even hinted that I was from Indiana originally, just to throw him off. But I told him about morning chores, and about the horses, and the sunsets, and my mother's baking . . ." He dropped his gaze. "I used to dream about brown buttered noodles. I didn't even like them that much. I mean, they were okay and I liked them fine, but they weren't my favorite. But for some reason I kept dreaming of my *mamm* serving this massive dish of brown buttered noodles."

"You miss her," Elizabeth said.

"She's my *mamm*." His dark gaze raised to meet hers, and the intensity in his gaze made her breath catch.

"What did you dream of last night?" she asked.

"What do you mean?" he asked warily.

"I heard you shout," she said.

"Oh . . ." He shrugged uncomfortably, but didn't seem inclined to answer more.

"What did you dream of?" she repeated. "Not brown buttered noodles this time."

"No. I dreamed of prison." Then his gaze softened and he shrugged. "I think I liked the dreams I had in prison better."

"Bridget is afraid you'll leave again," Elizabeth said.

"I have nowhere to go at the moment," he replied.

"But if you dreamed of coming home—" Wouldn't he stay? He'd achieved his deepest longing.

"I also dreamed of acceptance and somehow becoming a different man, and everyone being okay with that," he said. "It isn't going to happen."

"And with the *Englishers*?" she asked. "Will it happen there?"

Solomon didn't answer, but she suspected that it wouldn't. Once a man had been to prison, English or Amish, he wasn't going to be trusted anywhere.

Elizabeth moved farther down the garden row and started parting leaves again, looking for cucumbers. She spotted two smaller ones and left them to continue growing, then picked another large cucumber.

"Do you want help?" he asked.

"Sure," she said. "I have to get all the cucumbers and squash that are ready."

Solomon stepped over the rows of green beans that separated them and squatted down on the other side of the row of cucumbers. He parted some leaves and she reached in for the vegetables. For a few minutes they worked in silence, moving up the row until they'd half-filled the bin and gotten to the end.

"You never did like me much," Solomon said as he stood up.

Elizabeth rose, too, putting a hand to the small of her back. "That isn't true, Solomon."

"Come on . . ." He gave her a tired look. "You didn't."

It seemed cruel now to point it out, but he was right. "You were cocky," she said with a shrug.

"I still am." He shot her a grin, but there was something in his smile that made her stomach flutter just a little. She looked away.

"And you teased me a lot," she said. Her mind went back to those years when the boys used to pester her. They'd make up rhymes to go with Lizzie, they'd drop grasshoppers in her lap, they'd ask her stupid questions until she was filled with fury.

"It was fun," Solomon said.

"Not for me," she said. "I hated it. You'd do anything to make me angry."

"I was young and stupid. I would have done anything to make you blush," he said. "There's a difference."

"I don't believe that. You picked on me," she said. "You never teased the other girls like you did with me."

"They weren't half as pretty as you were." A smile quirked up one side of his mouth.

"As if that's how you get a girl's attention," she said, refusing to be charmed. "Pestering a girl isn't okay, you know. We don't like boys who drive us crazy."

"I'm sorry." He sobered. "I'm not going to do it again. Believe it or not, I'm wiser now. I'm no longer a teenager."

"Thank you," she said.

"You're prettier now," he said, but there wasn't flirtation in his voice this time. Just quiet honesty. She looked over at him and found his gaze locked on her—no bashfulness on his part. He was just looking at her, his eyes roving over her face, down her dress. "Do you have a boyfriend? A fiancé?"

"No," she replied, and she instinctively crossed her arms.

"How come?"

There were several rather good reasons, the chief of which was her father's criminal history, but she had no desire to discuss that.

"That's my business," she replied.

He smiled at that, then laughed softly. "All right. Fair enough."

She turned to pick up the plastic bin of cucumbers and Solomon beat her to it. He hoisted the bin easily, his muscles flexing in that way that drew her eye in spite of her best efforts to ignore them.

"Squash, you say?" he said.

She nodded and went to retrieve a knife from the grass where she'd left it. "There are a few that are ready. They were popular last year, your grandmother said."

Solomon slipped the knife out of her fingers and tested the blade against his thumb. Then he squatted down next to a section of acorn squash and reached into the leaves

THE PREACHER'S DAUGHTER   27

with the knife, biting his bottom lip as he sawed at the vine. Then he passed her a nice, fat squash in the palm of his hand. She took it and headed back down the row to grab another plastic bin. When she looked back at him, she saw his strong back and narrow waist, those *Englisher* jeans fitting snugger than was proper for their people. He reached into the wide leaves of the squash plant, his muscular physique on display.

Solomon was back, for a while at least. And he was even less of a romantic option now that he'd been to prison, but there was something about him that made her take notice—something almost feral and definitely masculine. He seemed to have more swagger about him than usual Amish men had, and the memory of the way his eyes had moved over her made her pulse speed up.

And he'd said she was pretty . . . Her face warmed at the memory. Amish men didn't flirt like that. They had some reserve. They were more careful.

Did he really think she was pretty?

Elizabeth grabbed the tub and headed back up the dirt row to where Solomon had three squashes waiting. He looked up as she bent to pick them up and passed another squash into her hands, his fingers, blackened by dirt, brushing over hers.

"I have to find some proper clothes," he said, looking down at himself. "The ladies in there will be scandalized to see me in blue jeans."

"They're more scandalized by your time in prison," she said. When the words came out, she heard how barbed they sounded, but Solomon only shrugged.

"Probably," he said.

She'd been too blunt and she knew it. It wasn't as if she had much right to lecture anyone anymore.

"They'll probably survive the shock," she added with a conciliatory smile. She settled back down to look through the squash leaves for any that might be ripe.

Maybe it had been a long time since she'd been flirted with . . . or maybe she was just missing being treated as if she was worthy of any attention at all. Because anyone who knew what had happened to her *daet* had long since stopped.

Solomon cut the vine of another gourd and pulled it out of the leaves. It felt good to be useful after a year of sitting in a cell. It felt good to clean out a stall, brush down a horse, harvest some vegetables . . . It felt good to breathe fresh air.

"I missed this," he said, and his knife made it through another vine.

"Work?" she asked.

"It's more of a luxury than people realize," he replied. "Prison is far from boring, but it's also far from useful."

All he'd had to do in prison was read his Bible, work out at the gym, and attend pretty much any religious service they offered. It was calmer in the chapel—no fighting, at least. It was a safer space, and he'd been anxious to find anywhere that let him just breathe for a little while. Prison was full of social obligations to other inmates— loyalties, feuds, demands. A church service, a Bible study, a talk with a reverend or a priest—it was a respite from the other pressures. There, a man was allowed to acknowledge his own soul.

He'd dreamed of regular Amish men's work again—hard work that required his muscles and his brain, that let him stand outside in clean air and not have his shoulder blades tickle, wondering who might be coming up behind him. When he was locked up, he was so certain that *here* he would feel safe again.

But even kneeling outside, harvesting squash, he still felt as if he should be watching his back. It was like his body had learned that response over the last year and it didn't know how to stop, even back home with a bright summer sky, a grass-scented breeze, and the nicker of horses grazing in the field. His shoulder blades still tickled.

"Was it hard in prison?" she asked, and that drilling gaze of hers swung back to his face.

"Yah. Of course it was hard. It was punishment."

"Is there a way to be safe there?" she asked. "If you were honest and good, would it make it easier? Maybe you could just sit quietly in your cell and it would be . . . okay?"

"Not really," he replied.

She pressed her lips together, and he saw tears mist her eyes. Sympathy for him? That surprised him.

"Did you feel Gott with you at least?" she asked hopefully. "Did Gott give you some special comfort?"

He thought back to the hours of darkness when he'd lay in bed, tears filling him up but not daring to let them fall. He remembered listening in the night to the other inmates' snores, coughs and muttering in their sleep.

"Yah," he said. "Gott did bring comfort. You hear Him better when you've got nothing else. Maybe you listen harder."

"That's good." She nodded quickly. "I'm glad."

Had she spared him a thought while he was in prison? Was it dumb of him to hope she had? He'd figured that the girls back in Bountiful would have forgotten him by now, and he eyed her uncertainly as she took the squash from his hand and put it into the bin without meeting his gaze.

Solomon had been working outside since breakfast with the sun warming his back. Sweat trickled down his spine, and he squinted against the glare. He missed a proper hat. Amish clothing not only set them apart, but it was practical.

"Are you thirsty?" he asked.

"Hmm?" Elizabeth's mind seemed to have been else-where.

"I'm going in for a drink," he said. "Do you want water?"

"Yah. Also, there are some more plastic bins I left on the front porch, if you wouldn't mind grabbing those," she said.

"Sure."

Solomon pushed himself up and handed the knife over to her. Her fingers felt soft under his, and he tried not to give it much notice. A girl like her—even if he stayed in Bountiful—would never lower herself to the likes of him. He knew better than to toy with those kinds of disap-pointments. Teasing her was one thing, but letting himself actually hope for something more . . . that was stupidity.

As Solomon came around the house, he wiped some

sweat from his brow. He was thirsty—this being his first actual break since he started cleaning out the stables that morning. He spotted the plastic containers on the porch, pulled open the screen door, and headed into the house. The soft murmur of women's voices came from the kitchen. They'd been polite enough when he unhitched their buggy for them a couple of hours earlier. One of the women was his friend, Seth's, grandmother, Edith. He'd never known her well, but he knew who she was. As he headed through the short hallway toward them, their voices became clearer.

"I don't know why you'd bring her here," one woman was saying. "You know that family—"

"Her father, not the family," his grandmother cut in. "Abe Yoder might be a bad one, and he might have done our community wrong, but should his *kinner* have to pay for that? Elizabeth is not her father. She doesn't need to pay for her father's sins."

Solomon froze. He shouldn't be eavesdropping, and in a minute, he'd start making some noise to announce his presence, but what was this about Abe Yoder? Abe was a preacher—a very popular one. At least he had been back before Solomon left. How much had changed over the years he'd been away?

"He'll come back eventually," the other woman said. "They'll let him out of prison and he'll have nowhere else to go."

Prison? Solomon's breath caught. Abe Yoder was in jail? He felt like the air was squeezed out of his lungs. It wasn't just the shock of another man from this community having been locked up—it was the thought of Abe Yoder, the charismatic preacher who could bring the very rafters to salvation, so they said . . . It would seem that Elizabeth's concern about prison time was less about him than he'd fancied.

"If his *kinner* are just like him, though, it might be wise to keep some distance from them." This was another female voice. "He raised them. And he was too permissive with them—I always said. Didn't I, Lydia? I always said it. He encouraged Elizabeth to be mouthy and rude."

"She was never rude to me," Mammi said. "Not once."

"She didn't keep her opinions to herself either," the woman retorted. "And who wants to hear what a girl that age thinks? No one. She needs to be listening and learning, not spouting off about her own views. Youthful ideas might be very pretty, but they change over time—and it's only when those shiny ideas have gained some balance and wisdom that they're useful to anyone else."

Lizzie had been forthright with her views, Solomon would admit to that. She'd been judgmental, too, arching a brow and staring him down when he used language she didn't approve of, or spouted off about his own changing views . . . but her *daet* was in prison? His brain was still trying to wrap around that one. . . .

"It was an awkward time," Mammi said. "I'll agree to that. But those teenage years generally are."

"The thing is, you don't have anyone else here to protect you," the first woman said. "Does she have access to your personal papers or your banking information?"

"No!" Mammi sighed. "Look, I asked her to come and help me, and . . . and . . . I wasn't going to say this, but she's the only one who might understand Sol's situation right now. Or be sympathetic. Or . . . make him feel welcome."

There was silence, and his heart beat so loudly that he could hear it in his head. If Lizzie was his best chance of being accepted or welcomed, he was in trouble indeed.

"Bridget, you aren't safe around Sol either," the first woman said quietly. "You know that. . . ."

Solomon's chest constricted and anger thrummed up inside of him.

"I'm perfectly safe!" his grandmother said firmly. "He's home. He needs to find his place again, that's all."

"He's been in jail!" the second woman said. "Even I don't feel perfectly comfortable visiting you while he's here. Bridget, it is possible to have a heart that is too big, you know."

"He's my grandson!" Mammi said. "Edith, what if this was Seth? What if Seth had gotten into trouble and come home again?"

"This wouldn't be Seth. He's married with three *kinner* of his own right now. And he's always been responsible—"

"And he couldn't possibly have gone off?" Mammi demanded. "I remember a time when he was awfully keen on an *Englisher* girl."

"We nipped that off," Edith replied. "We took care of it."

"We're just saying," the other woman interjected, "you've got the daughter of a criminal helping you in the house and your grandson who was just released from prison sleeping under this roof. This isn't safe, Bridget. We're worried, and you can't be offended that we care."

Solomon cleared his throat, and the women went silent. He pasted what he hoped was an easy smile on his face and sauntered the rest of the way down the hallway and into the kitchen. The older women sat around the kitchen table with Mammi. They were both his grandmother's age, their hair white and their hands gnarled and stained by garden soil. He didn't know these women well, and they both looked away uncomfortably.

"I'm thirsty, Mammi," he said. "Sorry to interrupt."

"It's no bother, Sol," Mammi said, rising from her chair. "I'll get you some water."

She went to the sink, and the kitchen fell into silence. The women at the table looked at each other.

Solomon cast a look in the women's direction. "You'll have to tell Seth I say hello."

They murmured something in reply. Solomon drank the water down in several gulps and handed the glass back.

"We really should go," Edith said, pushing back her chair. "I've got my own housework to attend to."

"Yah, so much to do today still," Lydia said, and she rose to her feet. "Bridget, thank you for your lovely pie. It was delicious."

"Elizabeth made it," Mammi said, but her smile looked tired now. "I'll let her know you enjoyed it."

They didn't say anything more to Solomon, and he watched as they headed outside. He looked over at his grandmother and she widened her eyes and nodded toward the door. It was his job to go hitch them up again.

"I heard what they said," he said quietly.

Mammi's face fell. "Oh, Sol . . . I'm sorry. They don't mean it."

"Don't they?" he asked. Of course they'd meant it.

He'd never heard such deep sincerity in his life. They were afraid of him and they were afraid for his grandmother. What did they think he was going to do?

Bridget looked around feebly, then looked up at Solomon and gave a weak shrug.

"Please hitch their horse," she said at last. "Or they'll never leave."

Solomon smiled bitterly at that. "On my way, Mammi."

What was he going to do, let two old women hitch up their own buggy? This was a man's job—to help the womenfolk and do the jobs that required bodily strength. And Solomon might be a great many things right now— an outcast, an ex-con, untrusted and disliked—but he was still a man, and these muscles were good for something.

Chapter Three

Elizabeth carried the tub of squash toward the side door. Solomon had finished hitching up the older women's buggy, and he held the horse's bridle while they hoisted themselves up into the seat. The entire process was wordless, and Elizabeth put the heavy bin onto the porch. These women visited often—they were Bridget's good friends. They'd never been terribly warm to Elizabeth— and she knew why—but they were normally warmer than this. The women were both tense and grim, their eyes fixed on Solomon with sharp distrust.

Elizabeth forced a smile and raised one hand in a wave, and when Lydia looked up, she smiled hesitantly.

"Have a good day," Elizabeth said. "I didn't realize you were leaving so soon or I would have come in to say hello."

Not that they would have wanted that, of course. She'd been staying out in the garden for a reason. The old women liked their time alone together, when they could talk without reservation.

"Goodbye," Edith said briskly, and she flicked the reins three times as the horse started to pull the buggy around to head back out. The buggy wasn't moving around very quickly, however, and Elizabeth watched as Edith's expression slipped into a scowl before she was out of sight.

"Are they always that friendly?" Solomon asked bitterly. "Or am I just lucky?"

"No, that was especially sour," Elizabeth replied. "You must remember them—that's Seth's *mammi*."

"Yah, I know," he replied. "And they couldn't get out of here fast enough once they set eyes on me."

"They're older," Elizabeth said evasively. "They'll get used to seeing you around again."

"Have they gotten used to you yet?" he asked, giving her a pointed look; then he turned and headed into the house. Something had changed.

The buggy reached the end of the drive and turned onto the road. Elizabeth sighed. Not everyone in Bountiful was like those old women. There were people who had softened to the Yoder *kinner*, realized that they weren't their father and that they deserved a chance to choose something better than he had. Bishop David Lapp was open and kind. And her brother, Isaiah, had married and was a new *daet* now. It was possible to move on . . .

She headed around the porch and up the stairs to the side door.

"His name was Rueben Miller," Bridget was saying as Elizabeth came inside. "He spent some time working on the bishop's farm when he was a teenager—do you remember him?"

Elizabeth let the screen door bounce against her hand to stop the bang and she glanced uncomfortably toward Solomon who stood next to the kitchen table. He didn't look at her.

"Do you remember him?" Bridget turned to Elizabeth. "Rueben Miller. He's from Edson—that area."

"No, I don't think I ever met him," Elizabeth replied and headed toward the sink to wash her hands.

"Well, he's dead."

Elizabeth blinked. "Oh, I'm sorry to hear it."

"It was a terrible accident," Bridget said. "He was working with a baler, and something went wrong and he got his arm caught in it and—" Bridget winced. "Apparently, it was very painful, and he didn't survive."

Elizabeth turned on the water, then looked over at Solomon, and he met her gaze for a second.

"Is there a funeral you want to attend, Mammi?" he asked.

Elizabeth soaped up and washed her hands.

"No, it isn't that," Bridget replied. "I do remember him, though. He was at a service Sunday one summer and he chatted with me a little bit. I knew his grandmother— she was a school friend of mine. The thing is, he's left behind a wife and two little girls."

"That's very sad," Elizabeth murmured as she turned off the water and reached for a towel. "She must be crushed."

"Yah, she is," Bridget agreed. "But she's got those two little girls, and while she can stay with family for a little while, she's going to need a new husband. And the bishop is thinking about a man here in Bountiful for her. We might have a wedding in the family."

That was the way—there were already *kinner* to provide for. But there were women like Elizabeth who needed a husband, too. A young widow of good character had better luck with these things than the daughter of a criminal, though. If Elizabeth stayed in Bountiful, that was. She had other plans, but she hadn't breathed them aloud to anyone yet.

Solomon shifted uncomfortably. "Mammi, I might be single, but—"

"Oh, not you, Sol," Bridget said, and then she winced. "And I don't mean that as an insult, my dear boy, but you have your own challenges right now. No one is looking to you to take on a family. You can rest easy. They're considering your cousin—Johannes Miller."

"As long as I'm not the one being suggested," he said with a faint smile.

Elizabeth felt the blood leave her face. Johannes was not only Bridget's great-nephew and Solomon's second cousin but, more importantly, he was her younger sister's fiancé . . . or he had been until Lovina left.

"No, he's not free," Elizabeth said, and as soon as the words were out, she knew they were silly. Technically, he was very free, even if he was still in love with Lovina.

"I know that he and Lovina were engaged," Bridget said slowly. "But she's gone now, and he's left here in Bountiful. Is he supposed to stay single and mourn that relationship forever?"

"No, but—" Elizabeth licked her lips. "When she comes back—and I'm sure she will—"

Elizabeth knew it sounded feeble, but they were all hoping that Lovina would change her mind and come home and everything could be set right again. With Johannes single, that still seemed possible.

"Lovina and Johannes got engaged?" Solomon interjected, and both Elizabeth and Bridget turned toward him. "Mamm didn't tell me that . . . Mammi, you didn't either."

"We thought that family gossip might . . . hurt," Bridget replied. She adjusted her glasses. "It felt cruel to rub your cousin's happiness in your face. And then she left him and went English, so the wedding was off. There was nothing to tell."

Elizabeth looked down as Bridget and her grandson exchanged a long look.

"Johannes told me personally that if she came back, he'd be willing to marry her still—" Elizabeth said.

"I think the bishop sees what a good man Johannes is," Bridget said. "He's stable, he's helping his *daet* run the dairy farm, he's pious and has a good heart . . ."

"And he's in love with my sister still!" Elizabeth retorted. "What if Lovina comes back?"

Bridget was quiet for a moment. "I don't know. It wasn't my idea."

"But the bishop told you about it," she said.

"He wanted my opinion," she replied. "We all know what a kind, gentle man Johannes is. He's got such a big heart and he's wonderful with *kinner*. It takes a special sort to take on a whole family. And Sovilla is a good match for him, actually. She's kind and sweet. She's a good mother and she's very devout. She's an excellent cook, too. Johannes could do worse."

"Is the bishop bringing it up to him?" Elizabeth asked.

"I think so." Bridget paused. "I'm sorry, dear. I didn't mean to upset you. I know that Johannes has almost been a part of your family. I didn't realize that you were still . . . holding out hope."

"He's in love with Lovina still," Elizabeth said firmly. "And I don't think that fact would make for a happy marriage, no matter how good this woman is."

Bridget nodded. "I see the point."

Not that it mattered what Bridget thought. She was only the relater of news. If the bishop thought that Johannes was a good match for this young widow, he and the elders would bring it up. And while Elizabeth knew that Johannes wasn't really theirs, letting him go felt like letting go of Lovina, too.

Bridget sighed. "I thought I'd go lay down and have a little rest, if you two don't mind."

"No, that's fine," Elizabeth said. "I'll get started on some bread while you sleep."

"Would you?" Bridget said, and she gave a hopeful smile. "It is such a relief to have you here, Elizabeth. Thank you. I hope there aren't hard feelings between us, dear—"

"Of course not," Elizabeth replied. "It was just a surprise. That's all."

As Bridget went slowly up the stairs, Elizabeth caught Solomon's eyes locked on her.

"You still think your sister will come back," Solomon said.

"Yah, I do," Elizabeth replied. "She left because of—" She stopped, and tears misted her eyes. Was she still going to try to hide the truth to protect her own pride? "—my father."

"I overheard the old women talking about it," he replied.

She nodded, swallowing back the rising tears. "She left because of that."

"What did your *daet* do?" he asked. "I can't imagine him breaking any law. . . ."

Elizabeth's chest tightened and she turned away. She

hadn't believed he was guilty for the longest time either, until he'd confessed it himself in a letter.

"He helped some *Englishers* defraud our community with a bogus charity fund," she said. She glanced toward him, waiting for a response.

Solomon stood there watching her, his brows furrowed. "Seriously? Why would he do that? He was a preacher— he was Amish. Stealing from his own neighbors?"

"Why would *you* be involved in a robbery?" she shot back.

It was the old protectiveness. She'd been defending her *daet* for so long now . . . Solomon didn't answer her. He just watched her warily.

"My *daet* was angry," she said with a sigh. "Before my *mamm* died of cancer, he went to the community for more money for some treatments that might have helped her. The community turned him down. So he'd carried that grudge."

"So he got revenge?" Solomon eyed her, the disbelief in his voice. It was ironic that of all people, Solomon could be shocked by this.

"He didn't start out wanting to defraud everyone. He was tricked into it by *Englishers* claiming to have investments that would benefit us, and when he found out what he was involved in, he didn't stop."

Solomon was silent.

"He was sentenced to three years in prison," she added, her voice tight.

"So when you were asking about prison out there"— he jutted his chin toward the garden— "that was because of your *daet*. Not me."

Shame flooded through her. He'd opened up to her,

and it wasn't because of her worries for him. "Uh . . . yah. He was on my mind."

"Right." He nodded.

"You'd know better than any of us what my father is experiencing right now," she said. "No one else knows! *I* don't know! We get his letters, but he won't say what he's going through. Mostly, he just preaches at us like he always did . . . Solomon, how else do I find out if he's okay?"

"You visit him?" Solomon's voice was sharp and she froze. "That might be a start."

"I can't," she breathed.

"No, the Amish don't like visiting prisons," he said bitterly.

"It's just that—" She sucked in a breath. She didn't want to visit him there. She couldn't see her *daet* like that—humbled so low. And she didn't want to see the shame in his eyes. "I write him letters, though."

They both fell silent and Elizabeth turned toward the kitchen and pulled down a bin of flour. She didn't need Solomon's judgment, too. No, she hadn't visited her father. She'd hardly forgiven him.

"Those old women don't trust you, you know," Solomon said.

She felt her face heat. "I know. No one does anymore. People judge us by our *daet*."

"They think you'll rob my *mammi*," he added. "That was their main concern this time around."

Elizabeth froze, her heart speeding up in her chest. No matter how many times she came up against this, she felt the same surge of anger. She couldn't defend herself.

It wasn't about *her* good reputation, it was about her father. And she couldn't defend him either.

"I wouldn't do that," she said sharply. "I'm not my father."

She pulled down a bowl, then reached for the yeast. Her hands were trembling and she tried to still them.

"They think I will, too, for that matter," he said.

"But you did something to lose their trust," she said bitterly. "I didn't. That's the difference."

Elizabeth spooned some dried yeast into the bowl and added a teaspoon of sugar. She didn't need to think to make bread. Her hands knew the work. So today, she would bake bread and sustain a home. That was what a good woman did, and Elizabeth would go through the motions of being a good woman. The community's opinion was a powerful drive. She would do the things that calmed a good, Amish woman, even if they failed to calm her.

Solomon watched Elizabeth as she worked. Her cheeks were flushed and she moved with careful certainty—measuring cups full of flour and using a butter knife to smooth the top of each cup to a perfectly flat finish before she dumped it into the bowl.

"I didn't do it, you know," he said.

Her gaze flickered up toward him. "What?"

"The robbery. I didn't do it."

She frowned and paused, the cup measurer in one hand and the butter knife in the other. "My *daet* said he was innocent for a long time, too. I've heard those stories before."

Somehow it mattered to him that she believe him. He wasn't the man she thought.

Solomon shook his head. "So, you don't care if I did it or not."

"How could you be arrested, charged, found guilty, and put in jail for something you never did?" She turned back to measuring flour. "This is one thing I've been through before."

"I was caught up with some bad people, but I'd never been involved in anything like that before. They asked me to meet them at a certain intersection, and when they got there, they jumped in the car and told me to drive. That was it."

"Then you could have told people that," she said.

"I did." He shot her an annoyed look. "And they didn't believe me. You probably don't either, but it's the truth. I had no idea I was helping them escape after a robbery. I had no idea they were armed that night."

"Did you know they had guns at all?" she asked.

"Yah . . . but some people have them. We Amish have guns for hunting. *Englishers* do, too. Sometimes they collect guns, or they use them at a gun range. It's perfectly legal to own a firearm."

She was silent for a moment, the large bowl of flour in front of her, and she very gently lay down the measuring cup on the counter with a soft click.

"Every action is a choice," she said slowly, but as the words came out, her confidence rose. "You made a hundred choices that got you there and I won't be feeling sorry for you because you didn't know that the one time they were going further. You should have pulled away when you saw weapons that were more than hunting rifles. You should have pulled away when you saw their character!"

Advice about English living from an Amish girl who'd

never been past the fence. This all sounded very good to her, didn't it? It wasn't so cut-and-dried on the other side.

"Have you been alone out there?" he asked. "Do you know what it's like to live English, to be the odd one out all the time? Do you know how lonely it is?"

"No," she admitted. "I don't. But if it was so bad, you should have come home! It isn't like you didn't have that option!"

She turned away, then reached for a smaller bowl. She pulled a wire basket of eggs toward her and cracked three into the bowl, then started to whisk. She didn't stop— didn't slow down. And watching her reminded him of all the things he'd missed most all those years away. The absolute certainty the Amish had—an answer to everything. He missed feeling right about everything, too. Funny, how there was no going back with things like that.

"I couldn't just come back after that fight with my *mamm*," he said. "We both said things, and . . . it wasn't that simple."

"You're here now." She looked up, her gaze locking defiantly onto his.

"And my mother isn't," he replied. "She came to see me in prison three times, and the last visit was to cut me off. To tell me she was done with me."

Elizabeth blinked at that, then she shook her head. "You still came home. . . ."

But she had no idea how much courage it had taken to come, even now. He watched as she poured the wet ingredients into the dry and began to mix, and as the wooden spoon moved round and round, she kept her gaze locked on the bowl.

"What is my *daet* going through?" she asked, and she looked up.

Her concern wasn't for him, or for his traumatic experiences behind bars, but she looked at him so dismally that he felt a tug toward her anyway.

"It's scary," he said quietly. "You're scared all the time. Because the guards keep order generally, but they don't catch all the little things that happen. There's always someone to knock you down or punch you, and there's always some threat or other. The inmates make weapons of their own, so if someone who has no hope of getting out gets angry with you, he'll use it on you. What does he have to lose?"

Elizabeth swallowed. "You said you went to church there, though—"

"Yah," he said. "It was the safest place, a worship service. I didn't care who was putting it on, I'd be there. But it was also the place where a lot of drug handoffs happened. Even a worship service wasn't untainted. You get so that you miss having just one innocent, unblemished thing in your life."

Her stirring slowed. "Did you eat okay?" Her voice shook with that question.

"Sometimes," he said. "When you get used to things, your appetite comes back. But then there's always someone who wants what's on your tray, and you've got to decide what you want more—peace or your pudding cup."

"What did you want more?" she asked, her voice catching.

"Depended on the day," he replied. "Sometimes you're hungry enough to fight for your meal."

"My *daet* wouldn't fight," she said, shaking her head.

"You don't know that," he said. "It's not the same as here. There were things I'd fight for in prison that I'd never even raise my voice for here in Bountiful. There's no desperation here."

"What is our faith if it ends at the edges of the farm?" she said, her gaze clouding.

"It's not faith that ends," he said. "But your ideals get rather shaken."

He looked around the kitchen—at the clean, polished wooden table, the solid chairs pushed in underneath it. The kitchen was neat and tidy, the only clutter on the counter that of the dishes required to make bread. She had never experienced anything but order and plenty. Food was healing in a place like this. Food in prison was not.

Elizabeth finished mixing with the spoon and then poured some oil into her hands and began working the dough with her fingers. Her hands were slim and pale, and he caught himself watching her, mesmerized.

"Is it all punishment and fear?" she asked, looking up, her eyes filled with pleading. She wanted hope now. She wanted him to make her feel better.

"No, it's not all bad," he said quietly. "You learn to value the little things. You look forward to things like cherry pie, and lemonade, and the sound of cattle lowing on a warm summer morning. You're thankful for the small things, like a new undershirt, or a new comb, or the sound of rain pattering against glass. Prison changes you—it's like pickling a cucumber. You can't undo the ways it changes you. But that's not all bad either."

She continued to work the dough, kneading it, rolling it, kneading some more. She worked methodically, and he watched her in silence. Then she pulled her hands free and poured a little more oil into her fingers, rubbing the dough from them, and patting the pieces back onto the ball of dough in the bowl.

"Are you different now?" she asked. Her hands stilled and she fixed him with that dark gaze of hers.

"Yah. Very."

She put a clean, white towel over the bowl and then headed to the sink. She turned on the water, and he watched her as she washed her hands. She was slim, and a tendril of chocolate-brown hair fell down her neck, drawing his gaze. Prison made a man dream of simple things. . . .

Elizabeth opened a cupboard. "Solomon?"

"Yah." His voice sounded tight.

"Could you reach the baking stone down for me?"

It would be a flat disk made of stone that the *Englishers* used to make pizza, and it gave a nice base for loaves of bread, too. He knew what she was talking about, and he headed around the counter to her side and looked up. It was just out of her reach, and it would be heavy. He stretched and pulled it from the shelf and lowered it to the counter. She was close to him—so close he could make out the soft scent of her shampoo and he could see a faint dusting of flour on the tip of her nose.

"Thank you," she said.

He reached out and brushed the flour from her nose with one finger, and she pulled back in surprise.

"Flour," he said.

"Oh . . ." She smiled faintly.

"Are you scared of me?" he asked.

She didn't answer at first, and his stomach dropped, but then she shrugged.

"You're rather English now," she said. "Look at you—

you even look English. And an Amish man wouldn't do that. . . ."

"Touch you," he said.

"Yah." Her cheeks pinked.

"Okay," he said, taking a step back. "I'll cut that out. I just wanted to make sure that you knew I'm not a dangerous man. I know I'm telling you stories that probably scare you."

"A little," she admitted. "But I did ask."

She lifted her shoulders, and he saw veiled humor in her eyes. He wasn't sure why he was trying to explain himself to Lizzie Yoder, of all people, and it wasn't just because she was in front of him either. But even if she disagreed with him, or even disliked him, he didn't want her to be afraid of him. He'd faced enough of that in prison. Part of surviving had been acting tough and he didn't want to do that anymore.

"I'm not someone you have to worry about, you know," he said. "Yah, I did something wrong. I probably won't be able to make a life here, but I'm"—he cast around for a word to describe himself now—"I'm safe."

Elizabeth's gaze flickered up at him, and for just a moment he saw the swirling uncertainty in those deep, brown eyes. Her lips parted, and he couldn't help but catch his breath. She was beautiful . . .

"I'm not scared of you, Solomon Lantz," she said.

He let out a careful breath, not wanting to betray his own relief at those words. "Good. That's what I wanted to hear."

"But I'll feel better around you when you're in some proper Amish clothes," she added.

He looked down at himself with a rueful smile. He was wearing the same thing he'd worn yesterday—he'd washed out the shirt in the sink and hung it in his room overnight. There had been a few pants and shirts left from before he'd gone English, but they were far too small now. He'd outgrown so many things that he'd left behind, his clothes were the least of it.

"I'll be sure to find some," he said.

She smiled at that. "I've got some cooking to do now."

"Yah. All right." She was booting him out—that was how women got people out of their kitchens. "I'll go wash the buggy. It looks like no one has done that in a year."

He'd easily find ways to stay useful while he was here, but he still found himself oddly drawn to the preacher's daughter, who'd always rebuffed him. Maybe he wanted a bit of respect, some acknowledgment of what he'd endured.

Or maybe he just wanted some human connection.

Chapter Four

Elizabeth was already in the kitchen starting breakfast the next morning when Solomon came downstairs, shirtless. She looked over her shoulder, and when she saw his bare chest and stomach, both well-muscled, and his abs flat and his shoulders and arms bulky with strength, she felt the heat hit her face. She turned again quickly—seeing him like this wasn't proper.

He wore his jeans again, and outside the side door, flapping on the clothesline, was that T-shirt Elizabeth had hand washed for him. She'd forgotten to bring it up and leave it by his bedroom door. It had slipped her mind.

"Just getting my shirt," he said.

"Yah." She allowed herself one quick look as he headed for the side door. He was no longer that skinny, teenaged boy who used to pester her. Now he was a hefty man, muscular, with jeans that rode a little too low on his hips.

It wasn't modest, but in his defense, he did look embarrassed.

Solomon came back inside, pulling his shirt down as he did, and he stopped at the kitchen table.

"So, we're going to Seth Stuckey's farm today?" Solomon asked.

They'd discussed the plans last night. The Stuckeys were sending flowers to be sold at the roadside stand along with the Lantz produce, so Elizabeth and Solomon would go to pick up the load of freshly cut flowers in buckets of treated water to keep them fresh, and bring them back in time to open the produce stand for the first time that year.

"Yah," Elizabeth said. "They'll be expecting us. Well, they'll be expecting me more precisely, but all the same."

"Who is Seth married to?" Solomon asked.

"Jodie Beachy," she replied. "They have three *kinner* now—two boys and a girl."

Solomon nodded. "Good for him. Jodie is a surprise. Wasn't she the skinny girl who giggled all the time?"

"She grew up," Elizabeth said. "She's not the girl you remember."

Jodie was now a sweet, quiet mother with a house of her own to use up her energy and a husband to cook for. She wasn't a fluttery girl anymore—she was a wife and a *mamm*. None of them were the same people they were five years ago. Life had changed the young people of Bountiful as much as it had changed Solomon. He'd hardened—physically and in other, deeper ways, too, which she wasn't sure was good news. It seemed more like emotional scar tissue in Solomon than strength.

"Maybe Seth will lend you some clothes," Elizabeth said. "And we'll get your grandmother's roadside stand started up today. There's a lot more traffic lately—the *Englishers* are waiting for the produce stands, I think."

Solomon nodded. "Yah. Back into the routine, right?"

She wasn't sure if he was glad for it or not, but work didn't wait for people's emotions. That was part of the sanctity of Amish work—it kept them all moving, growing, and healing, even if they wanted to indulge themselves. The work didn't wait; self-indulgence wasn't possible.

After breakfast, Bridget said she'd clean up. Elizabeth and Solomon had to make it to the Stuckey farm and back before nine.

"I'm sure Seth will be glad to see you, Sol," Bridget said, but her tone was just a shade too bright. She had doubts, it seemed. And so did Elizabeth, for that matter. The whole community would be shocked to see Solomon again, especially in his *Englisher* clothes, looking every inch the ex-con he was.

"Don't worry, Mammi," Solomon said, bending to kiss his grandmother's cheek. "It'll be fine."

Apparently, Solomon saw through Bridget's cheeriness, too, and Bridget adjusted her glasses—a nervous habit.

"Where does he live now?" Solomon asked.

"At his parents' place," Elizabeth said. "His *daet* passed on. His *mamm* and *mammi* live with him and his wife."

"Just down the road," he said.

"Yah."

"Let's go, then," he replied, and he pulled out a straw hat and tucked it under his arm. It was one of his old ones, it would seem, and Elizabeth glanced at it but didn't say anything.

They headed out to hitch up the buggy, and a few minutes later they were on their way, the horses clopping along cheerfully enough, the wagon wheels crunching over the gravel-strewn road.

The day was already heating up, and Elizabeth plucked her dress away from her body, trying to get a little extra ventilation. Solomon caught her eyeing his hat and gave her a grin.

"I missed a proper hat. The *Englishers* don't know what they're missing in having something to shade your eyes, as well as your neck."

She smiled at that. "You're enjoying being back."

"Yah." He flicked the reins, but the horses didn't speed up at all. They had one speed and they didn't tend to vary from it.

"What are your plans?" Elizabeth asked.

"After this visit home?" he asked.

"Is this still a visit?" she asked.

He shrugged. "I need to find work. In prison, I was learning about engines. I figured I might be able to be a mechanic."

She felt her earlier optimism wane. "You don't mean for generators, do you?"

"No, I mean for cars," he said. "There's a living to be made that way, and it takes a keen mind and being good with your hands."

"What do you know about car engines?" she asked.

"Not enough, but that doesn't mean I can't learn it," he said. "Does it?"

She sighed. Still the rebel.

"What are your plans?" he asked.

"Uh—" She hesitated. "I want to gain the community's

trust again. I want to get married, have some *kinner*, and raise them well."

She wanted to start over, away from here. She wanted to go somewhere else where they didn't know her *daet*, where no one had had their finances drained by him. But she couldn't tell anyone that. A fresh start had to be kept under wraps until she was ready to make her move.

"Is that going to happen here?" he asked. Too perceptive.

She felt a surge of annoyance. "I don't know, I can hope."

"Your *daet* did something bad, and people aren't going to forget it. Are you willing to stay and just shoulder the burden of being his daughter?" he asked.

"I don't have much choice at present," she replied. She'd have left already if it weren't for her sister's disappearance. She couldn't quite bring herself to leave town without knowing Lovina was okay. It felt like abandoning her.

"Yah, you do have a choice," he countered. "There is a whole world out there, you know. There are schools and jobs and communities. There are other ways to live a good life—"

That sounded a little too tempting coming in his bass tones, and she didn't like that. Who had tempted him to leave the safety of their Amish life?

"Is that coming from your prison chaplain?" she asked, hearing the bitterness in her own voice. "Going English didn't work out so well for you. If you're going to go somewhere, it has to be with Gott's blessing or you'll only end up with more trouble."

"I'm not saying you should leave the Amish life or that

you should stay," he replied, his voice low. "I'm saying you may have more options than you think."

Ironically, Elizabeth was only too aware of that. She did have other options if she was willing to leave Bountiful. She wasn't mired here, but she'd have to make her move before it was too late. She couldn't waste too much time. . . .

The Stuckey farm was a few yards ahead, and she glanced over at Solomon to see if he'd noticed. His gaze was already locked on the old mailbox. The horses carried them down the twisting drive that led to the farmhouse. The barn was down a hill from the main house and the greenhouse was right next to it, the summer sunlight glinting off the glass. The Stuckeys had a large vegetable garden, but their summer flower garden was larger still, row upon row of long-stemmed flowers that were sold in the *Englisher* flower shop in town. The floral scent drifted along the breeze toward them, and when they came around the turn, Elizabeth could see the white buckets of paper-wrapped floral bouquets waiting for them by the house.

Jodie opened the side door, an armload of more bouquets in her arms. She smiled a hello and bent to drop the flowers into the waiting buckets, jostling the bouquets to make room for just a few more.

"They're ready to go," Jodie called, and when she straightened and her gaze landed on Solomon, Elizabeth saw her stiffen.

"How many bouquets altogether?" Elizabeth asked, hopping down from the buggy. "I'll keep track of the sales to pay you the proceeds."

Seth came around the side of the house, two older boys

trailing after him. These were Seth's nephews, come to help and learn the work. Seth straightened his shoulders and headed in Solomon's direction.

"He's back, is he?" Jodie asked softly when Elizabeth reached her.

"Yah." Elizabeth glanced over her shoulder. The men were shaking hands; then Solomon pushed his thumbs into his jeans pockets. Amish men didn't have pockets, so it made him look even more English.

"And Bridget is letting him stay?" Jodie asked, raising her eyebrows. "My husband's grandmother tried to warn her. Sol might have dangerous friends, and now that he's out of jail, they might be inclined to look him up."

"Bridget is a woman who knows her mind," Elizabeth said. "And she knows her heart. She loves her grandson and wants him to have a chance."

"Hmm." Jodie crossed her arms under her breasts. Funny, Elizabeth seemed to be the lesser of their worries with Solomon here to distract them.

"Did he see your *daet* in jail?" Jodie asked after a beat of silence.

Elizabeth felt her face heat up. "Different prisons."

"Oh." Jodie nodded. "Well . . . just as well."

Elizabeth didn't know what she meant by that and she wasn't going to ask. Instead, she opted to change the subject. "Did you hear about the death in Edson?" she asked.

"Rueben Miller?" Jodie said.

"Did you know him?" Elizabeth asked.

Jodie's face pinked and she shrugged. "A little. He was nice. I spent some time in Edson before Seth started courting me, and . . . I got to know him."

Some time in Edson . . . yes, Elizabeth remembered

that. Jodie had never been considered beautiful and she'd wanted to get married. So she'd done the exact thing Elizabeth was planning for herself: she'd gone to see if she might have better luck a little farther from home. Jodie hadn't; she'd come home after a year away, still single. But in that year, Seth's serious girlfriend had broken up with him, and Jodie's compassion had been perfectly timed.

"Was Rueben a boyfriend?" Elizabeth asked, lowering her voice.

"We got to know each other, but there were no promises," Jodie said. "I was looking for a husband. He was looking for a wife. He took me home for a couple of months. That was all."

"Yah." Elizabeth nodded quickly. It seemed to be that easy for other people, but it never had been for her. She'd never had a boyfriend and she'd certainly never talked marriage compatibility with a man before.

"I'm sad to hear of his death," Jodie said softly. "Rueben was such a good man."

"I hear they need to find a husband for his widow," Elizabeth said. Maybe Jodie had heard more—maybe there were other available men for Sovilla Miller to consider besides Johannes.

"Yah," Jodie said with a nod. "They'll need to find her someone. Two little girls to feed and clothe, and Sovilla's still young. She could have another five *kinner* easily enough. And she comes from a good family. Her *daet* is really well-respected in Edson."

Elizabeth licked her lips and dropped her gaze.

"Oh, you know what I mean," Jodie said, seeming to sense that she'd said too much. "But I also know that

Rueben was only starting his fencing business. He left behind some debt and not much else. It's not like Seth. If something happened to him, I'd still be provided for. Sovilla's in trouble."

"She'll find something," Elizabeth said. "We all sort something out."

Jodie smiled faintly. "You will, too."

Giggling, chattering, skinny, and too pale—Jodie hadn't been the pick of the marriage market, but she'd landed a good husband anyway. Elizabeth had thought she could afford to wait and find the best man she could. She wasn't so sure anymore.

"I don't know why you turned down Oliver Wagler," Jodie added. "He has a good business, and he's honest, too."

"He's almost sixty," Elizabeth said. "And he didn't propose."

"He was asking about you, though," Jodie said. "We all know what that means, especially to a man of his generation."

But Elizabeth hadn't responded favorably to his "asking about." Her brother, Isaiah, asked her what she thought, and she'd told him plainly. Her brother would have cleaned up her answer before he passed it on, but Oliver stopped asking around. He married a widow closer to his own age from a nearby community. An old man who'd been widowed twice seemed to be the best option Elizabeth could get right now, and given that choice, she would rather stay single.

Seth and Solomon went past them into the house, and Jodie nodded in that direction, too.

"I have to help Edith clean up, if you want to chat until

they're done," Jodie said, and then she called to her own younger *kinner* who were playing by the garden. "Don't touch the flowers, now, boys!"

Elizabeth followed Jodie up the stairs. Jodie didn't seem to mind Elizabeth so much. Perhaps it was just the relationship between two women of the same age where one of them had obviously come out on top. Jodie didn't see a threat in Elizabeth—not anymore at least. Jodie had it all; she could afford to let a few crumbs fall from her table.

"Lots of *Englishers* on the roads today," Jodie commented. "Hopefully, with some blessing, the sales will be good."

Elizabeth followed Jodie into the house. Edith was in the kitchen, standing at the sink washing a load of dishes. The kitchen table was cluttered with rolls of brown paper to wrap the flowers. Edith rapped on the window over the sink and shook a finger.

"Out of the flowers, Nathan!" Edith called to her great-grandson through the glass.

"Good morning," Elizabeth said, casting a smile in Edith's direction, and Edith eyed her back distrustfully.

This was Elizabeth's life now . . . so different from a couple of years ago, when she had options as the daughter of a prominent preacher.

"So tell me how you all are doing," Jodie said, casting her a smile. "How's Bethany and the baby?"

The conversation would turn to other people—ones who had succeeded in starting their own families, the ones with "news." One day, Elizabeth hoped to join their ranks, but it wouldn't happen easily, and it likely wouldn't happen here.

"Moses is growing so fast," Elizabeth said. She knew the kind of conversation required of her. "He's so big and strong. And Bethany has recovered well from the birth . . ."

Solomon was right—there were other places where she could forge a life for herself, and in moments like this one, her escape couldn't come soon enough.

Solomon stood in the upstairs hallway of the Stuckey farmhouse, listening to the soft murmur of female voices below. It was polite chitchat, and he could make out Elizabeth's voice in the mix and found himself trying to make out her words. He couldn't, though . . .

He felt foolish standing here in someone else's upstairs hallway, waiting for charity, but he didn't have much choice right now.

"This should work," Seth said, coming out of the bedroom he shared with his wife. He had some clothes in his hands. "The pants are a little worn. I'm sorry about that. But one of the shirts is new. My wife just made it."

So generous. Too generous. Seth was the irritatingly perfect Amish man, it seemed.

"No," Solomon said. "Don't give me the new shirt. If you would part with an old one, I'd be grateful."

"You should have something nice for service Sunday," Seth said.

"I'm not going to service Sunday!" Solomon bit back a bitter laugh. "Thank you for your kindness, Seth, but a couple of pants and shirts would be enough. And nothing your wife has just painstakingly sewn for you. I just need something to get me started so I can get a job. I'll make it up to you."

Seth nodded and pulled the top shirt from the pile, handing the rest over. "I hope they fit."

"They'll be fine. Thank you." Solomon accepted the clothes. They felt clean and smelled like laundry soap and sunshine from a line dry.

"If there's anything else I can do to help you out, just let me know," Seth said.

"Actually—" Solomon licked his lips. "I—uh—I need a job."

Seth froze for a second, then cleared his throat. "If I hear of someone hiring, I'll pass it along."

"Do you have any hired labor here?" Solomon asked.

"Yah, but—" Seth cleared his throat. "I don't need more."

"Even with harvest coming up?" Solomon pressed. "Normally, there are some seasonal hires, right? I know the work. I can harvest corn and build shocks as good as anyone. I'm better than an *Englisher*, right?"

Seth looked toward the stairs but didn't answer.

"Have you hired your seasonal work yet?" Solomon pressed. He doubted he would have. It was only the end of July. There were still two or three weeks before that hiring started, and if Solomon could count on an income then, he could find something small in between times.

Seth glanced back, then looked away. "I can't hire you, Sol. I'm sorry."

"Why not?" Solomon asked. "You know me!"

"You've got a criminal record—"

"Yah, but I'm back. And I'm not some stranger out of prison. I'm your old friend."

"'Friend' is a strong word," Seth replied, and his tone firmed. "We knew each other. We haven't been close since we were *kinner*. And I certainly didn't go English with you."

He could feel the heat in his face. Did Seth want him to beg? "I'm not a danger, Seth. I made some mistakes and I've learned from them. I got caught up with the wrong people—"

"I have a family, Sol!" Seth's voice rose, and the women's voices downstairs suddenly hushed. Seth lowered his voice again. "The answer is no. I'll give you clothes. I'll give you food if you need it. But I can't give you a job. That's where I draw the line."

They were silent for a few beats, and Solomon searched the other man's face. Seth rubbed a hand through his beard and averted his gaze. Seth didn't trust him around his home and around his children. Maybe he was worried about Jodie, too. Who knew? Did they really think he'd hurt people? Did they think he'd be stupid enough to bring old associations back to Bountiful?

"Right," Solomon said gruffly.

"Wait—you'll need suspenders," Seth said.

"I have some at home," Solomon replied. "I'm fine."

"Okay, well . . ."

"Thanks all the same," Solomon said, forcing the words out. Being humble when a man had everything he needed was easy. Ducking his head and being humble when he was already desperate was a different feeling entirely.

Solomon headed down the stairs first and emerged into the kitchen. The women all looked up at him, and the side door opened, the *kinner* coming back inside at the same moment.

"We'd best get back," Solomon said to Elizabeth, and she immediately stood up from the chair at the table where she'd been sitting. Was she as uncomfortable as he was? Hard to tell, but he wanted to get out of here—away from the humiliation.

"Bridget says to thank you for the flowers, and we'll be sure to keep track of the sales and bring you the money," Elizabeth said.

"Be sure you do," Edith said quietly, and Solomon saw the pink bloom in Elizabeth's cheeks.

"Do you think my grandmother would shortchange you?" Solomon snapped. "Or are you wondering if Elizabeth and I might?"

Edith didn't answer. She didn't have to. Everyone knew exactly what she'd meant.

"Let's go." Elizabeth put a hand on his arm and pushed him in the direction of the side door. Her hand was gentle but insistent. At least they were together in this—both of them being looked down on. Though there was small comfort in that.

"Thank you for selling them for us," Seth said. "We're always glad to work with neighbors—" The words seemed to evaporate in his mouth.

Solomon shot Seth a quick glance as he reached the door, and Seth looked away.

"I'll help you load up the flowers," Seth said quickly.

Solomon erupted into the sunlight, Elizabeth so close behind him that he felt the rustle of her dress against his jeans. He'd honestly thought that Seth would give him a job, just for old times' sake if nothing else. If Seth could look him in the face and offer clothes, he didn't think that a job was too much to ask.

Solomon and Seth loaded up the buckets into the back of the buggy, pushing some old blankets between the last of the buckets so they wouldn't tip. Then Solomon hoisted himself up next to Elizabeth.

"Take care now," Seth said, hooking his thumbs behind his suspenders. Solomon didn't answer, and he flicked the reins, the horses easing the buggy forward and plodding up the drive. He glanced back once and saw Seth still standing there watching them with his arms crossed over his chest, as if he were standing guard, Jodie in the doorway behind him.

They headed up the drive, both Solomon and Elizabeth in silence until they turned onto the road.

"You could have been more polite," Elizabeth said. "Seth did give you clothes, after all. And you never know—he might hire you."

"I asked for a job," Solomon said. "He said no."

Elizabeth glanced over at him. "Oh. I'm sorry."

"Whatever." He didn't want her pity either. "They insulted you, too."

"Maybe I'm more used to it," she replied.

He shot her a veiled look, but Elizabeth was looking away from him, out at the Stuckeys' rippling fields of oats.

"And this is the life you want?" Sol asked incredulously. "Where old women question your trustworthiness?"

"No, it isn't." Her voice was low.

"But you're willing to accept it," he retorted.

"I'm not staying." Her voice was so low, he almost didn't catch it over the rattle of the buggy.

"What?" he said.

Elizabeth turned toward him. "I'm not stupid, Solomon. I'm not staying. But I'm not going English either. I want to find a job in an Amish community in Indiana, maybe. Or Oregon. Or Ohio. Far from the gossip. I want to start over."

"So why haven't you done it yet?" he asked.

"Because I'm waiting for my sister to come home!" She shot him an irritated look. "Or to write. Or something."

Solomon eyed her in surprise. Elizabeth had more bravery in her than he'd given her credit for. She had a plan after all.

"So you think I should stay but you're leaving?" he asked.

"I do think you should stay Amish," she said. "I want to leave Bountiful and you want to leave *everything*. I disagree that there are many ways to live a good life. You were born Amish, and the narrow path isn't easy, but it's necessary. It takes strength to live out our beliefs, but an Amish life doesn't have to be in Bountiful."

For her, maybe. Not for him. She hadn't spent time in prison.

"And what makes you think you'll find getting a job easier than it is for me?" he asked.

"Your grandmother can give me a reference," she replied. "And maybe the bishop will, too. He's really tried hard to help my brother and me since Daet was arrested. The bishop wants the young people to find a way to stay . . . and that includes us."

Right. She did have more support than he did.

"I don't think it includes me," he said.

"I think it does—" But she didn't sound confident in that.

"I didn't just jump the fence," he said. "I went a whole lot further."

Elizabeth was silent for a moment. He normally liked being right, but not this time. The bishop might hope to keep his young people in the community, but he wouldn't want to keep a man like Solomon. Solomon was a threat and he knew it.

"You have your grandmother," she said at last. "And when your *mamm* comes back—"

But he didn't want to talk about his mother right now. She wasn't much of a comfort at the moment.

"I'm fine," he interrupted. "Let's just set up the produce stand for my grandmother."

Solomon didn't need her to reassure him or point out what he did have. Elizabeth was still the girl who'd caught his eye . . . the one he'd teased just to be close to back in his more immature years. And she was still a step above him, even now, when they'd both hit rock bottom. Ironic, wasn't it? Even with her father in prison for defrauding the community, he was still less acceptable than Elizabeth Yoder was.

Did Solomon really need more humbling than he'd already endured? Wasn't Gott finished with that yet?

Chapter Five

Elizabeth helped Bridget and Solomon set up the produce stall that morning. The stand had a little shack attached to it where they could stand in the shade while waiting for customers. Outside the shack, there were slanted displays that held the fruits and vegetables, and some wooden bins to the side that held new potatoes and carrots.

Solomon, after he'd changed into his Amish clothing, did the heavy lifting of setting up the displays and unloading vegetables, and Elizabeth and Bridget set the produce out on the shelves and lined up the buckets of cut flowers so they could be seen from the road. Word would spread—the *Englishers* and their social media were a powerful combination.

Bridget hummed a hymn as she laid out some squash on the wooden display table. The squash were big and uniform this year, and Bridget's hands worked with practiced steadiness. Elizabeth glanced down the drive. Solomon was loading up some more baskets of vegetables into the wagon to bring up to the stand, and she watched him for a moment. He looked better now—more appropriate—but there was still something wild about him, even wearing some proper Amish clothes again.

Elizabeth carefully filled cardboard baskets with fresh tomatoes, the softest of which went on top. She worked quickly, and as Bridget arranged the squash, a car stopped and an *Englisher* woman came out with her wallet in one hand and a smile on her face.

"I'm so glad to see you opening up," she said. "We've been waiting for the Amish produce."

"Yah, it's that time," Bridget replied with a smile of her own. "What can I get you today?"

The sun was still low in the sky and shone golden across the nearby fields and warm on Elizabeth's back as she turned her attention to the cucumbers next. The *Englisher* woman bought two baskets of tomatoes and a bouquet of flowers with promises to return again the next day for more when she had more cash on her. She took a picture of their stall, and Elizabeth looked down uncomfortably while the phone was held in front of them.

"I'm just going to post this on Facebook. We have friends who've been waiting for the Amish roadside stands, too. They'll be glad to know you're open," the woman said.

"Thank you," Bridget said. "Spread the word. More is ripening every day, thank Gott."

"'Bye now," the woman called, and the car's tires crunched back up onto the road as she sped away. Elizabeth watched the car go, and Bridget's humming started up again.

This was a lovely life—Elizabeth never ceased to be thankful for the Amish community, for the Amish ways.

And yet how thankful would she be if she never did have a family of her own? At twenty-two, she wasn't quite an old maid yet, but soon . . .

The wagon came back up the drive, Solomon at the reins and the back of it filled with more produce to finish filling the stands. Hopefully, it would all sell this morning so nothing would wilt or wither in the afternoon heat. Solomon reined in the horses and hopped back down. He hoisted down a tub of potatoes and tossed some plastic bags on top of it. He worked efficiently, his muscles bulging with the effort, but she could see less of his imposing physique under the more modest Amish clothing he was now wearing. He looked more relatable this way—a white shirt rolled up to the elbows and a few more buttons open at the neck than was strictly proper, but it was still an improvement.

"This is the book for keeping track of how many bouquets you sell," Bridget said, pulling out a worn notebook. Elizabeth pulled her attention back to the old woman. A fresh page had the day's date at the top, and Bridget passed her a stubby pencil. "Don't sell them for less than the price the Stuckeys set, because we have to pay them back."

"Of course," Elizabeth said. "I'll make sure."

"This is the change pouch—" Bridget passed over a heavy, zippered canvas bag. "And come inside the shack so I can show you the box for the bills."

Elizabeth followed Bridget inside, and made note of the metal box the older woman pointed out.

"I'll come back in a couple of hours to pick up the money to bring back to the house so you don't have too much money out here at one time," Bridget said. "It's safer for you that way."

Elizabeth nodded.

"And thank you for helping me, Elizabeth," Bridget added with a smile. "I do appreciate it."

"It's a pleasure to be needed," Elizabeth replied, returning her smile.

"I'm going to head back to the house," Bridget said. "It's still washing day."

"I can help with that, too," Elizabeth said.

The old woman batted her hand. "It's fine. I'll get it done. I appreciate this."

They both went back outside the shack again, and Bridget carried on down the drive toward the house, her gait slow but steady. The horses nibbled at the tender roadside grass, and Solomon lifted down the last plastic tub of vegetables, this one only partway filled with beets.

Elizabeth glanced over at Solomon. His hat was cocked to one side to better shield his face from the low light.

"You look better in Amish clothes," she said.

Solomon looked over at her. "Less scary?"

She shrugged. "Yah. No one's really comfortable about the English, are they?"

Solomon's gaze rested on her for a few beats longer than was comfortable. A car pulled up to the stall, giving her an excuse to turn away.

This was an older couple, and they bought two heads of lettuce and eight baskets of tomatoes. The old woman chattered about the pasta sauce she'd make, and while she paid, Solomon helped her husband to put their purchased food into the trunk of the car. They drove on, and Elizabeth tucked away the zippered bag of change once more.

"Will you really leave here?" Solomon asked.

"Eventually," she replied.

He nodded. "I shouldn't be surprised, but I am. When I think of Bountiful, it includes you."

"It's not like you're planning to stay," she replied.

"I have less than you do to hold on to," he replied.

"Well, I want more than a house and a community—I want a family of my own," she said. "I want a husband."

It felt terribly brazen to say that to a man out loud, but Solomon didn't exactly fit into things here in Bountiful. He wasn't another Amish man following the same Amish social codes.

A smile tugged at Solomon's lips. "Yah, high time, young lady. You always were picky."

She rolled her eyes. "Because I wasn't encouraging you?"

He sobered. "You weren't encouraging anyone. No one could match your high standards. Even after your Rumspringa, I heard of three different men who asked you home from singing—and you turned them all down. When I'd come back to visit my cousins, they used to joke about it. You wanted a man who could preach like your *daet*, provide a comfortable farm for you to live on, be as handsome as Adam in the garden, and have a spotless reputation. Oh, and not ever have been married or engaged before either. No man could attain that."

Elizabeth eyed him for a moment. "You all talked about me?"

"Men talk, too," he said.

"If me not being interested was offensive," she said, "I don't really care. Being courted is serious. If I couldn't see myself marrying a man, I wasn't going to encourage it."

Solomon shrugged. "I don't have a right to tell you what you should want, but I can point out that men aren't perfect. Not one of us. That's just my humble opinion, for whatever it's worth."

But some men were better than others—some were *safer* than others. There were women who couldn't ask for much because they didn't offer much in character. But Elizabeth had been a woman who'd kept herself pure, who'd stayed to the narrow path. She'd put her focus into learning to cook and sew as best she could, because one day she'd have a family relying on her. It was the Amish way, and if she could ask for more in a husband, why wouldn't she? But she wasn't going to argue feminine standards with Solomon Lantz. What would he know about that?

"I don't need your opinions, Solomon," she said.

He eyed her for a moment, then angled his chin toward the buggy. "I'm going to bring the horses to pasture." He paused. "Are you mad at me for speaking my mind?"

"A little, yah," she said.

Solomon shrugged. "Okay. Well, I'm not apologizing. I meant what I said."

Anger simmered up inside her, but it only masked her deeper misgivings. She had been prideful in her youth—she knew that. And she'd lost everything when her father was arrested.

"I didn't do anything wrong, Solomon," she said, softening her tone. "My *daet* did, but I'm not him!"

"Even before your *daet*'s fall from grace, you weren't going to find that perfect man," Solomon replied. "And you can wander as far as you like—all the way to Oregon or Ohio, if you really want to. You won't find him, because a perfect man doesn't exist."

Solomon took the lead horse by the bridle and led them around until they were headed back in the direction of the stables.

"There are good men!" she called after him.

"Yah. You turned a lot of them down," he replied, then he hoisted himself back up into the seat and flicked the reins.

The empty wagon rattled down the drive toward the stable. What did he know about the kind of man she'd been waiting for? There were men who didn't want to rebel, and who longed for the same simple Amish life that she did. There were men who'd saved themselves, who had standards, too. But Solomon had always been rebellious and stubborn. He'd been the kind of teenager she'd known to steer clear of, and when he'd jumped the fence, she'd been proven right in that.

She knew what she wanted back then, and while life had certainly derailed her options here in Bountiful, her longing for a proper Amish home with a truly good man she could love with all her heart hadn't changed.

Would it happen now? Only Gott knew. But her hope wasn't dead yet.

A pickup truck came hurtling down the road toward her, music blasting out into the morning air, and Elizabeth watched it approach, her breath bated. She hated these fast drivers—whooping it up while they entertained themselves over the summer. It was dangerous.

The truck slowed as it passed the stand, and just when she thought it would carry on past, it suddenly screeched to a stop and started to reverse. Her heart skipped a beat and then pounded hard in her throat. She was alone out here, and she looked over her shoulder toward the house.

The windows were open and the truck, once red, was covered in mud. There were three young men in the cab, and the one nearest the window leaned out. The music was turned down, but it wasn't turned off, and the sound of it was like the shriek of metal, and the men seemed to be shouting out the song. It made her breath catch and she tried not to wince, but she wasn't sure she managed it.

"Hey, there."

"Hello," she said.

"You're cute," he said.

She didn't answer that, but she swallowed and eyed them warily.

"What're you selling?" The doors opened and all three men got out, the engine still running, the music still going, and her pulse sped up in response to it. They were dressed in blue jeans—a whole lot like the ones Solomon had been wearing until recently—but on them it looked different—more frightening. They wore T-shirts with ugly pictures on the front of skeletons and pain. The one who'd been talking to her wore a baseball cap on backward.

"Hey!" He raised his voice. "I said, what are you selling?"

She sucked in a breath.

"Don't you speak English?" he said, louder still, coming closer.

"Vegetables," she said, then cleared her throat. "I'm sure you aren't interested."

"What?" The second man was wearing a cowboy hat and he took it off, revealing sweaty hair, and then re-placed it. "I like vegetables. I like—" He reached out and picked up a head of lettuce with one dirty hand, then dropped it back in the bin with the others. "I like lettuce."

"Nah, you don't." The third one laughed. He was smaller than the other two. "When did you last eat salad?"

They came closer, fingering every vegetable in reach, and then the biggest man reached into the bucket of flowers and pulled out a bouquet. He slapped his friend on the chest with it and laughed. Elizabeth's gaze was locked on the bouquet—Bridget would owe the Stuckeys for every single bouquet that was lost—

"Hey, give me one!" The other man grabbed another bouquet, and her heart sank. She needed out of here— she needed help! She moved out of the shade of the stand. If she could just get clear, she'd run. The men seemed to have lost interest in her for the time being as they laughed and beat each other with the flowers until petals were scattered over the dusty ground and the stems hung limp and bruised, then they tossed them on the ground.

Elizabeth slipped out from under the shelter, but just as she got out into the sunlight, she found the largest man blocking her path. He smelled of sweat, sausage, and the sour smell of alcohol, and he spat on the ground in front of her. He'd been drinking early.

"Where are you going?" he growled.

With every panicked beat, her heart sent up a wordless prayer. Elizabeth stared at him, then lunged to the side, but she wasn't fast enough. The big man's meaty hand slapped down on her wrist and she let out a cry of pain.

"I said, where are you going?" he demanded. "We aren't done here yet."

Solomon pulled the brush down the horse's flank as the big stallion swung his weight from one hoof to another. It was hot inside the stable, but once the horses were brushed, he'd send them out into the open air and finish cleaning out the stalls.

He'd meant what he said to Elizabeth—she never had been realistic, and she'd been so filled with pride for her preacher *daet* that she'd seen herself as above pretty much every available man in Bountiful. She never could acknowledge her own pride either, because pride was perhaps the worst sin for an Amish person. The Amish were humble people . . . but there were some Amish who were humbler than others. It wasn't irritation that she'd never been interested in him either. He'd been rebellious and full of attitude. Frankly, he didn't blame her. But she should have moved on with a decent man and started that family. Her own pride had held her back and he could see that plain as his own boots.

In the distance, a blast of heavy metal music filled the air. He straightened and listened, and the music suddenly dropped. It didn't die away like the vehicle had driven off either, it just disappeared. Like the driver had flicked the knob and turned it down.

He put the comb onto a window ledge and opened the stable's sliding back door. The stallion plodded out into the sunshine, and Solomon watched him go, then listened again. He couldn't make out music, but he heard a high-pitched cry that broke off suddenly, and he didn't have to process another thought. He broke into a run through the corral, jumped the fence, and headed up the drive toward the sound of that cry.

Solomon spotted the men before he saw Elizabeth. One was looming over her—the biggest of the three by far. He was huge—a mountain of a man—and if this were prison, Solomon might rethink it. But prison had taught him a few skills he hadn't thought he'd have to use again quite this quickly.

"Hey!" Solomon barked as he reached the road.

The men turned, the biggest one looking him up and down with a glance of disdain. He had one meaty hand on Elizabeth's arm, and she looked so pale he was worried she might pass out.

"You okay, Lizzie?" he said, his voice low.

She didn't answer, but she sucked in a breath, and Solomon realized that the man's grip on her was tightening. Talking wasn't going to fix this one, and prison had one rule when facing down a bully and his cronies: beat up the biggest one and the others would back off.

And the big one was probably going to kill him if he managed to get a punch back . . . Surprise would have to work for him, because if he didn't act now, he'd lose his advantage.

Without another word, Solomon launched himself at the man, slamming a boot into the side of his knee, catching him by surprise and knocking him off-balance. There was a crack, and the man shouted in pain and went down.

Logic faded away and Solomon was left with the pounding of his own blood in his ears and the deafening certainty that he wasn't letting this animal touch Lizzie again. His body knew what to do—and this brute had never faced the kind of thing Solomon had faced again and again when he was behind bars. This idiot had size—Solomon had experience.

His fists slammed into the man's dense face, and when one of the smaller men came at him, he stood up and grabbed the man's throat, pulling him forward and then slamming him back so that he hit the ground with a gasp and a thud as his breath went whooshing out of him. Solomon planted a knee in the center of the man's chest, and he was about to start the same process on the second man when he felt a different touch on his shoulders and Lizzie's voice came piercing through the fog.

"Solomon! Stop!"

Solomon sat poised over the man on the ground, his fist shaking with the desire to teach this other man a lesson he'd never forget, but Elizabeth's hands encircled his upper arm, pulling him backward.

"Solomon!" Elizabeth's voice shook him out of his reverie. "Solomon, you'll kill him!"

He could easily have thrown her off, but he allowed her to pull him back and he stood up. The smaller man writhed backward, out of his reach, one hand on his throat and his terrified gaze locked on Solomon's face.

Solomon reached back, and his hand connected with Elizabeth's warm side. He nudged her gently back and turned to look at the big man rolling over and groaning as he stumbled to his feet.

"He's crazy—" one of the men squeaked. "You're crazy, man! What's wrong with you?"

Solomon's breath was coming in hot pants, and he sucked in a breath, trying to calm his heart. He kept himself between Elizabeth and the other men as they crawled back into their vehicle, and the wheels spun before they took off down the road.

"I wasn't killing anyone," Solomon said, turning toward Elizabeth for the first time, and he found her staring at him in wide-eyed shock. "Lizzie? You okay?"

She shook her head and tears welled up in her eyes. Some color had come back to her face, and he could see something in her gaze that wrung out his heart—she was terrified.

"Oh . . . Lizzie . . . come here," he said, but she took a step back.

"What was that?" she breathed. "You were . . . you were . . ."

She didn't finish, but she didn't have to. He was preparing to beat a man—and he had to admit that was the case. He would have done it. Prowling after an unprotected Amish woman? Men like that got more than a beating in prison—they often ended up dead. Even convicts had girlfriends, wives, daughters. But Solomon wasn't killing anyone, or even coming close. But he'd have hurt him rather badly—that he'd admit to.

That was another lesson he'd learned in prison—when to stop.

"Lizzie," he said softly. "You're safe with me, okay? Those guys weren't, but you are. You hear me?"

Elizabeth's face crumpled and he pulled her into his arms and leaned his face against her *kapp*. Her hairpins slid sideways and her *kapp* came loose. He could smell the soft scent of her sun-warmed hair and he pulled her close against him, as if he could physically absorb the experience and take it away from her.

Elizabeth grabbed handfuls of his shirt in her fists and hot tears soaked against his chest. The adrenaline was seeping out of his system, and it was then he noticed the stinging ache in his knuckles. He looked down to see blood from his split skin. Maybe not all his blood either. There was a patch of accusing blood on the dusty ground, too, and he kicked at some dirt to cover it up. Elizabeth pulled back and wiped her face with the heels of her hands. Her wrist looked bruised.

"Who were they?" he asked. "Did you know them?"

"Them?" She looked at him incredulously. "How would I know people like that? I've never seen them before in my life!"

Elizabeth seemed to notice her *kapp* then, because she plucked it from her head where it hung by one pin and looked down at it through tearful eyes.

"Did he hurt you?" Solomon asked.

Elizabeth ran a hand over her wrist and she looked around herself at the debris of crushed flowers.

"Let me see—" He reached for her hand and she pulled it against herself. "Hey . . ." He softened his tone. "Lizzie, you know I'm not going to hurt you. Let me see your wrist."

He slipped his fingers around her arm and tugged it gently away from her so he could get a better look. There were red fingerprints left on her flesh, and the joint was already swelling. Yah, he didn't feel bad for what he'd done now. What would that brute have done to her if he hadn't shown up?

"Does it hurt?" he asked softly.

She nodded, and he felt another wave of anger.

"What was that?" she breathed.

"I don't know—'townies' is what they called men like that in prison. Just local idiots who get drunk and get into trouble."

Elizabeth shook her head. "No—you. What happened to you there? You changed! You were someone different!"

He felt the heat hit his neck and face and he shrugged. "I'm not different."

"You are! You're not Amish anymore, Solomon."

He felt her words like a punch to the chest. "Hey, the only difference between me now and me five years ago is that I know how to take care of myself now. That's it. I wasn't going to let him hurt you."

"Where did you learn to fight like that?" she asked.

"You probably don't want to know," he said quietly.

"And if they'd ganged up on you?" she asked, her voice shaking.

"If they'd ganged up on me?" He laughed softly. "Nah. They had their leader—that big animal who had your wrist. The other two were just followers. That's how it works—you get the big one and the other ones fall into line."

"You learned that in jail?" she asked.

"Yah. I did. And I know that scares you, but that was in defense of you, and I hope you'll never have to see it again. Ever. Okay? But I wasn't standing passively by and waiting to see what he had in mind—" He didn't want to even think about it, but Gott hadn't left Elizabeth unprotected either. Solomon might not be the proper Amish man anymore, but he was capable of stopping those creeps.

Elizabeth eyed him with a strange look on her face, and Solomon sighed, then looked up and down the road. Nothing. They were alone and the truck was gone. For the time being at least, they were safe.

"Okay, let's get you back to the house," he said.

"The money," she said.

"Right. Hold on." He grabbed the money box and the change bag from inside the stand and then caught her hand in his as they headed down the drive together. He held her hand firmly, and she closed her fingers around his just as tightly in return.

"It's okay," he said, half to her and half to himself. "They're just some town guys who had too much to drink. They'll sober up."

"You know how people like that work?"

No, he didn't. Not really. He knew from stories he'd heard—some in prison, some from his less savory friends. He'd never hung out with men like that. He'd spent his time with the types of people who used their brains more than their brawn . . . even if their brains led them in less legal directions.

"Sure," he lied. "It'll be fine."

Because he wanted her to feel safe, even if it lowered

her opinion of him. Besides, he wasn't leaving her on her own at that stand again. He was lucky this time—but the Amish didn't believe in luck. They believed in divine intervention.

Did Gott help an Amish man beat an *Englisher* into submission? It hardly seemed likely, and yet if Solomon had learned one thing in his time away, it was that Gott worked outside of their boundaries just as powerfully as he worked within them.

Gott wasn't caged.

Chapter Six

Elizabeth sat at the kitchen table, a cold cloth on her wrist, watching as Bridget bathed Solomon's hands. She was only now seeing his bloodied knuckle, and she winced in sympathy when he flinched. Solomon's gaze moved up toward Elizabeth, and a smile flickered at one corner of his lips. His muscles were relaxed, but they still appeared to be filled with latent strength. He closed his fingers into a fist and the blood started seeping again.

"Stop that," Bridget said, swatting his arm.

"Just checking," he said.

"Checking for what? If you're actually mortal?" the old woman muttered.

Elizabeth smiled at that, adjusting the cold cloth on her wrist, and Solomon glanced her way with a twinkle in his eye. The fear all felt so far away now that they were in the kitchen with Bridget fussing over them. The door to the basement hung open and a laundry basket filled with wet, clean clothes sat next to it, ready for the line.

"You did this to another human being, Sol," Bridget said, shaking her head. "I know he was a bad man and I know he'd have done worse given the chance, but we are

Amish, and our way of life is not because other people deserve it! We don't fight, Sol. We don't kill. We don't pick up arms in times of war and we certainly don't beat the life out of men at our gates!"

"He's fine," Solomon said.

"No, Sol, he isn't." Bridget pressed the cloth against his knuckles. "You punched him in the face until your knuckles bled. That man is not okay! And whether or not he deserved that treatment is not for us to judge."

"Mammi, it's better than what he had in mind—"

"Gott does not ask us to punish, and I won't debate that with you," Bridget replied. "There are other ways, Sol, and if you don't find them, you'll end up in prison all over again."

Bridget exchanged a serious look with Solomon and Elizabeth dropped her gaze. It wasn't comfortable to watch a grown man lectured by his grandmother, but Bridget was right, of course. Their ideals didn't change because of evil men. The Amish believed in the sanctity of all life, created by Gott.

"I can start hanging laundry," Elizabeth said, starting to rise.

"Sit!" Bridget said, waggling a finger in her direction. "You need more cold on that wrist before you try to use it. Just be still."

Elizabeth sank back down. It was hard to refuse an order like that—the maternal authority ringing in the old woman's voice.

"Should we call the police?" Elizabeth asked.

"We don't dare call the police," Bridget replied. "Sol's on parole and fighting for any reason will get him locked back up. We'll shut down the stand. That's all we can do."

"No," Solomon said. "What about the money you'll make? You need it!"

"Gott will provide," Bridget replied.

"Mammi, I know I'm already disappointing you, but I asked for a job this morning with Seth, and—" He swallowed. "He turned me down. It might take a little while for me to find someone who will hire me."

"I'm not leaning on you, Sol," Bridget replied. "And while I am disappointed right now, I haven't given up on you either. I meant it when I said that Gott will provide. He hasn't let us down yet."

Outside, Elizabeth heard the sound of horses' hooves, and Solomon pulled his hand away from Bridget's ministrations and headed to the window.

"It's Johannes," he said.

Elizabeth exchanged a look with Bridget and Solomon got up from his seat at the table, pulled open the door, and headed outside.

"He must be here to see you, dear," Bridget said to Elizabeth.

Elizabeth had stayed friends with her sister's ex-fiancé, but he didn't tend to come visit per se. Her heart sped up. Was there news from Lovina?

Elizabeth headed to the door. Outside, Solomon was filling some buckets with water for the horses to drink, and Johannes looked up when he saw Elizabeth. He was a tall man with sandy-blond hair and a solemn expression.

"I won't take too long, so I won't unhitch," Johannes said. He went over and picked up a bucket from Solomon and carried it to the first horse. They worked easily together— and side by side, Elizabeth could see the family resemblance between the two.

"Go on in," Solomon said. "I'll take care of this."

Elizabeth noticed Johannes's gaze linger on Solomon's hands for a moment, then he turned his steps toward the house.

Elizabeth stepped back to let Johannes come inside. He gave her a nod, but his expression remained sober.

"Hello, Auntie," he said when he saw the old woman at the kitchen table. There were bloodied cloths in a pile there, and Johannes looked at them, then shot Elizabeth a questioning look.

"What happened?" Johannes demanded. "Did Sol hit you?"

"What?" Elizabeth shook her head. "Do I look like it? No! It's a long story—well, maybe not so long. Some *Englishers* came by the produce stand and started hassling me. Solomon . . . um . . . he took care of it."

Johannes didn't look appeased by that story, and he looked over his shoulder in Solomon's direction before shutting the door.

"He was fighting?" Johannes said. "That's what you mean, right?"

"We'll sort it out," Bridget said firmly. "Leave it to me."

Johannes pressed his lips together, and Bridget swiped the cloths off the table. She went to the cupboard and pulled out some disinfectant and wiped down the table. Then she gestured for Johannes to sit and headed to the sink to wash her hands.

"Have you heard from Lovina?" Elizabeth asked, leaning forward and lowering her voice.

He shook his head. "No, I haven't."

"Oh . . ." The hope that had started to well up inside her seeped away.

"I came by to talk to both you and Aunt Bridget, though. It's about Lovina . . . a little bit at least," Johannes said. "I got a visit from the bishop this morning and . . . and, well, he has an idea."

"He wants you to marry," Elizabeth said dully.

"You heard?" he asked with a frown.

"Yah," she admitted. "Sovilla Miller, the woman who was widowed recently, right?"

"That's the one," he said, and he heaved a sad sigh.

"What did the bishop say?" Elizabeth asked hesitantly.

"He said that with Lovina gone, I couldn't throw away the rest of my life on a woman who left me," Johannes replied. "He said that she's living her life and I owe it to myself to live mine."

"With Sovilla," Elizabeth said bitterly.

Bridget came back to the table with a blackberry pie and three plates. She put it down and then pulled out a chair.

"Please have pie," she said gently, putting a hand on Johannes's arm.

Johannes smiled wanly, then nodded. Bridget served him a piece of pie and he sank a fork into the crust but didn't lift the bite to his lips. He stared at his plate for a moment or two, then looked up at Elizabeth.

"Sovilla needs a husband," he said.

"There are other men, aren't there?" Elizabeth asked.

"Yah, I suppose," he replied.

Elizabeth felt her stomach tighten. "Are you considering it, then?"

Johannes sighed. "I don't know. The thing is, if I thought Lovina would come back, I'd never do it. But I'm not convinced she will come back."

Elizabeth sucked in a wavering breath. "I think she will. I know my sister—and when she left it was because of my father's crime, not because she no longer believed in our way of life. She might need to sort it out in her head, but I can't imagine that everything we were raised to do would go out the window."

"Everything your father raised her to do," Johannes said, and he met her gaze.

"I can't believe that she's just . . . gone," Elizabeth said, shaking her head. "You knew her, too, Johannes. Do you really think she'd stop loving all of us? Do you think she could change that much, permanently?"

"Other young people jumped the fence, too," Johannes said. "All for the same reason—they'd trusted your father. And when he was proven to be—" He swallowed.

"A crook," Elizabeth supplied. "I know. My father was supposed to strengthen people's faith, and instead he caused a great many to lose it. But I still don't think Lovina will stay away forever."

"How long would you have me wait?" Johannes asked, his voice low. "There are days when I'd be relieved to get a letter that told me that she's marrying some *Englisher*! I would, because it would set me free."

They were silent for a moment. Johannes had a different relationship to Lovina than the rest of them. He'd belonged to her by choice, not by blood. No matter what happened, Lovina would be Elizabeth's younger sister, but it wasn't the same for Johannes. People who'd been in love had a more delicate balance, and perhaps a more exquisite pain.

"Could you love this . . . Sovilla?" Elizabeth asked.

He shook his head. "I don't know. But I know I could

be useful to her. I could support her and take care of her *kinner* like my own. At least I wouldn't be alone."

"You should pray about it," Bridget said quietly.

They both turned their attention to the old woman, and Bridget shrugged weakly. "There is no saying how Gott is working right now. Look at Ruth in the Bible. Her husband died and she left everyone she knew to go to her mother-in-law's home country, where she met Boaz. Look at Isaac—his father sent a servant to bring a girl for him and he fell in love with her as soon as he saw her—"

"Yah, I know," Johannes said. "Gott works in strange ways sometimes. And trust me, I've been praying, but I don't have an answer from Him yet."

Bridget nodded. "Best get one. It might be time to let go of how we thought things would turn out and accept how they are."

Except that sounded like giving up, and Elizabeth wasn't ready to do that yet. Was Johannes?

The side door opened and Solomon came inside. Johannes stood up.

"I have some thinking to do," Johannes said.

Johannes gave Solomon a nod and then headed out the door. Solomon stood there for a moment.

"I'm going to bring the produce back from the road," Solomon said.

"Thank you, Sol," Bridget said.

What would they do without the men who protected them and cared for them? But one by one, the men Elizabeth had come to count on were drifting away. Her *daet* had started it all when he proved that he wasn't the reliable man they all believed him to be. Her uncle, who had always been gruff, proved himself to be cold and unwelcoming when she'd needed a home most. And now Johannes, who rightfully deserved to move on, was considering doing just that. Elizabeth knew it would change things between them all. A new wife wouldn't welcome this close relationship with his old fiancée's family.

Bridget had mentioned Ruth of the Bible, and how she'd traveled far to find her noble husband, Boaz. Maybe it could be the same for Elizabeth, and she could find a man she could trust in with all her heart, whose integrity and goodness would be her support, and she could put her uncertainty behind her for good.

Solomon had said she'd never find it, but she disagreed. She wasn't looking for perfection anymore, she was looking for character. Her *daet* had told her that she deserved that much. He used to sit in the kitchen with Elizabeth and Lovina and tell them of the kind of men they deserved to marry—kind, considerate, faithful men.

"You are not only my daughters, you are Gott's," her father had said earnestly. "And you cannot accept less than what you deserve. Too many girls make that mistake, and they live to regret it. Do you understand?"

Elizabeth had always insisted that she did. She was older than Lovina, after all, and that meant that she should be wiser. She'd always been the more serious sister, too. But she'd only really understood what her father meant once her friends started getting engaged and married, and she'd seen a few girls make very big mistakes in their choices.

"Choose better than she did," was all her father would say.

And while her father had let her down in every other

way in these last couple of years, she had to believe that he'd spoken *some* truth . . . didn't she?

Because if she couldn't believe in something, she'd end up like Lovina and she'd have nothing left at all.

That evening, after his grandmother had nodded off in her chair in the sitting room, Solomon headed outside. His excuse was that he needed to fix a fence on the far side of the pasture, but while it had gotten rickety, it wasn't a dire emergency either. He just wanted space.

That fight had upset him more than he wanted the women to know. He was shaken, and every time he closed his hand, his knuckles stung. That feeling of pounding on another man—it was like he'd materialized back in the prison again. That spot in the middle of his back began to prickle as if he was being watched, and he pulled off his straw hat and scrubbed a hand through his short-cropped hair. He could almost feel the chill of cement walls closing in around him.

Solomon shivered, even though the air was warm and it hummed with the sound of night insects. The sun had set, and as he trudged back toward the house through the long grass, he slapped at a mosquito on his arm.

Gott, will I react like an inmate for the rest of my life?

The adrenaline had long since worn off, as had his certainty that he'd handled that situation correctly. Had there been a way to get Lizzie away from them without resorting to violence? He wasn't even sure. What he did know was that the man who had surged up inside him was no better than a convict, fighting for dominance, or for respect, or just to make some massive thug leave him alone.

And that brute with his hand on Elizabeth had reminded him of a particular inmate in the prison . . . except this hadn't been prison, and there weren't any guards turning a blind eye.

The sky still glowed crimson at the horizon and a couple of stars pierced through the dusk. He headed back toward the house, a bag of tools from the shed slung over one shoulder. The house was dark upstairs, but the kitchen and sitting room windows shone with the light of two kerosene lamps.

Funny how years ago, trudging back toward this old house, he'd felt so cooped up and hemmed in that it had filled him with a simmering anger. Now, that old house with the creaking hinges on the door and the white paint flaking off the siding represented a comfort he wasn't even sure he deserved anymore.

When he was a boy, Solomon's mother used to tell him the story from Genesis about the Garden of Eden, and how Adam and Eve had everything they could possibly want. But they'd wanted to know more—dangerously more—and that was the start of an eternity of misery.

You're being like Adam and Eve, his mother used to tell him. *You want to know what's out there in the world, but you have no appreciation for your life right here. I pray that you'll come to your senses before it's too late, Son.*

Solomon had missed his *mamm* something fierce when he was in prison, and he'd told himself that when he got out, he'd make it up to her. He'd prove that he could make her proud. But sitting in a cell, he hadn't been very realistic about his options after he came back. Getting a job wasn't going to be easy and gaining trust might not be possible anymore. So making it up to her? He might not be able to.

As Solomon came up to the side of the house, he heard the familiar squeak of the clothesline in the darkness, and the line of fluttering dresses and towels leaped to the side.

"Solomon?" It was Lizzie. She leaned forward to get a better look at him.

"What are you doing out here?" he asked.

"Bringing in the laundry," she said. "I put it off too long."

He could make her out on the porch, the clothes on the line dancing in the night air as she pulled them toward her. She plucked off the pins and folded another shirt and dropped it into the basket at her feet.

"I'm sure you could leave that until morning," he said.

"I wanted the fresh air," she replied.

Yah, he could sympathize with that. He'd just fixed a fence that didn't need fixing for the same reason.

"You want help with that?" he asked.

"This is women's work," she said with a short laugh.

"I don't care. I want the fresh air, too," he replied.

She smiled faintly, then shrugged. "All right, then."

She was beautiful standing there in the faint light that came out from a side window. Her white *kapp* caught the light, and there was a deep glimmer in her dark eyes that made his pulse speed up. Solomon dropped his tool bag on a step and headed up the four stairs to the porch where Lizzie stood. She folded a towel and dropped it into the basket. He pulled on the line and it squeaked as the clothes danced closer. The next item was his *Englisher* T-shirt. He pulled it down and folded it roughly, tossing it aside, away from the other laundry.

"Did you fight like that in prison?" Lizzie asked quietly.

"Yah." He took down his jeans next and shook them out, dropping the clothespins into the bag at her feet.

"Why?" she asked softly.

He looked down at her and found Lizzie looking up into his face with a searching expression on her face.

"Because I had to," he replied, and he felt his throat tighten with emotion. "It's different in there. It's more violent, for one. And the guards don't always stop it. There are some men who have been in prison for decades and they run everything. You have to go along with them, and if you don't—" He sucked in a breath.

"What did they want?" she whispered.

"Sometimes it was to deliver something to another inmate, or just to choose sides in a fight. . . . There was one big guy who wanted me to grovel for him and I just couldn't. So my cellmate started teaching me how to fight out in the yard. And the next time that big bully came at me, I hit him first."

Stories like this one felt out of place out here on his grandmother's porch. They felt dirty, wrong.

"That isn't Christian," she said.

"Nope, not really," he agreed. What did she want to hear? That he could defend his actions from the Bible? It was laughable, really. It wasn't a regular life in there—it was survival.

"Did it work?" she asked after a beat of silence.

"Yah. He left me alone after that. Started saying he liked me after all." That had almost been worse. That had been a very scary man who'd done some very bad things.

Solomon hadn't wanted to be associated with him at all. But at least he'd earned a certain type of peace.

"It was lonely in there," Solomon went on, his hands moving automatically to fold the jeans he was holding, and then he reached for a towel. "You're surrounded with men constantly. You can hear them snore at night, you can hear them eat, talk, argue, breathe . . . You can smell them. And yet you've never been more alone in your life."

"Because no one cares about you," she said.

"I suppose," he agreed. "But prison changes you . . . and you can't help it. I think my *mamm* noticed. The last time she visited, she said her visits weren't helping me and she wasn't going to come again."

"What?" she breathed.

"The funny thing is," he went on, "she thought her visits weren't helping because I suppose she could see me changing, becoming more like the other inmates. While her visits might not have been keeping me the same, they were keeping me sane." Elizabeth looked up at him and he cleared his throat. "And even being let out of prison, I'm not exactly free yet."

"Why not?" she asked with a frown.

"I have a parole officer. I have to meet up with him day after tomorrow."

"What does he do?" she asked.

"Makes sure I'm behaving myself," he replied.

"And not fighting . . ." She sucked in a breath. "What if he found out about that?"

"I'd end up in jail again," he said.

She nodded. "Then we can't speak of it, can we?"

"That would be kind," he said, and he smiled faintly.

Elizabeth took down the last towel and folded it, but neither of them moved. Her gaze dropped to the wind-dried towel in her hands and then she dropped it into the basket. They were done with the chore—it was time to go inside. He would make some tea, his grandmother would wake up, and then she'd insist upon a family worship, all together. She'd done it every night since he'd returned. But he wasn't ready for that . . .

"Should we go in?" he asked. She didn't answer at first, so he added, "Or do you want to sit?"

The words were out before he could think better of them. He just wanted a few more minutes with her outside in the soft darkness. Whatever it was that kept loosening his lips to make him say things he'd never said aloud before, he wanted more of it. He nodded toward the stairs and he let her go first, and then he sank onto the step next to her. For a moment, they sat in silence, listening to the chirp of crickets. She felt warm next to him and smelled faintly of baking.

"That really scared me today," she said softly.

He reached over and took her hand. "I meant it when I said you were safe with me. But I know. I'm sorry I scared you."

"If you hadn't fought them, if you'd been more Amish—" She stopped.

"Are you saying you're grateful I wasn't more Amish about it?" he asked with a rueful smile.

She smiled faintly back and shrugged. "That's terrible, isn't it?"

"It's nice to be appreciated, all the same," he replied.

There was a wisp of hair hanging down across her

cheek, and he reached to move it, her skin soft against his rough hand. She moved her cheek against his hand, just for a moment, and he swallowed.

"Are you glad I came back now?" he asked.

She looked over at him, a smile turning up her lips. "Yah. I am."

He felt his reserve crumble. It had been a long time since he'd been alone with a woman, and even longer since he'd felt a wave of tenderness like this. . . . She made him want to be better than he was, to be more worthy of her respect. Because right now all he could offer was this beefy body of his, and this unsettling instinct to protect her.

"I'm sure you know it, but you're beautiful, Lizzie," he murmured.

She dropped her gaze, and in this low light, he couldn't tell if he'd made her blush or not. He was hoping he had. This was one thing that made him feel like a man again, made him feel human—being able to make her react in some way. This was the grown-up version of his youthful antics, he realized ruefully. Except as an adult, his feelings sank a whole lot deeper. He should move away, stand up, stop this now before it got out of hand, but he couldn't bring himself to do it.

"Solomon, I—" She lifted her face just as he was turning toward her, and he found himself mere inches from her. She stopped, and when his gaze moved down to her lips, she didn't move away either.

He wanted to say something to her, but no words came to mind. He knew what he wanted to say . . .

He lowered his lips over hers in a gentle kiss, waiting to feel her recoil or stiffen, but it didn't come. Her eyes fluttered shut and as his lips moved over hers, his pulse sped up. It was like the night around them disappeared and all that was left was the two of them, their hands clasped, their breath mingling out there in the grass-scented air, and an overwhelming urge to pull her closer.

He released her fingers and slid his arm around her waist, feeling the softness of her form, and she leaned into his arms. She was both fragile and strong, and when she pulled back, he tipped his forehead against hers, trying to catch his breath.

"Oh . . ." she breathed, and one pale hand moved up his arm and rested on his biceps, and he doubted she knew what that movement was doing to him.

"Yah . . ." He didn't have any words for what had just happened. He pulled back so he could look into her face, and her eyes glistened and her lips were plump from the kiss.

"We shouldn't do that," she whispered.

"I know," he said. "But there's a whole lot I shouldn't have done, and I can assure you, this is the thing that brings me the least guilt right now."

She pulled back her hand and smoothed it down her apron. She seemed to be trying to mentally rearrange herself.

"You look fine," he whispered. No one would know.

She stood up and he stayed seated, watching her. He wasn't going to chase her down or force himself on her. But he wasn't going to apologize for that kiss either.

"I need to take in the washing," she said.

He chuckled softly. "All right."

She went back up the stairs and picked up the laundry basket of folded items and dropped the little bag of clothespins on top. She looked back at him once and then disappeared inside, leaving him alone with his thoughts and the sound of the crickets.

No, he wasn't a good Amish man, and he never would be. He'd never achieve whatever heights of goodness Lizzie would require from the man she married, and he didn't care to either. Because if he'd been a better man, he wouldn't have been able to defend her as efficiently as he had.

He wasn't a good man, but he was here. That would have to count for something.

Chapter Seven

Lizzie lay in her bed that night, her breath bated. Solomon had kissed her . . . and that was no gallant peck either, although what did she know about kisses? He'd smelled like musk and fresh air, and those muscular arms that had only recently been used in pounding on her assailant had encircled her so gently . . . and yet it was the gentleness of steel—he'd stopped when she pulled back, but she'd never felt such strength.

She'd never run her hands over a man's arms before either . . . so she didn't really have any comparison. Nor had she ever been kissed.

So she lay there remembering what his lips had felt like against hers, the sandpaper of his stubble and the tickle of his breath.

That was her first kiss . . . and that was likely a very bad thing. She'd just let Solomon Lantz kiss her. Whatever it was about him that seemed to draw her in had to be resisted. Yes, he was strong and handsome. And he did make her feel safe just because he was close by, but was it a sin to be relying on a man's baser instincts to protect her? Should she feel bad for being grateful that he wasn't just a little more Amish?

Probably.

So she rolled over and shut her eyes.

Gott, forgive me, she prayed. *Give me self-control with him.*

And then she fell into a fitful sleep in which she dreamed of threatening *Englishers*, except she was at service Sunday, and her father was preaching, and those terrifying men stomped through the congregation and right up to where he stood. Her *daet* shut his eyes and began to pray. Her father always had prayed beautifully, whether he'd been in front of a congregation or if it had simply been around their humble table. Abe Yoder had always had the words that made a person feel that Gott was leaning in close. And in the dream, the prayer he began to say was the one he'd prayed with her before bed every night when she was very small: *Dear Gott,* as we go to sleep, we thank Thee for this day. We ask Thee to help us choose the right in work as well as play. Make us humble and kind, grateful and good. Give us only enough so that we choose what we should. And when we awake, give us strength for the rest, and keep us together, happy and blessed.

It was the prayer that always made her feel so cherished, but then the *Englisher* raised his fist, and Elizabeth woke up with a start, her chest heaving and tears on her cheeks.

Only a dream . . . but when she rolled back over again in the hot bedroom, sleep didn't come for a long time.

* * *

The next morning Elizabeth stayed busy with Bridget. It was cleaning day and the bedrooms all had to be swept and mopped and the baseboards and window ledges wiped down. The bathroom needed to be scrubbed, too, and as Elizabeth worked, that kiss kept replaying itself in her mind. Somehow, she'd thought her first kiss would be different from that . . . maybe more chaste. She'd imagined a man would lean in and peck her lips, then maybe compliment her cooking . . . but Solomon's kiss had been filled with something deeper, something more powerful, and it had tugged her in against every better instinct of her own. He wasn't complimenting her cooking—he was vowing to protect her.

When she got to Solomon's bedroom with her bucket and her mop, she paused at the threshold and looked inside. The bed was made, although a little rumpled, and his English clothes lay folded on the end of the bed. The room smelled like him—like that faint musk and the outdoors. She paused at the bed and let her fingers run over the blue denim and the soft T-shirt. They'd washed those clothes, hung them to dry, and those *Englisher* items weren't going anywhere. Solomon wasn't done with them yet.

Elizabeth cleaned his room quickly and then left. But before she did, she looked back at that rumpled bed and those *Englisher* clothes laying there in the open. He wasn't staying. He'd told them both that very clearly. This was a visit, and one of these days soon, this bedroom would be empty, and those *Englisher* clothes would be gone. So would his reassuring strength. She felt safer with him around.

By the time Elizabeth finished cleaning the upstairs,

Bridget had finished with the kitchen and had some egg salad sandwiches sitting on a plate on the counter.

"I don't know how I'd do all this without you, Elizabeth," Bridget said, wiping her forehead with the back of her hand. "There's still the sitting room to be done, and the laundry room in the basement, and I meant to wipe down the canned goods shelves down there—they're so dusty, and they're nearly empty, so it's a good time . . ." Bridget's voice trailed off. "But there's time for that tomorrow."

"I can get started on it after lunch," Elizabeth offered.

"But Lydia and Edith are coming over to do some crocheting for the NICU at Erindale Hospital," Bridget countered. "And I happen to know that you're very good at crochet. You used to make those church dolls, didn't you?"

Elizabeth smiled. "I'm surprised anyone remembers that."

"They were very well done," Bridget replied. "And with you helping us, I'm sure we could finish that many more caps for the babies there. And we're doing little blankets for them as well." Bridget looked at her hopefully.

"Yah, I can help," Elizabeth agreed with a smile.

Bridget smiled back and put the bowl where she'd mixed the egg salad into the sink and ran some water into it. "How is Sol doing?"

"I'm sure you'd know better than I would," Elizabeth replied.

"I wouldn't count on that," Bridget replied. "There are things a man won't say to his grandmother."

"I—" Elizabeth felt her cheeks heat. "I talked to him after he had that fight, and he had a very good point that if he'd been just a little more Amish, I might have been badly hurt."

"Yah . . ." Bridget took off her glasses and used the corner of her apron to wipe them. "I know. But is he using that as an excuse to stay English?"

"I don't know," Elizabeth admitted softly.

"If only he'd come home properly—at heart, you know?" Bridget said, and she put her glasses back on. "He could find healing here. But he'd have to commit to coming home. There's something powerful in commitment."

Would a commitment to staying in Bountiful be enough for Solomon, though? She'd thought the Amish clothes would make a difference, but somehow they hadn't. He looked less jarring, but at heart, he wasn't a modest Amish man anymore.

"He's changed, though," Elizabeth said.

"Oh, he was always a little wild," Bridget replied.

"He's not . . . Amish now," Elizabeth said. "It wasn't just a fight. It wasn't just a punch. I saw what he did, Bridget. If I hadn't stopped him, he'd have beaten two more men senseless!"

And he was powerful enough to do it.

"He'll adjust," Bridget replied.

"I think it's more than adjustment, though," Elizabeth countered. "He's not staying in Bountiful. He's been clear about that—"

"Do you agree with Edith and Lydia, then?" Bridget demanded. "Do you think he's a danger to me?"

Bridget stood still, her gnarled hands clutched in front of her apron. Her eyes misted with angry tears and Elizabeth felt a wave of regret.

"No," Elizabeth said, softening her voice. "He's no danger to you or me. He'd protect us with his last breath. He loves you too much to be any danger to you, Bridget. I know that. But I wonder if he might be a danger to himself. He's struggling to find a place to belong, and now that he has a criminal record, that isn't going to be easy."

"No one said it would be easy," Bridget retorted. "But where else can a man be loved unconditionally than at home?"

Elizabeth nodded and dropped her gaze.

"What?" Bridget said.

"His *mamm*—" She licked her lips.

"My daughter-in-law is as stubborn as her son," Bridget said, and she pulled out a chair to sit down. "In fact, that's exactly where Sol got that wild, stubborn streak of his. He's just like his *mamm*."

"Did you know she visited him in prison?" Elizabeth asked.

"Yah, of course." Bridget put a sandwich on Elizabeth's plate using only her fingertips. They'd eat at the counter, it seemed. "He's her son. I went once, too, but they limit how many visits the men there can have, so I didn't want to take that time away from Anke."

"Did you know that she refused to visit him again?"

Bridget froze in the act of getting her own sandwich, then looked up. "What?"

"That's what he told me. He said she walked out on

him and said she wouldn't come back. I think it"—
Elizabeth sucked in a breath—"broke his heart."

"Anke wouldn't do that—"

"Would Solomon lie about something like that?"
Elizabeth asked. Because she didn't think he had. He'd
opened up.

Bridget shook her head and put down the sandwich on
her plate, staring at it mutely for a moment. Then she
looked up. "They had a difficult relationship, those two.
Anke had trouble raising him after my son died. Sol
was always so hardheaded, and Anke was prone to over-
reaction. They both were, honestly. My son was the one
who brought balance to that family, and when he died, I
tried to be an influence, but it wasn't the same. Any little
thing Sol did, Anke would lecture him about how it would
ruin his entire life. I told her that she was going too far,
but she wouldn't listen. She said she was his mother
and I needed to respect that. And I did! But she went
too far . . ."

"Was she . . . harsh?" Elizabeth asked. "Did she beat
him?"

"No, no, not like that." Bridget sighed. "She just
thought that every little thing was a sign of him going
down the wrong path."

"In her defense, he did jump the fence," Elizabeth said.

"Did he do that because he really wanted to, or because he believed he was halfway to hell already?"
Bridget asked. "I love my daughter-in-law—I do. She
stayed with me even after my son's death, and we've taken
care of each other. Most people would support her trying
to use a strong hand with Sol—in fact, most of the family

encouraged her in that. But Sol was more sensitive than his brother and sisters."

"Yah?" Elizabeth frowned. "He always seemed . . . tough."

"That's just on the outside," Bridget replied. "He was always very tender. He felt things deeply. His *mamm* didn't see it."

Elizabeth shrugged weakly. Obviously she hadn't either. The Solomon she'd known back then was stubborn and constantly teasing. The Solomon she'd become reacquainted with recently was gentler, even after that time in prison.

"This is why I wanted you to befriend him," Bridget said. "He needs to feel like he belongs with someone— he needs to see the potential here."

There was movement behind them and Elizabeth and Bridget both turned to see Solomon standing in the doorway, his hat in one hand and a streak of dirt down his white shirt. His dark gaze flickered between Elizabeth and Bridget, and she could read the betrayal in his eyes.

"You asked her to be my friend?" Solomon asked, his voice low.

"We didn't hear you," Bridget said feebly.

"I oiled the screen door this morning," he said, and he shook his head. "Maybe I shouldn't have. You could have had some warning. Is that what this was—you were pretending to care?"

"Sol, this isn't what it seems," Bridget said. "I'm sorry to have been talking about you."

But Solomon's gaze was locked on Elizabeth. That accusation had been for her, and she could only imagine that he was remembering the same thing she was—a kiss on the steps, shared confidences . . . That hadn't been because his grandmother asked her to be nice.

"Never mind," he said.

Solomon turned and headed down the steps—and this time, Elizabeth could hear his footfalls. She rubbed a hand over her face.

Bridget hurried across the kitchen and pushed open the screen door. "Sol! Come back, Sol!"

The clatter of a buggy brought Elizabeth to the door, too. Edith and Lydia had arrived, but it was Seth who was driving them. Seth reined the horse in and his wary gaze followed Sol as he disappeared into the stable. The he looked back at Elizabeth and Bridget at the door.

"Everything okay?" Seth called.

"Yes, fine!" Bridget replied, forcing a smile.

"I'll go talk to Solomon," Elizabeth murmured.

Bridget caught her arm. "We don't breathe a word about that fight, Elizabeth, do you hear me?"

"Of course."

Because if word got out about that, Solomon could be sent back to prison. He'd made mistakes and he'd likely leave the Amish life for good, but he didn't deserve more punishment.

Solomon grabbed a bale of hay and hauled it across the stable. He'd kissed her. Maybe it had been a stupid thing to do, but he'd at least thought it was mutual! He'd thought that Elizabeth had been talking to him because she wanted to. But his grandmother had pushed her into it? If it weren't for Bridget, would Elizabeth have spoken to him at all?

He dropped the bale next to a stall, his brain spinning.

He'd said a lot—he'd opened up. It was only occurring to him now that she might have been reporting back to his grandmother. He'd thought it would stay private. Was he the fool here for having thought a girl like Elizabeth could actually care for him? Maybe.

He grabbed a utility knife from a shelf and cut the twine on the bale of hay. It popped, but the hay stayed compressed—an older bale, apparently. He pushed the pitchfork into its depths and twisted the hay loose.

The stable door opened and Solomon looked up to see Elizabeth. She stood in the doorway, eyeing him uncertainly for a moment, and he hated that he still thought she was beautiful.

"What part were you mad at?" Elizabeth asked, the door falling shut behind her.

"It doesn't matter," he replied. "I'm up to speed now."

"So what do you think you know?" she asked.

"My grandmother asked you to keep an eye on me . . . something like that?" he said.

She was silent.

"So, what was that last night?" He dropped the pitchfork tongs against the cement floor with a clang.

Her cheeks tinged pink.

"Did you actually want that kiss? Or did I just surprise you?" He shook his head. "Do you feel like I forced that kiss on you?"

"No—" She shook her head.

"When I told you about jail and what it was like . . . did you care, or was that so you could tell my grandmother where I was at in my head?"

"Of course, I care!" she shot back.

He met her gaze, and for a moment, they just stared at each other.

"I feel a little stupid," he admitted. "I thought there was something genuine between us."

Elizabeth's gaze dropped. "Your grandmother did ask me to be your friend. That part is true—"

"I should have realized that," he muttered. Of course, Mammi was trying to make things easier on him. He should have sensed her influence on this.

"But that isn't why I was talking to you, or why I . . . why we . . ." Elizabeth looked up at him helplessly. "It doesn't explain that kiss."

"No?" he asked, and he couldn't help the hope that seeped through his tone. He hated it—wished he could hide it better.

"I started to get to know you again, Sol, and you're not the boy who used to pester me." She swallowed. "You're . . . a man."

There was something in her voice that gave him pause. She wouldn't meet his gaze.

"You mean years have passed and we've both grown up, or you're seen me . . . *as a man*." He leaned the pitchfork against the wall and walked out to where she stood. She didn't move, and when he reached her, she looked up at him. She licked her lips.

"They're the same thing," she breathed.

Did she really think so? It was almost sweet that she'd be that naïve.

"No, they aren't." He glanced toward the window, then back down at her. "One is a friend. The other is . . . on a different level. It's like when I look at you, I don't just see little Lizzie who I mercilessly teased. I don't see a pal, or a buddy. And to be clear, I'm not asking for anything, but if I have to be honest, when I look at you, I see . . . a woman."

Elizabeth sucked in a breath, and for a beat, she met his gaze. Then she looked down.

"Does it matter?" she asked. "It's not like you're staying."

"Yah, it matters," he said quietly. "Because you kissed me back."

She looked away, annoyance shining in her eyes.

"You felt something with me," he went on. "You saw me as a man, and you felt something—"

"I . . . did." She shrugged. "I shouldn't have, though—"

"I don't think there is a lot of control over those things," he said with a short laugh.

"There'd better be!" she retorted.

"Yah, over our actions, absolutely," he replied. "But over attraction? You think you can muscle up your virtue and stop feeling even that?"

"I should try, at least," she said, her voice faint.

He ran a hand down her arm, and he felt the goose bumps rise on her flesh. That was from his touch, he realized. His fingers on her skin made her shiver like that. He caught her hand and she didn't pull back.

"If you didn't want to kiss me, you should have stopped me last night," he said, and he dropped her hand.

"It's just—" Her gaze flickered up to meet his, and then she looked away, closing her fingers into a fist. "I'd never been kissed before."

Solomon's heart thudded to a stop. "What?"

"I know it sounds ridiculous at my age, but . . . I've been careful."

Very careful, it would seem. And that kiss might have meant something to her that he hadn't realized.

"Then why kiss *me*?" he asked.

She didn't answer and he caught her hand again. "Lizzie—"

This mattered. If she'd never kissed a man before, why had she deigned to kiss him?

"Because you saved me!" Tears misted Elizabeth's eyes. "Because I was terrified, and then you were there, and you defended me! And when we were talking, you felt like a real person again instead of just the boy who jumped the fence, and—"

"And?" he breathed.

". . . I wanted to."

He couldn't help the smile that tickled his lips. "Yah?"

He'd sparked something inside her, too, and he liked that. She'd seen the man in him, and she'd responded. He wasn't just some foolish teenager anymore.

"I don't want to kiss you again," she clarified.

"Of course not," he said, but he couldn't help the mild sense of victory. "That would be debasing, and a mistake."

She gave him an annoyed look. "There's no future between us, and I don't toy with those things. If I waited that long for a first kiss, I'm not about to fool around. I'm looking for a husband, not a boyfriend."

"Yah . . ." He let the joking go. "I know. And I'm not exactly husband material. You don't have to point that out. I just needed to know that you weren't out there with me because of my grandmother. That would have been wrong—on too many levels."

"No, it wasn't because of your grandmother," she replied quietly.

"I won't kiss you again," he said quietly. "You can spend time with me and not worry that I'll try."

"Okay." She nodded.

What was it about Elizabeth that brought out the nobility in him? He wanted to be the kind of man she could relax around. He wanted her to be able to lean into him, to let down her guard. And that would mean exercising his self-control. With her hand on his arm, he was tempted to step closer again and close that distance between them. But he wouldn't.

"Look," he said, clearing his throat. "I can go man the roadside stall with you to make sure you'll be okay, but I'd rather find a job so that my grandmother can just leave the stand closed this year."

Elizabeth nodded. "I'm sure she'd appreciate that."

"But getting a job isn't going to be easy," he said. "If Seth wouldn't hire me, I doubt there's some Amish farmer just waiting to bring an ex-con onto his land."

"There has to be somewhere," Elizabeth said. "Where do other men with your . . . history . . . work?"

"For the most part, they don't. They get back into crime and go back to jail," he replied.

Elizabeth didn't answer.

"But something did occur to me," he added. "Your family is the one that might actually understand me. With your *daet* in prison, you've got a more personal connection to all that, and you might understand a man who made a mistake and is trying to go right."

"I'm not sure we understand my *daet* at all," she said.

He was silent for a moment. "But you'd want him to have a way to keep himself when he gets out, right?"

"Yah. Of course."

"Do you think your brother might be willing to help me get a job, then?" he asked. "He works with his father-in-law at the book bindery, doesn't he? I mean, I can do pretty much anything they asked of me, and then I could hand my wages over to my grandmother. And I have a feeling she'd like that—some Amish-earned money."

Elizabeth smiled faintly. "Yah, she would like that."

"Will you ask him?" Solomon asked.

She sucked in a breath. "I can't promise that he'll do anything, but I'll ask."

"Thank you." It was something.

He wasn't trying to use her tenderness toward him for his own gain. This was different—he was trying to be worthy of it. Because whatever had sparked between them on a chemical level, he craved something deeper than her touch. He wanted her respect.

Was it too much to ask?

Chapter Eight

The next morning Elizabeth looked out the side of the buggy, watching the birds flit from fence post to fence post as the horses plodded along. The sun shone hot already, without even the faintest of breezes. Elizabeth plucked at the neckline of her dress, looking for some cool air.

"What will happen at your parole meeting?" she asked.

"No idea," Solomon replied. He rubbed a hand over his healing split knuckles.

"Are you nervous?" she asked.

"A bit," he said, and he cast her a smile. "I'll be okay."

Was he as confident as he looked, or had he gotten good at faking it? Elizabeth eyed him for a moment, watching him fiddle with the reins.

"Do you believe in Gott still?" she asked.

He raised an eyebrow. "Yah. Hard not to."

"Do you believe Gott wants you to live a good, moral, Amish life?" she asked.

He smiled ruefully. "Good and moral, yah. Amish? I don't know. There is more out there than we ever knew, you know. My *mamm* used to tell me about Adam and

Eve, and how they were given everything good, and they still wanted to see what was beyond it," he said. "She said I was just like that, always wanting to peer beyond the fence."

"Do you agree with her?" Elizabeth asked hesitantly. "That it's dangerous out there?" Because she did.

"No," he said. "I don't. I think there is good and bad right here in the Amish community, and there is good and bad outside it. And we can choose the apple from anywhere."

"But when you left, you ended up with wicked people," she countered. "That must mean something . . ."

Could he not see it? He'd been safe here in Bountiful, even if he felt a little restrained or bored. But when he left, that was when all his misery had begun. Would he still defend that one choice that started it all?

"Jesus talked about pleasing Gott. He said we need to feed the hungry, give water to the thirsty, visit people in prison." Solomon's gaze stayed on the road ahead of them. "It was a Catholic priest who sat with me and talked to me about my soul, about how I could be a different man if I chose to be. Do you think that priest is part of the wicked world out there? According to our own Bible, he was doing right."

Elizabeth sighed. "It's just safer here . . ."

"Even if you go another year or two unmarried?" His glaze flicked in her direction, and she felt the prick in his words. "What if you get too old, and your hopes of finding a husband dry up? What then? What if you could choose between living an English life with a husband who loved you and as many babies as you wanted to have or an Amish life as a spinster?"

That was every woman's fear in this community, and it felt cruel for him to point it out.

"That isn't fair," she said.

They were approaching Isaiah's drive and she pointed to the mailbox with block letters spelling Yoder.

"It's perfectly fair," he said quietly. "It just might be reality."

"We don't know how anything will work out," she said. "Gott doesn't give us choices like that."

Solomon reined in the horses and the buggy came to a stop at the top of the drive under the dappled shade of some trees that tickled the hard top of the buggy with their branches.

"If you looked at things as they are," he said quietly, "you might realize that is your choice exactly. Or it will be if you don't find your perfectly Amish, deeply spiritual, obnoxiously attractive husband very soon."

Elizabeth stared at him, her breath coming shallow.

"Who says marrying *Englishers* is any easier?" she asked.

He reached out and ran the back of his finger down her cheek, and she felt a shiver down her back in response to his touch.

"You don't know how beautiful you are, do you?" he murmured.

Her breath caught in her throat, and for a heartbeat his eyes locked onto hers. Then she heard the slam of a screen door behind her and she looked over her shoulder and saw her sister-in-law, Bethany, on the step holding her infant son in her arms.

"I have to go," she said.

"Yah," he agreed. "I'll come by again on my way back."

"Thank you." She scooted to the edge of the seat and hopped down. Her heart was beating at a quicker pace and she looked once over her shoulder as she headed down the drive to find Solomon watching her with a solemn expression on his face.

Was he really suggesting that she leave the Amish faith? Was her snake in the garden none other than Solomon Lantz? Because there was no life for her but an Amish life, and she had to believe that Gott would provide a husband for her with her own people. She had to.

Bethany smiled and stood back as Elizabeth came up to the porch.

"I saw the buggy stop through the front window," Bethany said. "It's so good to see you, Elizabeth. Here—hold Mo. He's getting heavy."

Elizabeth scooped up the baby into her arms and smiled down at the plump little boy as she followed Bethany back into the house.

"How is Bridget faring?" Bethany asked. "And don't mind me, I'm just going to finish up the dishes and then I'm all yours."

"Go right ahead," Elizabeth replied. "I can help—"

"He's teething," Bethany said. "And he refuses to be put down. Trust me, that *is* helping."

Elizabeth sat down at the kitchen table and dandled Moses on her knee. The little boy's chin was slick with drool and he picked up the corner of her apron and pushed it into his mouth to gnaw on it.

"Bridget is doing well," Elizabeth said. "That was Solomon who drove me here."

"Solomon's back?" Bethany whirled around, her eyes wide. "I thought he was in prison!"

"He was," Elizabeth said. "He's out."

There were more questions, and Elizabeth answered what she could, keeping Solomon's more private experience to herself. It wasn't right to share that . . . but he was back in the community, and word would start to travel now.

"What's Solomon like now?" Bethany asked. "Does he seem . . . changed?"

"It's been five years," Elizabeth said. "So, yah. He's grown up."

He'd grown up, and he'd gained an attractiveness that she couldn't deny. Would the other girls see it soon enough? Maybe . . .

"I suppose it happens to us all," Bethany said softly, and she turned back to the sink. "Did you hear about Rueben Miller's passing?"

For the next few minutes they exchanged information about the unfortunate accident and the young widow who was left behind. Bethany had heard more about the specifics of the accident, and about who had found him, and how some *Englisher* lawyer had tried to get Sovilla to sue the company that had made the baler, but she wouldn't.

"I don't think it's right to ask Johannes to step in like this," Elizabeth said.

"No?" Bethany let the water out of the sink and dried her hands. Then she pulled some muffins out of a cupboard and brought them to the table.

"I really don't," Elizabeth replied. "You know how much he loves Lovina. He's been in love with her since

he was a young teen, and asking him to marry someone
he's never met in order to provide for them—"

"She is a good woman, though," Bethany said.

"Still, a stranger," Elizabeth replied. "You got to
choose your husband, Bethany. And you've told me more
than once that being deeply in love with a man makes
everything easier."

"Look, you might not see this," Bethany said quietly,
"but the way Johannes loves Lovina isn't healthy. Love
has to be practical, too. You can't give your heart to an
Englisher, for example, because it would never work.
Love is important, but if it isn't rooted in some practical-
ity, it's useless."

"If I found a man who loved me like Johannes loves
Lovina, I'd marry him in a heartbeat," Elizabeth said.

"Yah," Bethany said. "I know. But you'd *marry* him.
You'd love him back. Johannes is alone."

"I know . . ." Elizabeth sighed. "I suppose there's
comfort in someone else missing her like we do."

"Yah," Bethany agreed. "And I know that marrying a
stranger isn't what we dream of, but I could see how it
might work for them."

The baby squirmed and started to cry, and Bethany
reached over and picked up her son. Mo stopped crying
the minute he was back in her arms again, and Elizabeth
smoothed down the sodden corner of her apron.

"They've both loved others deeply and had their hearts
broken," Elizabeth admitted. "I can see that."

"And it might help Johannes to pull out of this grief,"
Bethany added. "Besides, when Lovina does come back,
she won't be the same girl who left. I saw Micah last

week. He came to visit and he . . . he's different. He looks different, he acts differently, he's . . . he's *Englisher* now. And he seems to have forgotten all the things that used to come as second nature."

"And you think it'll be the same for Lovina," Elizabeth said.

"It will be, Lizzie," Bethany said softly. "She can't help but change. And if she didn't contact Johannes, it's for a good reason. I don't think we should hold him back."

"What does my brother think?" Elizabeth asked woodenly.

"The same," Bethany said with a sad shrug. "We all want Lovina home again, but there is no way any of us will be able to pick up where we left off."

The comfort of an Amish life was that things didn't change. The way of life they followed was the same one their grandparents had followed. The *Englishers* might move on with technology and newfangled ideas, but the Amish didn't. They embraced tradition. And yet relationships couldn't be slowed down along with the rest of their culture.

"I told Solomon that I'd ask my brother and you about a job," Elizabeth said. "He's one who *has* come back and he needs work."

Bethany didn't answer for a moment, then she said, "But he was in prison for robbery."

"Yah." Elizabeth dropped her gaze.

"I don't think my *daet* will like that idea," Bethany said. "It's dangerous. If his old friends came back—"

"He isn't in contact with them," Elizabeth replied. "He's determined to turn his life around."

"I'll talk to Isaiah and my *daet*," Bethany said. But by the look on her face, Elizabeth wasn't encouraged.

"Thank you for that," Elizabeth said. "People might change for the worse out there with the *Englishers*, but I think it's possible to come home. I really do."

She had to believe it. Because if Solomon couldn't come home, neither could Lovina. There had to be a place for them here, for all of them. People had to find forgiveness in their communities, because Solomon's warning was hanging heavy in her heart.

What if her beloved Amish life left her single and paying for her father's crimes for the rest of her life? Forgiveness had to be possible for all of their sakes.

Solomon sat in the parole officer's small, bland office on the edge of downtown Bountiful. It was located within walking distance from the buggy parking. The room felt claustrophobic, even though there was hardly any furniture inside. A middle-aged man with a receding hairline sat behind a desk that had no personal photos or anything on it, just a desktop calendar, a stapler, and a mishmash of paper.

"My name is Jeffrey Sparks," the man said with a cordial smile. "We'll be seeing a lot of each other. You can call me Jeff."

Solomon nodded, mute. He glanced around the office once more. It was almost cell-like, and that thought made the part in the center of his back tingle again.

"So, how does it feel to be out?" Jeff asked.

Solomon jerked his attention back to the man behind the desk.

"Good."

"It feels good," Jeff repeated, then fell silent, watching him. What did he want to hear?

"Yah, I mean, it's nice to be out," Solomon said, and when Jeff still watched him expectantly, he added, "but it's hard."

"Hm. It would be," Jeff agreed. "What part is hardest?"

"No one trusts me," Solomon said. "In the Amish life, trust is what makes our community function, and I've lost that. It leaves me on the outside."

"I have news for you," Jeff said. "It's the same with us regular people, too."

Solomon smiled faintly, then nodded. "Yah, I can see that."

"So what are your plans to make sure you don't commit any more crimes and you are able to rejoin society?"

"I . . ." Solomon felt his mouth go dry. His plan had been to go home for a little while and eat some home cooking, maybe repair his relationship with his mother. He hadn't really thought much beyond that—just a few basic comforts. "I don't really have one."

"I'm glad you're willing to admit that," Jeff said. "Do you think you'll be able to successfully restart your life and stay out of trouble without a proper plan?"

"Um—" Solomon shifted in his chair. "I'll come up with something."

"Thinking things through on the fly is what got you in prison to begin with," Jeff said, fixing him with a flat look. "You think it'll work better the second time?"

"Maybe not," Solomon admitted. "But I am thinking things through, and I will come up with something."

"Well, luckily for you, that's why I'm here—to help you adjust to life again, and to help you get a start. I'm here to help you formulate a plan."

"That would be nice," Solomon said. He'd assumed the parole officer was more like a prison guard, making sure he kept to the straight and narrow and willing to toss him back into jail if he didn't. Maybe there was still a fair amount of truth in that assumption still.

"How much schooling do you have?" Jeff asked.

"Eighth grade."

The man nodded, pressing his lips together. "That's fine if you're going to live Amish, but that won't be enough anywhere else."

"Yah." Solomon knew that. He'd felt the pinch of his limited education when he'd jumped the fence five years ago.

"Are you planning on staying Amish this time?" he asked. "I mean, you're dressed Amish."

Solomon glanced around the bland office. He missed the outdoors already—sunshine, fields, horses, and cattle . . . "I'm staying with my grandmother, so I'm dressed the part right now. It makes people more comfortable." An image of Lizzie rose in his mind. It made *her* more comfortable . . . "But I'm not sure I can live Amish now. Like I said, I'm on the outside now. No one trusts me. I'm looking for work, but it's not going to be easy."

"Do you want help with that?" Jeff asked.

"Yah. I do. If I can get it."

"I do have a few options for you," Jeff said. "But none of them are Amish. If you want to go back to your Amish life, I don't have any contacts to help you get work or anything like that."

"I understand," Solomon replied, leaning forward. Any job at all right now would be helpful.

"But I do have options that might interest you if you want to stay . . . English. Isn't that what you call it?" Jeff said.

"Yah," Solomon said with a nod.

"First of all, there's a program for adults looking to get their GED," Jeff said, pulling a pamphlet out of his desk. "That's a high school equivalency diploma. And after you get that, there are programs that will help you get further education in fields that are hiring. There are jobs in operating large vehicles, in computer maintenance, in technical fields like the oil and gas industry . . . There are opportunities out there so that you can restart your life and make a decent living."

But would that schooling take place in stifling rooms like this one? He wasn't keen on more school, but what choice did he have? A good income was tempting. And maybe there was a place for him with the *Englishers* if this man seemed confident.

"That sounds helpful," Solomon said.

"I'm glad," Jeff replied. "The first step is to get your high school diploma, though. Is that something you're willing to do?"

"What would it take?" Solomon's educational experience had been in a one-room schoolhouse with ample time outside and relatively low expectations from the teacher. He'd seen some TV shows that depicted a high school experience, and it all looked rather intimidating on a social level. All those people, all the expectations . . .

"There are two different programs offered in Bountiful," Jeff said. "I can get you set up in one of them. Normally, there are evening classes to allow people to work during the day. It's a lot of bookwork and you'll have to study hard, but others have done it before you."

Solomon nodded. "Okay . . ."

"Can you read? Any trouble with numbers or anything?" Jeff asked.

Solomon frowned. "Yah. I can read. I'm fine. Why?"

"I'm just checking," he replied. "There are other supports if you can't. The next GED class doesn't start for another month, but I can get you on the list. Is there anything else you need?"

Solomon shook his head. "I don't think so."

"And you said you're looking for work, and you have a place to stay, right?"

"Yah, I already started looking. I'm going to check the help wanted ads on the hardware store corkboard today," Solomon replied.

"Excellent. Well, best of luck. And I'll see you next week," Jeff said. "I'll mark you down as compliant and in good standing."

Solomon rose to his feet and exited the office. A young woman was waiting in the plastic chairs just outside, chewing on her thumbnail. She looked up at him and they exchanged a silent look before she headed into the office, and Solomon pushed outside into the summer air.

He sucked in a deep breath and put his straw hat back on his head. He started down the sidewalk and noticed a police cruiser at the traffic lights. Funny—cops still made him nervous. He'd been warned by the other inmates that once he got out, if anything happened in the community, the cops would come looking for him first. He was no longer just an innocent civilian, going about his business. He was now labeled as trouble.

The cruiser crept forward again and disappeared around a corner, and it was then that he spotted a familiar, meaty face across the street—the *Englisher* who'd had his hands on Elizabeth—and Solomon's blood ran cold. The man's face was bruised beneath that dirty baseball cap, and his nose looked swollen and painful.

The big man seemed to spot him at the same time, and for a moment their gazes met. Solomon's heart thudded to a stop. At first, neither of them moved, and then the big *Englisher* angled his steps across the street, sidestepping an oncoming car and continuing straight toward Solomon.

Gott, help me—

Did he deserve that prayer after what he'd done to the man? Did he deserve protection? Solomon wasn't even sure right now, but his heart raised upward anyway.

The man stepped up onto the sidewalk and stopped in front of Solomon.

"I knew I'd see you again," the man hissed.

Solomon didn't answer and he stepped to the side, eyeing him warily.

"Hey!" The man thumped Solomon in the middle of the chest.

"I don't want trouble," Solomon said.

"Not now, huh?" the man barked. "You don't want

trouble? What about the other day? You sure wanted it then!"

The man wanted to fight, and again, Solomon felt like the jail walls were starting to rise up around him all over again. Men were the same—on the inside of prison walls and out here in the free air. They were all the same. And when a bully wanted a fight, he would have it.

"You were hassling a woman," Solomon said. "And you were drunk. You wouldn't stop. I'm sure it's different now. Neither of us are drinking and we can be reasonable here—"

"'Reasonable.'" The man mimicked Solomon's Amish accent in a mocking tone. "Try to hit me now, you Amish puppy. Try it now!"

There was a part of Solomon that was tempted to do just that. Because for all this man's size and strength, he didn't have a teaspoon of Solomon's experience, and there was a good chance that this bully hadn't spent any time behind prison walls yet either. Give him a good prison term to hone his baser instincts and this man would go from bully to downright dangerous. But right now, Solomon would have the upper hand.

"I said I don't want to fight," Solomon said.

The man thumped him again, and Solomon felt his anger simmer.

"Don't touch me," Solomon said, his voice low, and he knew that his response had just crossed a line. He'd gone from peaceful to warning, and that was a breath away from a full-out fight. This was it—if he stood his ground now, he'd be grappling with this man again in the middle of Bountiful and he would be behind bars within the hour.

Gott, help me!

He didn't want to fight and he felt a surge of helplessness. This wasn't the life he wanted—fighting with local thugs and trying to intimidate hooligans. He'd come home for the Amish calm, for the slower pace, for the ability to think, but life wasn't going to go back to that, was it? He'd never just be an Amish man again.

A siren's whoop drew the big man's attention, and Solomon nearly sagged with relief. But he couldn't show weakness. There could be no fighting in front of cops . . . but the danger wasn't past yet.

"Hey!" a cop called out the window of his cruiser. "There a problem here, Alphonso?"

The *Englisher* shrugged extravagantly. "No, no, just talking to my buddy here."

"You okay?" the officer asked, turning his attention to Solomon. It took Solomon a second to realize that the cop only saw an Amish man being harassed on the street—nothing more.

"I am, but I wanted to go about my business, Officer," Solomon said.

"Go on, then," the officer said. "Alphonso, we're going to have a chat."

The police officer opened his door and got out, hand hovering around his belt, and Alphonso put up his hands in a sign of surrender.

"Nothing going on here," Alphonso said. "Honest, Officer. It was just a friendly talk, that's it—"

"I'm sure," the officer retorted, and Solomon gave the police officers a nod and then picked up his pace and headed for the intersection.

When he looked over his shoulder, Alphonso was too busy defending himself to the Bountiful police officers that he wasn't even looking.

Thank you, Gott, Solomon prayed silently.

He'd gotten out of this without a fight . . . Would he be able to next time? Alphonso knew where he was staying. But another realization chilled his blood. Alphonso also knew where to find Elizabeth.

Chapter Nine

When Solomon returned to pick up Elizabeth, she pulled herself up into the buggy next to him. It had been a nice visit—she'd missed her brother's family. Solomon glanced down at her and gave her a tight smile, then flicked the reins. His knee bounced with repressed energy.

"How did it go?" Elizabeth asked.

"Good." Solomon's voice was terse.

She smiled hesitantly. "You sure? You look tight enough to snap."

"Yah. It was good." He glanced over at her. "I'm fine."

He leaned forward to look in the side mirror, then checked the other one. He leaned back with a sigh.

"Are you looking for someone?" she asked.

"I saw that *Englisher* in town."

Her stomach sank. "The one you fought?"

"Yah, and he tried starting a fight in town, too. The police saw it and questioned him a bit and let me leave."

Somehow she'd hoped that those *Englisher* trouble-makers would simply go away and it would be over, but they did live in the area obviously. So it wasn't going to be so simple, was it? She felt a shiver run up her arms in spite of the heat of the day.

"The police could see that you were trying to be peaceful?" she asked.

"What they saw was an Amish man," he replied. "And they assumed I was peaceful because of these clothes. If they knew my record—"

"But they didn't," she cut in quickly. And that was something to be thankful for right now.

"No, they didn't." His knee kept jiggling and she put her hand on it, meaning to point out his nervous tick. As her hand touched his knee, he stilled, and she felt the warmth of his leg move up her arm. Solomon took the reins into one hand and put his warm palm over her fingers. She didn't move. Her touch had stilled him, and it seemed that his touch had done the same for her.

"We were taught that Gott would give us protection, blessing, even," he said softly.

"Yah." It was a fact.

"Does that still count for me?" he asked. His fingers closed around hers and he pulled her hand farther up his leg to a more comfortable position.

"If you've come back—" she started, but the words evaporated on her tongue. He'd already told her this wasn't permanent. "If you're doing what Gott wants of you, I think you'll have His blessing."

"I think I've gone so far away from what Gott wanted for me that a simple sidestep isn't going to get me back to it," he said, and she heard the sadness in his voice.

As they rode together toward Bridget's house, she allowed herself the luxury of leaning against his strong shoulder. He was warm and solid, and as a grass-scented breeze blew through the buggy, she felt a wave of sympathy for him. They said that when people went English, they no longer cared what Gott wanted, but Solomon seemed to care still.

"I asked Bethany about a job at her *daet*'s bookbinding shop for you," she said.

He looked down at her, and for a moment they were so close, his gaze locked on hers, then he looked back to the road. "What did she say?"

"She said she'd talk to my brother," she replied.

"Hm." He nodded, and she felt his grip on her hand tighten ever so little.

"And I'll talk to my brother myself tomorrow at service Sunday," she said.

"Thank you," he said, but she heard the doubt in his voice. "I have a backup plan, too."

"You do?" She straightened, but he kept her hand firmly in his. Should she pull back? She didn't want to. His strong grip was as much comfort to her as it was to him, it seemed.

"I'm going to finish high school," he said. "I can start next month, the parole officer says. After that, there could be more job training. There are more jobs available for a man with a diploma."

"But Amish don't do that," she said weakly. "We stop at the eighth grade. It's best that way—we have enough."

"Amish don't tend to spend time in prison either," he replied.

"Are you really wanting to do things the English way?" she asked.

"Do I want to go back to school?" he asked. "No. I don't. But I do want a job that I can count on. I don't need anything too fancy. I need to pay my bills, and buy my food, and maybe have some friends in my life."

"English friends," she breathed.

"I need people, Lizzie," he said softly. "I'm on my own."

Her heartbeat sped up. He had a point here—he needed a job, and he needed a community.

"I'm here," she said, and her voice sounded strange in her own ears.

"Yah—" He looked over at her and smiled. "You are."

"If you're patient, maybe things will get better here," she pressed on. "People might need time, but you might find a job yet."

Solomon didn't answer, but he tugged her closer to him again and she leaned back against his shoulder.

Solomon wasn't a regular Amish man anymore, and his future was with the English. She could feel it in the pit of her stomach. He was going to be forced to find a job somewhere, and if the *Englishers* were willing to help him, give him solutions, even hire him, and not his Amish brethren, he'd have little choice.

People would talk—they always did. They'd retell the story of the boy who jumped the fence and ended up in an *Englisher* jail. They'd tell how he came back for a little while, and they'd say that he'd given up on Gott because they wouldn't see any other way to explain it. In the kitchens across the county, and maybe even all the way to Indiana, people would talk about the destructive *choice*

Solomon made, and they'd never once take responsibility
for their own part in pushing him out.

The next morning dawned cool and overcast, and after
chores were completed and breakfast was eaten, Solomon
drove his grandmother and Elizabeth to service Sunday.
He'd told Seth that he wasn't going to attend, but then his
grandmother had asked him so sweetly if he'd drive them
there and Elizabeth had looked at him in silence, but there
had been hope in those dark eyes . . . and he couldn't turn
them down.

It was different being in the buggy with his grandmother between him and Elizabeth. He'd hoped to have
Elizabeth beside him. He wouldn't be able to hold her
hand, but to have her next to him, her arm brushing against
his, would have been a simple pleasure in the midst of a
difficult morning. . . . Apparently, his grandmother had
thought of that, however, and she'd tactfully inserted
herself between them.

"I'd best sit in the middle," she'd said gently. "You
know . . . appearances."

This Sunday's service was being held at a neighboring
farm owned by Hezekiah Beachy, one of the local elders.
It felt good to be back in an Amish role again this Sunday,
reins in hand, driving his family to service. The morning
was overcast, giving them a break from the heat of the
last few days, and he was grateful for that.

The horses plodded along at a leisurely pace, and the
closer they got to the Beachy farm, the tighter the knot in
his stomach grew. He'd be judged today—there was no

getting around it. People who hadn't heard he'd returned yet would find out, and there would be talk—most of it behind his back if he was lucky. The last thing he wanted was a lecture or three from older men who thought he could use a dose of wisdom.

"Word is going to spread when people see me," Solomon said.

"Yah," his grandmother agreed. "Someone is bound to write to your *mamm*, too . . . gossip being what it is."

Solomon sighed. "Should I have written to her myself?"

It was what his grandmother had wanted him to do from the start. But the thought of it still put his teeth on edge. What could he tell her without sounding pathetic? What could he say that was worth a stamp that wouldn't end with giving her yet another opportunity to tell him that he was a disappointment?

Bridget angled her head to the side in a half shrug. "I don't know, Sol. But she'll know soon enough that you're back. And she'll be angry with me for not having told her."

He hadn't considered that—his grandmother's relationship to his *mamm*. He'd taken the pair of them for granted growing up—their bickering and their solidarity. Mamm and Mammi had butted heads at times, but they'd always been there for each other.

"Sorry," he said quietly.

"It's all right." She leaned back and folded her hands in her lap. "The Lord works all things out for good for those who love Him. And He's working now."

"She'll understand, if you tell her that I didn't want you to write to her," he said. "Won't she?"

His grandmother gave him a rueful look. "No. She won't."

"She's the one who turned her back on me," he countered. "She doesn't really have a right to be offended."

"And she's still your mother," his grandmother replied. "Besides, when have you found that to work on people— telling them that they have no right to be upset?"

Solomon remained silent. His *mamm* hadn't come back to see him again behind bars. She hadn't cared to check on him to see if he was okay, if he was eating, if he was alive or dead. She'd treated him like a little boy being punished. She'd done that once when he'd complained that he didn't want to go to a prayer meeting with her and Mammi. She'd reined in the horses and ordered him out of the buggy about a mile from home and told him he could walk back, then, but they were going without him.

He could still remember that heartbroken feeling of watching the buggy carry on and knowing he'd go back to sit on the step alone, because they'd locked the house before they left. He'd been angry, and a little frightened, and he'd ended up spending the time waiting in the stables with the horses.

"There are codes between women, my dear boy," Bridget added, "and you don't know the half of them."

Solomon looked past his grandmother to Elizabeth on the other side of her. Elizabeth seemed to feel his eyes on her because she glanced toward him and gave him a small smile.

"Is it true?" he asked. "Is there a whole code here that I'm missing out on?"

"Yah, it's true," Elizabeth replied.

Well, maybe it was a good thing that his *mamm* would know he was home. At least when she found out, it wouldn't be because he was pleading with her for anything. He hadn't asked her for a thing this time around—not her forgiveness and not her love. Maybe she'd come home for him—come face him. And maybe she wouldn't . . . but it wouldn't be an outright rejection this way, at least.

An Amish family walked along the side of the road—a husband and wife and six *kinner* trailing along behind. They strolled along, and Solomon had to look a little closer to recognize them. He knew them—Thomas Hertzberger was a few years older than him and had married a girl from another community when Solomon was a young teen.

Another buggy was coming up behind them, moving faster than they were, but it wouldn't overtake them. The Beachy farm was coming up on the left, and an oncoming buggy was already turning in. Solomon guided the horses past Thomas's family and stayed back, his face shielded from view. But the oncoming buggy was driven by an older couple who had been kind to him when his *daet* died—and the old woman did a double take, staring at him in surprise. Her mouth silently formed his name, and then she disappeared from sight as the buggy went around the corner.

She was the first one to recognize him . . . and there would be more to come.

Solomon guided the horses down the drive. The field was already filled with gray buggies nestled in lush, green grass.

"Maybe you'd let me write a letter to your *mamm* now?" his grandmother asked, putting a hand on his arm. "I do care what she thinks of me, Sol. Maybe my letter can beat some of the others with a little blessing to speed it along."

"Yah," he said. "Okay."

Bridget smiled. "Good. Now, let's worship. Gott is still working among us, Solomon. I can promise you that."

When they parked the buggy and Elizabeth got down, she waited and gave Bridget a hand down, too. Bridget was spry for her age and didn't need much help as she came down to the soft grass at their feet. Solomon stood by the horses, ready to release them to graze for the day, but his gaze was locked on her. He looked nervous, and his usual cocksure bravado had faded. Why was it that facing down a massive *Englisher* bully looked like it took less bravery from him than facing down his own community?

"It'll be okay," Elizabeth said.

"Yah." He dropped his eyes and started undoing some buckles.

Elizabeth looked over to find Bridget eyeing her speculatively. Elizabeth looked down uncomfortably. It was Bridget's idea that she be friendly with him, wasn't it? Was Bridget changing her mind on that now?

"I need to find my brother," Elizabeth said. "I wanted to talk to him, and now is probably better before the service starts."

"You go on," Bridget said. "We'll be fine."

Elizabeth looked over at Solomon again, but he hadn't looked up again, his lips pursed as he unhitched the horses. She hesitated for a moment and then turned and headed out across the grassy field used for parking and toward that familiar old farmhouse.

She didn't know what she'd been doing lately. She felt a powerful draw toward that wounded ex-con, and it didn't make sense! She knew she had no future with him. Elizabeth was a pragmatic woman. She'd turned down better men than him over the years because she had an image in her mind of the life she wanted.

And yet there was something about Solomon Lantz that tugged at her . . . She'd held his hand, she'd kissed him, she'd talked with him outside in the darkness. She'd gone further with Solomon than she had with any other man who'd pursued her, and Solomon wasn't staying. So why was she letting this physical draw between them keep going? The strength he exuded, the vulnerability in his eyes when he met her gaze, and the way he kissed her so that every inch of her body tingled . . . that wasn't so easy to forget.

And she was realizing after all these cautious years that she was longing for some connection, too. Was that her problem—something as simple as loneliness?

Elizabeth spotted her brother out by the tent that had been erected for the service. His arms were crossed over his chest and he was talking with another man from the community. Bethany wasn't anywhere to be seen—likely inside the house with the baby. If she wanted to speak to her brother without his wife present, she'd need to take advantage of this.

She headed across the farmyard, nodding at some friends—if she could even count these women as friends anymore—and a few acquaintances. It was easier to walk past on a mission than to stand around looking for someone willing to chat with her these days. There were a few who were warming up again, but it was different. She wasn't the respected daughter of a powerful preacher. She was now a woman to be pitied. The shift had been palpable.

When she approached her brother, the man he was speaking with noticed her first. He gave her a nod, then reached out and touched Isaiah's elbow in a farewell before heading off. Her brother glanced toward her looking tired.

"I saw Bethany and Mo yesterday morning," she said, pasting a smile on her face. "Mo sure is growing!"

"Yah, he is." Her brother took off his hat and rubbed a hand through his hair before replacing it. "Bethany said that she'd seen you—"

"It was nice to visit," she said. "One of these days I need to come by when you're home so I can see my big brother, too."

Isaiah smiled at that, but it didn't reach his eyes. "She also said you wanted me to talk to her father about a job for Solomon Lantz."

So her sister-in-law had mentioned it already. Elizabeth hadn't been sure that she would. By the grim look on her brother's face, she could tell how this was going to go.

"It's hard for him, Isaiah," she said. "Even Seth Stuckey won't give him a chance. They used to be friends back in the day."

"There might be good reason for Seth not to hire him," her brother replied. "Solomon was involved in a violent robbery. People have to take care of their families. I wouldn't be bringing him to work within a mile of my wife either."

"He was tricked, though," she said.

"So he tells the pretty girl working with his grand-mother," Isaiah replied wryly.

"It isn't like that," she said. At least not all of it was like that.

"Lizzie, I thought you knew what you wanted out of life," her brother said. "I know it's been hard lately, but I managed to fall in love and get married. And I'm the one who was helping Daet find investors! So don't give up yet."

"Your situation was . . . unique," she said delicately.

His wife was already pregnant when he'd married her. Bethany's family had good reason to let her marry him.

"Still," Isaiah replied. "We said we'd help keep each other grounded, right? Well, I'm doing that for you right now. You've got to take a big step away from Solomon Lantz."

Elizabeth sighed. "Isaiah, if you talked to him, I think you'd see that he's still one of us. Or he should be. But if the community makes it impossible for him to stay, what choice will he have? Yah, we have to protect ourselves, but we also have to protect *our own*."

"Wait—" Isaiah cast her an annoyed look. "You aren't letting him court you, are you?"

"No, I'm not letting him court me!" she shot back. "I understand how complicated this is—trust me, I have my own future in mind, too, and it isn't with him. But he's staying at Bridget's house, so I see him! Bridget wanted me to be friendly with him, help him settle back in. So this is all by Bridget's request and with her blessing. Solomon and I have talked quite a bit. This is incredibly hard for him, and I know what it's like to have my community turn their back on me. You know what that feels like, too. How is he supposed to get another chance if no one will give it to him?"

"Lizzie, you need to be careful around that man," Isaiah said, lowering his voice. "He's an ex-con. He's done a crime bad enough for *Englishers* to put him in jail, and he's back. He has nowhere else to go! But how long until he ends up in his old habits?"

"You got a second chance with a job at the book bindery," Elizabeth said softly. "That job made all the difference for you."

"It was our *daet* who broke the law, not me," he replied.

She sighed. "So you won't help him, then?"

"No." Isaiah shook his head. "I have a family to protect, too, Lizzie. What if I asked my father-in-law to give him a job and Solomon's old friends robbed the place?"

"Where is he supposed to find a job, then?" she asked. "If his friends won't help—"

"I'm not his friend!" Isaiah replied, and he sighed. "Lizzie, you have a really good heart. You do. But you can't risk your own reputation with trying to help him. We have enough over our heads with our own father."

There was no point arguing. The problem was, she completely understood her brother's position. If she hadn't gotten to know Solomon again, she'd share it just as vehemently.

"I just thought I'd ask," she said.

"And speaking of Daet," he added, his voice lowering

further. He took a step closer and glanced around before continuing. "I got a letter from him in yesterday's mail."

"Oh?" She frowned, and the look on her brother's face made her pulse speed up.

"He's getting out of jail," he whispered.

Elizabeth's heart pounded to a stop and she stared, openmouthed, at her brother. "What?"

"He's getting out early on good behavior," Isaiah said. "And he's coming home . . ."

"There is no more family home!" she said. "The farm is gone. Where is he going to stay?"

"My place," her brother replied. "For now."

"Do you *want* him at your place?" she breathed. "Is Bethany okay with it?"

"What other choice do I have?" Isaiah asked.

"So she doesn't like it," Elizabeth concluded.

"Even I don't like it!" Isaiah retorted. "I don't think you would either. But we're doing our duty. The bishop says it's all right so long as Daet is ready to confess his sin and face the consequences. So you see why we can't be helping out the other ex-con in town. We have enough problems of our own, Lizzie. Someone else will have to help Solomon."

"When is Daet coming?" she asked weakly.

"Tomorrow. I'll pick him up from the bus depot."

Elizabeth nodded, and she felt her throat close off with emotion. She didn't want to see her father right now. She hadn't prepared herself for it. Sure, she'd read his letters and grappled with her feelings about what he'd done, and about trying to forgive him, but that was hard enough with her father locked up. But he was coming back . . .

very soon! Could she look him in the face? Could she even be glad he was out?

"What did he say in the letter?" she whispered. "I mean . . . what is he expecting from us?"

"He says he misses us terribly," Isaiah replied. "He reminded us about old times, when we were happy as a family. He asks for our forgiveness."

She nodded. "It won't be the same, though."

"Maybe once we face it, it'll be easier," Isaiah said. "That's what I'm hoping, at least. It'll be better than dreading it."

"Did you tell the bishop that he's coming?" she asked.

"I told him this morning," her brother replied. "Whatever I do is with the bishop's blessing. I've got a family reputation to protect, too, Lizzie."

"And if the bishop says he's shunned and he has to leave?" she asked.

Isaiah's eyes misted. "Then he leaves."

The families were starting to split up now, the women headed to the women's side of the tent and the men to the men's side. Elizabeth stood there for a moment, her legs feeling leaden. Would Bridget want her to stay and help her if her father was back in the community?

Isaiah reached out and squeezed her arm.

"We'll get through this," her brother said. "But we have to take care of our own problems. You get that, right?"

She nodded. "Yah."

There was no argument from her. Their problems had just multiplied. With Daet back, whatever bit of warmth had begun in the community would immediately be cut off because Daet had ruined the finances of more than one local family with that fraud. People might forgive on a spiritual level, but it wouldn't be happening on a personal one.

The Amish believed in their spiritual ideals, but at the end of the day they were human, too.

Chapter Ten

Solomon sat at the kitchen table that evening with a pair of leather boots courtesy of one of the neighbors. They were well worn, but with a good polish and buffing, they'd look better. He dipped the brush into the black polish and started brushing it over the leather in smooth strokes.

"It's Sunday, Sol," Bridget said reproachfully.

"I know, Mammi," he said apologetically. "But keeping my hands busy makes me feel better."

Shoe polishing wasn't necessary work, like caring for the animals, but it kept him from pacing a trench into the floor from his own nervous energy. Service Sunday had been difficult. The preaching had been long, and he wasn't used to sitting on a hard bench, his back straight, for that amount of time anymore. The sermon topic had been dry, and his gaze kept moving over to where Elizabeth sat next to her sister-in-law, who held the sleeping baby in her lap. Elizabeth sat perfectly still, her expression creased with worry. And that had only made him wonder if that was because of him. Was he making her life that much more difficult?

When they got back, they ate, and Solomon headed out to clean the stables only to find one horse had wandered off through a damaged part of the barbed-wire fence. He'd had to walk three miles down the road to find the mare and bring her back. After that he'd had to fix the fence, then there was dinner, and now he sat at the table with these boots in front of him, wondering if he looked as tattered on the outside as he felt on the inside. He hoped not. Tomorrow he needed to look for work and he didn't want to give anyone reason to turn him down.

Elizabeth was outside working in the garden, and for a few minutes at least he and his grandmother were alone.

"Sol, when we stopped at the Hertzbergers' place on the way home, I picked up something," Bridget said. She opened a kitchen drawer and pulled out a cell phone, then placed it on the table next to his boots.

"What's this?" It was a flip phone—an old one.

"I spoke with the bishop today, and he says that if Elizabeth used a cell phone in case of emergency at the stand, that would be all right," Bridget said.

"And you got one that quickly?" he asked with a frown. "Is there a rebellious streak in my grandmother I didn't know about?"

Bridget smiled at his wry humor and picked the phone back up. "Sarah Hertzberger used this when she had that difficult pregnancy. It's a phone that has time already paid . . . I don't quite understand it. But it's supposed to be easy to use. She wrote down the phone number for us, and we can call the police if we need to. You see? You just type in the number for the police in here—9-1-1—"

"What do you mean, 'we'?" he asked, plucking the

phone from her hands. "And don't press Send, Mammi. It'll call them. You can't do that if it isn't an emergency."

"I was just—" Bridget sighed.

"It's okay," he said. "I know how to use it."

Bridget brushed her hands down her apron. "Fine. You know how. That's good. All the same, if I'm there at the produce stand myself, I'm sure those young men would behave."

"I don't think it works that way for *Englishers*, Mammi," he replied.

"Do they hatch from eggs?" she demanded archly. "They have mothers and grandmothers. A nice, stern look goes a long way."

Solomon sighed, trying to cap his frustration. He needed to find work, but he couldn't leave them undefended here either. "Mammi, look, I'll do it. I'll man the stall. You and Elizabeth stay here at home. I'll take the cell phone."

"If I knew those men's mothers, I would take care of this easily enough," she said with a sigh. "But I don't. And I won't be chased into my house out of fear of a few hooligans either."

"They're grown men, Mammi."

"This is my life, Sol!" Her chin trembled. "This is my livelihood! What am I supposed to do, hide indoors? There will be no money for extras if I do that. We have a garden to harvest and produce to sell. That doesn't go away because of some troublemakers."

Was she even listening to him? Did she understand how dangerous these men were? If his mother were here, she'd be able to talk some sense into Mammi—she'd always had that gift. But she wasn't here, and Solomon was no authority figure in this kitchen.

"We'll figure it out," he said.

"I also wrote that letter to your mother and mailed it," Bridget said. "I told her that you'd arrived, and that you're looking for work. And that . . . you miss her."

"Mammi, stop speaking for me," he said with a sigh.

"You do miss her," Bridget replied. "I won't apologize for telling the truth."

Would his mother come back? This was about more than his need for her forgiveness now. They needed someone with a level head to make some decisions around here again.

"You've come home, Sol," Bridget said. "This is what your mother wanted—you back on the proper side of the fence. I'm sure she'll be satisfied."

"I take it you didn't tell her that this isn't a permanent solution?" he asked.

She batted her hand through the air. "Who knows? Maybe it will be. Who can say for certain?"

"I could," he replied.

His grandmother shot him an annoyed look. "Gott might have other plans for you, young man. There's a reason why we always say, 'if Gott wills it.' Do not tempt the Most High, Sol."

Why did he feel like he was being lectured for telling the truth? His grandmother looked out the window in the direction of the chicken house, where Elizabeth was gathering eggs. A light glowed warm and golden through the small windows. His grandmother yawned, and he felt a surge of sympathy for her. She was an old woman now, and while Solomon wanted to help her, he knew that his presence caused her more work and worry, too. They both needed his mother to return.

"You can go up to bed, Mammi," he said.

"I should wait until Elizabeth gets in," she replied. "It really is my responsibility to make sure that Elizabeth isn't in a compromising situation, and with you staying here— you're both young and single and . . . available. . . ."

"What am I going to do, Mammi?" he asked with a wry smile. "I'm going to wash dishes. I'm going to wish her a good night and I'm going to finish polishing these shoes. Her reputation will be safe in the same room as me, I'm sure."

His grandmother stifled another yawn. "Be sure that it is, Sol."

How much did she suspect? Solomon didn't answer, and as Bridget made her way upstairs, he picked up the shoe brush again. Elizabeth was the bright spot in this difficult return to his boyhood home. She sparked something inside him, and maybe that was visible to others . . . but she gave him something else to focus on besides his own repentance. She was an unattainable goal, and maybe every man needed one of those. It kept him putting one foot in front of the other.

He buffed the first boot and then put it down on an old piece of newspaper—*The Budget*. As he picked up the second boot, he saw a smear of black polish on the front of his white shirt and he let out a moan.

This was one of three shirts—he couldn't afford to ruin it. He put down the boot and the brush and looked from his smudged hands to his soiled shirt.

He muttered irritably and headed to the kitchen sink

where he washed his hands thoroughly with soap, gray suds going down the drain, and then shrugged off his suspenders and unbuttoned his shirt. He slipped it off and poured a dribble of blue dish liquid onto the smudge.

Just then the side door opened, and he heard Elizabeth come inside. He couldn't see her past the cupboards.

"I think I must have missed some cucumbers last time," Elizabeth said, and she came toward the sink, "because I found a few more—"

She stopped short and he looked over his shoulder. Elizabeth's gaze moved over his torso, and then she looked quickly to the side.

"I've got a stain on my shirt," he said. "Shoe polish."

"Oh, that will be tough to get out." Elizabeth's gaze flickered toward the sink.

"I don't want to leave it for my grandmother to wash," he said. "Besides, I don't have many shirts. This one can't be turned into rags yet."

"Right . . ." Elizabeth came hesitantly up beside him and looked down at the shirt in his hands. "Let me—"

She took it, scrubbed the fabric together a couple of times, and then reached for the dish soap again, adding more. She laid the shirt inside the sink and glanced over at him, her cheeks pink. He noticed the way her gaze lingered on his chest before she jerked her eyes up to meet his.

"Sorry, should I cover myself?" he asked, whisking a towel from the counter and holding it in front of his bare chest teasingly.

Elizabeth rolled her eyes and turned away. "You're too English."

He dropped the towel. "What—should I have left this shirt balled up in my laundry hamper and let my grand-mother deal with it?" he retorted. "I need to get it clean."

"Let that sit for a few minutes and then I'll add vinegar and baking soda," she said.

"That's the trick?"

"Yah." She turned back again, but she looked res-olutely toward the sink.

He couldn't help but chuckle. He was flustering her, and maybe a small part of him liked it. With Elizabeth, he was no longer the bad boy trying to fit back in, it was on a more basic level—man and woman.

"What was bothering you today?" he asked.

"Hmm?" She allowed herself to look at him again.

"Today in service. You looked worried. That wasn't about me, was it?"

"No, it wasn't about you," she said, but her smile slipped. "I talked to my brother—" She swallowed. "My *daet* is being let out of prison. He's coming back."

Solomon let the words sink in, then he eyed her cau-tiously. "Is this good news?"

"You know what he did," she replied. "And I don't know if I'm ready to face him."

"Yah . . ." It was why Solomon hadn't told his family he was getting released either.

"The bishop says he can come stay with my brother," she went on. "So, as long as the bishop is supportive, my brother says he'll help Daet out."

"Where else would your father go?" Solomon asked quietly.

"I don't know," Elizabeth said, and her voice caught.

"You were worried about him suffering not so long ago and now he'll be out," he said. "That's a good thing, isn't it?"

"Yah—" She nodded quickly. "At least he'll be out of jail. But . . . he robbed his neighbors, Solomon, and he ruined our lives! And now he's coming back."

"Yah . . ." He could see the complications there, but he had no answers either.

"Do you know what it's like to be the child of a convict?" she asked.

Solomon was silent and her lips quivered. She met his gaze and blinked back a mist of tears.

"I know what it's like to be the convict," he said.

"I'm sorry—I'm complaining to the wrong person," she said, and she started to turn, but he reached out and caught her hand.

"No, you aren't," he said. "You have every right to be angry, and shocked, and resentful, and . . ." He couldn't think of anything else to name the swirl of emotion she must be holding inside herself. "You can talk to me, Lizzie. You always can. I'm not quite that fragile."

She hesitated a moment, then turned back, her eyes flashing with ferocity.

"My father ruined us!" she said, her voice shaking. "He ruined our good name, and he preached with such authority about morality and community, and the strength of our Amish faith. . . ." Her lips turned downward. "And now he's coming back, and I'm no longer the preacher's daughter, I'm . . . *his* daughter."

"And you love him," Solomon murmured.

"I love him, and I hate him, and I want him to be safe,

but I want him to stay away, and—I'm now the daughter of a criminal!"

"You're Lizzie Yoder," he said, and he tugged her closer, feeling the swish of her skirt against his pants. She had an unnoticed tendril of hair loose. "You're not just someone's daughter, you're a woman in your own right."

"Everyone is someone's child," she said. "Everyone."

And while Solomon had to agree with her logic, it wasn't her argument that had his attention. He wanted to soothe her, to protect her, to take this burden from her, but he couldn't. He tucked the tendril of hair behind her ear and her free hand fluttered up to touch it.

"Then be your mother's daughter," he said. "You have more than one parent."

Elizabeth blinked up at him, her hand frozen at her face, as if the thought were a new one, and he reached out and ran his thumb down her soft cheek. He didn't know why he was doing this—it was going too far, again, and he knew it. But she didn't pull away as he traced his thumb along her jawline and brushed it across her lips. She parted them, sucking in a breath, and when she swayed ever so slightly in his direction, whatever was left of his self-control shuddered and fell.

Solomon dipped down his head and caught her lips with his, but this time he didn't hesitate or wait for permission. He pulled her against him, inhaling the scent of her, drawing her as close against him as he could. The last time he'd kissed her had been her first, and this kiss may very well be their last, and he wasn't going to leave it halfway. He'd kiss her like he'd longed to, and at the very least she'd never forget him. When she let out an audible sigh, he deepened the kiss, and she tasted like vanilla. Her hands pressed against his bare sides, and as he kissed her, he moved his hands down her neck until he reached the collar of her dress. He could feel just the barest hint of collarbone, and he had to stop there, but just that much fired his blood until all he could hear was the pounding of his own heartbeat and the sound of her breath.

Elizabeth leaned against Solomon's bare chest, his skin cool to her touch. His fingers plucked at the collar of her dress, and then he dropped his hands to her waist and pulled her closer against him. He seemed to know exactly how to do this—how to kiss a woman, how to hold her . . . and what the next steps seemed to be. She'd never done this before, and her head felt like it was full of water—no coherent thought, just sensation and longing as his fingers splayed over the small of her back.

He pulled her closer and she let her fingers slide around his waist and up his muscular back. His lips moved over hers so purposefully, completely in control of the moment. And all her worries seemed to melt away. There was something about his height and his strength, his arms around her seemed to hold her up, even though her knees felt weak.

Solomon broke off the kiss and pulled back a couple of inches. He didn't let go of her, though, and she dropped her gaze, suddenly embarrassed. Why did she keep doing this?

"Lizzie . . ."

She looked up, and his eyes were filled with a kind of burning intensity she'd never seen before in any other man, but something deep inside her was responding to it.

She didn't want to move. He twined a loose tendril of her hair around his finger, then let it go.

"Your hair is loose," he murmured.

"Oh," she said, shakily pulling away from him. The cool evening air flooded between them, and she fixed her hairpins, feeling for any other loose bits. She licked her lips.

"That was worth messing up your hair," he said.

"That's something you've done before . . ."

"I've been in jail for a year," he said with a teasing smile. "Trust me, there was none of this behind bars."

"Before that . . ."

"Are you asking if I've kissed a woman before?" he asked, and the teasing melted out of his voice. "Is that what you're worried about?"

She looked up at him mutely. She knew the answer—of course he had. And this—whatever it was, was entertainment for him. The *Englishers* played with such things, but the Amish didn't. Kisses and cuddles were saved for a fiancé, a husband.

"Yah, I've had a girlfriend or two," he said slowly. "But it's never been quite like that . . ."

"I don't believe you—"

He sobered. "I'm many things, Lizzie, but I'm no liar. That was . . ." He reached for her hand and pressed it against the center of his chest, over the top of the swirl of chest hair. She caught her breath. His heart beat fast beneath her fingers.

"You feel that?" he whispered.

She nodded.

"I wasn't quite the world-wise *Englisher* you think I am . . ." He licked his lips. "I didn't know how to talk to

Englisher girls. I dated a few different women, but I certainly never felt quite like this. . . ."

"All the same, I believe in facing things," she whispered, and she pulled her hand back. It was too intimate to touch him that way. "And you're not staying—neither am I. You've experienced parts of life I can't even imagine. So let's not pretend that I'm your first anything. I don't want you to reinvent history."

"Lizzie, I squandered my firsts," he whispered. "It's true. I haven't made great choices, and a lot of my lessons have been learned the worst way possible. But I'm not lying to you either. You're . . ."

She hung on his words, waiting for him to finish. "I'm what?"

"I don't know how to explain this . . ." A smile curved his lips. "When I was a boy, my *mamm* used to make strawberry jam, and I wasn't allowed to just eat it. Of course."

"Of course," she murmured back.

"She'd work for days, jarring it and stacking it on the shelves in the basement, and she'd keep one jar in the kitchen. I used to sneak it one teaspoon at a time, and I'd eat that spoon of jam outside behind the chicken house. There was nothing quite so delicious . . . you're my teaspoon of forbidden jam."

Elizabeth couldn't help but smile at that. "Are you going to say I'm sweet? That's cheesy."

"No, you're addictive." He touched her cheek again. "And worth waiting for just a teaspoon."

She felt her cheeks heat.

"Did you get in trouble?" she whispered. "For the jam, I mean. Did you get caught?"

"Every time." A slow smile crept over his face. "I never licked my lips well enough, and Mamm would catch me. One day she found a stash of spoons out behind the chicken house, too."

"And you didn't learn your lesson?" she asked.

"I learned I liked strawberry jam more than I was afraid of a swat," he said with a slow smile. She remembered him as a teenager, unwilling to be curbed by an elder's lecture, or by any of the complaints sent back to his *mamm*.

"That might be your problem," she breathed. "You should have taken a few more of those swats to heart."

"Maybe. But my problem is the opposite of yours."

So she had a problem now? At the moment her problem was standing shirtless in front of her talking about strawberry jam, his voice low, and his fingers stroking the tender inside of her wrist.

"And what's mine?" she asked as a shiver of goose bumps went up her arm.

"You were told to avoid jam," he said. "And so you turned your back on it, and you never try it. Ever. And you think you're better for your sacrifice."

"What's the jam, then?" she asked with a teasing smile. "I feel like that changed."

"A kiss," he said.

"Is that what this was, a simple kiss?"

He shrugged. "Maybe not quite so simple . . . I'd like a little bit of credit for having done it well, but this was a kiss, yah."

His smoldering gaze met hers and her stomach flipped. He was thinking of doing it again, she could tell by the way his gaze moved down to her lips.

"You waited and waited for the perfect man," he said. "And I think you'll discover that when you find someone who's religious enough, respectable enough, serious enough, financially comfortable enough . . . that he won't be able to kiss you like I just did."

"What makes you so sure?" she breathed.

"Call it a hunch," he said. "I've never had a kiss like that before either . . ."

"Why do you hate that I want a good man?" she whispered.

"I don't hate it," he said.

"You seem to."

"I just . . ." He shrugged. "I think you were told the same kind of half-truths I was."

She eyed him uncertainly. "Like what?"

"I was told that out with the *Englishers*, there was freedom. And there was . . . but I ended up with even less when I went to jail," he replied. "I think you've been told that a perfect man exists out there, and if you're a very, very good woman, you can earn him."

Elizabeth dropped her gaze. "You make it sound like a business transaction."

"What if there isn't a payoff?" he asked. "What if there isn't some guaranteed ideal life for those who follow all the rules? What if we're all just doing our best, and the rain falls on the righteous and the unrighteous alike?"

Then everything she'd based her life on would be in vain, and the life she'd longed for would feel depressingly out of reach. If there was no difference between the good people and the bad, if there was no reward for doing things Gott's way, why did the Amish carry on so stoically down the narrow path?

But this sounded a little too much like a ploy to get her to go further than a kiss. She'd been warned about this—every girl was. And if he was using the Bible to try to convince her . . .

"Are you trying to talk me into something?" she asked hesitantly.

Solomon released her wrist and he winced. "You think that's what I was doing?"

"I don't know . . ." she admitted.

"Well, it isn't," he said softly, and he took a deliberate step back. "I told you. I only ever took a teaspoon of that jam. I wasn't asking for more than a kiss from a woman who isn't my wife. I never will."

He turned back to the sink and opened the cupboard. He pulled down a plastic jug of vinegar and a box of baking soda. He opened the vinegar, sniffed it, closed it again, and picked up the shirt.

"You just need to—" she started.

"I'll figure it out." He cast her a smile that still retained some of that earlier smolder. "I might be more self-sufficient than you think."

He was giving her an escape, and if she didn't want to regret this evening, she'd take it.

She nodded. "I'll head up to bed, then."

Solomon reached out and touched her cheek with the back of one finger. "Good night, Lizzie."

What was it about this man that one touch like that could make her start longing for more? She needed to get upstairs and clear her head. That was what she needed. So she turned and headed up the staircase, and she didn't allow herself to look back.

She could hear the water turning on for a moment,

though, and then off. Then on. He was scrubbing his shirt, and she did hope he got it clean.

The problem with stains, both the kind in fabric and the kind in reputations, was that they didn't always wash out, even with the best scrubbing and with following all the advice. Not every shirt was salvageable. There was a little faded discoloration that could take a church item of clothing and turn it into workwear. As quickly as that. It had happened to the Yoders already.

And if Elizabeth didn't want her own reputation to sink her, she'd best keep her head on her shoulders. His touch wasn't worth her entire future. She shivered. At least that was what she'd realize once she had some time to breathe. She knew it.

Chapter Eleven

The next morning Solomon was quiet over breakfast, but Elizabeth felt his sock foot touch her bare toes under the table. It was a casual touch, but he didn't move away either. She looked up at him over her bowl of oatmeal and he gave her a small smile.

His kiss wasn't quite so forgettable as she'd hoped. She shouldn't be playing with this . . . even if he wasn't pushing for more, those searing kisses were enough. His arms, his hands, the way his dark gaze could pin her to the spot.

"Did you get the stain out?" Elizabeth asked.

"Yah," Solomon replied. "My shirt is on the line outside."

"A stain?" Bridget asked, coming back to the table with a plate of toast. "What stain?"

"I got some shoe polish on my shirt," he said.

"I can take care of that for you," Bridget said. "You could have left it."

"I'm not leaving extra work for my *mammi*," Solomon said, shooting his grandmother a smile. "I scrubbed it out."

"Easy as that?" Bridget asked, raising an eyebrow.

"No, Elizabeth gave me some pointers," he replied.

Bridget turned her gaze to Elizabeth, her expression prim. She didn't look away either, and for a couple of beats Elizabeth felt the heat rise in her face.

"I . . . helped him," Elizabeth said.

"Ah. Well, let's finish eating and you two can get the produce set up. If you two can handle it alone for a few hours, I have some housework I want to finish up."

Elizabeth helped Bridget clear the table when they were done eating, and then they all turned their energy to getting the produce ready for the stand once more. Elizabeth had seen two police cruisers drive slowly down their road already, so maybe Seth had said something. Unruly *Englishers* were a danger to more than just the Lantz home.

Elizabeth and Bridget carried a plastic tub of produce up from the cool basement between them, and Solomon carried another one. They worked quickly, but no one spoke much.

"So, if we see them, we call the police?" Elizabeth asked as they deposited the tub on the kitchen floor and she rubbed her hands.

"Yah, I think so," Bridget said.

Elizabeth looked toward Solomon, who looked more sober than she'd seen him before, and her stomach sank. If Solomon was scared, she should be, too.

"It'll be fine," he said when he seemed to sense her eyes on him.

"And this is the phone," Bridget said, handing it over. It felt strange to have something like this. Some farmers in other communities had cell phones they kept in their barn in case of emergencies, but their community hadn't crossed that line, and she'd never seen one close up before.

Solomon picked up a tub of produce and headed for the side door, bumping the screen open ahead of himself and disappearing outside.

"Could you put the last tub on the porch for Sol?" Bridget asked. "Then come inside. I wanted to talk to you about something."

It was about her father, no doubt. Bridget knew he was returning and, very likely, she'd been thinking that over.

"Sure." Elizabeth sucked in a breath and headed for the last tub of produce. This had been a wonderful respite, and Bridget had her grandson now. But a wave of sadness washed over her as she carried the tub outside.

Solomon met her at the porch, and when he took the tub from her, his fingers brushed over hers.

"Ready to head up to the stand?" he asked, his voice low. His dark gaze held hers and she felt her face warming in response to him. She shook her head.

"No, I have to talk to Bridget," she said. "I'll meet you up there."

"Everything okay?" he asked, his gaze moving over her shoulder toward the screen door.

"I don't know. I'll see."

Maybe it would be good discipline to get her away from Solomon anyway. Whatever she was feeling for him wasn't helpful.

"Okay . . . see you at the road." His gaze lingered on her for a moment, and then he turned and trotted down the steps.

Elizabeth went back inside and found Bridget standing beside the kitchen table, her hands clasped in front of her and her gaze locked on a spot on the floor in front of her, glasses on the table beside her.

"Is it about my *daet*?" Elizabeth asked.

"Hmm?" Bridget shook her head. "No, it's not your father."

"Oh!" Elizabeth felt a weight come off her shoulders.

"It's about Sol." Bridget licked her lips. "And you."

Elizabeth's breath caught in her chest.

"What about us?" she asked.

"This is very uncomfortable for me to talk about, so please just let me say my piece," Bridget said. "I know that I asked you to be his friend and to make him feel welcome, but I only asked that of you because I was certain of your character and I thought you might be able to help him. So this may very well be my fault . . ."

"What?" Elizabeth asked, although she thought she knew.

"I saw you last night," Bridget said, and some pink tinged her cheeks.

"Oh—" Elizabeth's face heated, too.

"So as the one who is responsible for this home, it falls on me to speak with you about it," Bridget went on. "You have a reputation to worry about, just like every young woman. But you have more against you because of your father. Now, if you want to find a good husband and get married, you'll have to guard your reputation like a cow with her calf. You're a sweet girl with a big heart and you'll make a lovely wife, but that won't happen if you aren't careful."

"I know—" Elizabeth felt tears of embarrassment mist her eyes.

"Sol is a good-looking young man," Bridget went on.

"But he's not in a stable place right now either. He's only just back from prison. He might think he's ready for marriage and *kinner*, but—"

"He isn't ready for them. He doesn't claim to be," Elizabeth interjected.

"Then what on earth are you doing?" Bridget breathed, looking up at last and fixing her with an agonized gaze. "I thought at the very least he was making promises."

"I—" Elizabeth sucked in a breath. "I don't know what I was thinking. Not nearly enough, obviously."

"You grew up without a *mamm*, my girl," Bridget said. "But you know how things work. A good girl doesn't do those things! A kiss should be brief enough that it can be stolen through a closing door. That wasn't what I saw!"

"Bridget, I'm sorry," Elizabeth said. "And you're right. I know that!"

"Good girls *wait*," Bridget said firmly. "And so do good men. If you don't have things together enough to discuss marriage seriously, you have no business kissing each other or letting him hold you like that. Pregnancies happen—"

"We would never go that far!" Elizabeth cut in. "And we were both very clear on that."

"That's very sweet that you think so," Bridget replied curtly. "And many a girl has thought she never would either, until things tumbled too far in the privacy of a hayloft and she found herself pregnant. Young people think they are the first ones to have invented a passionate kiss, or even the act of procreation. You are not the first to have experienced any of these feelings, and you wouldn't be the first to fall pregnant either. You remember that."

"I will." Elizabeth swallowed hard.

"And one more thing," Bridget said briskly, and then her expression softened and she picked up her glasses from the table. "I don't think you're a bad girl. I think you're human. I think you have feelings, and a body, and hopes for your own future. And that combination can get out of control very quickly. I was young once, too, so I'm not trying to begrudge you your youth. I just need you to be more aware of what you're doing."

Elizabeth nodded. "I will be. I'm sorry."

"I'll never bring it up again," Bridget said, and she put her glasses back on. "It's over. We'll pretend this discussion never even happened. Now, off you go. And use that cell phone if you see that *Englisher*, you hear me?"

"I will." Elizabeth picked up the money pouch and turned toward the door. She escaped into the warm July sunlight and sucked in a ragged breath. To be lectured by Bridget Lantz—it was almost more than her pride could bear.

Bridget was right, of course. But she was wrong that they'd simply been playing around. Elizabeth wasn't the kind of woman to do that. . . . Somehow Solomon, with all the reasons to stay clear of him, had managed to soften her heart. So this might be more dangerous than Bridget feared.

As Elizabeth walked up the drive, the twitter of birds overhead were in stark contrast to the turmoil inside her. Solomon stood at the stall arranging a row of zucchini on the slanted display shelf. He looked up as she approached and silently went into the stall to put the money into the box.

"Everything okay?" Solomon asked.

She looked up to find him at the stall doorway. He met her gaze easily enough.

"Your grandmother saw us last night," she said woodenly.

Solomon's face paled and he dropped his gaze. "Oh . . . wow."

"Yah. And she gave me a very thorough lecture about what good girls do or don't do," she said. "I'm not sure she'll want me to stay."

"If she wanted you to leave, she'd have you out the door already," Solomon replied. "Trust me on that. My grandmother is a very decisive woman. She and my *mamm* have that in common."

"Great."

"Hey—" His voice firmed. "Lizzie, I kissed you and you kissed me back. That's it. Nothing more. I understand my grandmother's reaction, but—"

"Nothing more?" Elizabeth said. "So this is just a pastime for you?"

"Nothing more to be guilty about," he said softly. "That's what I meant."

She nodded curtly. Right—just some kisses that heated her blood and drained all reason from her brain. Just leaning into those strong arms, even when she knew it wasn't good for her. Only a few kisses that seemed to mean a great deal less to him.

"What did I say wrong?" he asked.

"Nothing." She licked her lips and raised her gaze to look at him. "You told me the truth. It was only a few kisses. No big deal."

"Hey." He crossed the few feet between them and caught her hand. Then he lowered his lips over hers in a tender, agonized kiss. "This isn't nothing, okay? I'm not kissing you to pass the time. I'm kissing you because"—he slipped his hand behind her neck and looked into her eyes—"because I can't help myself, because when I'm holding you, I feel alive. And I care about you—about your thoughts and your worries and your feelings. Okay? This isn't *nothing*."

"Okay . . ."

Elizabeth stood there for a moment, watching him. "But neither of us are staying here, Solomon. We both have plans—lives we hope to live that are very different. And this is quickly becoming very complicated."

"What do you want, then?" he asked. He hadn't backed up, and she could feel the heat of his body emanating against her. He looked down into her face. His mouth was a breath away from hers, but what she wanted was very different from what she needed.

"I need to stop this," she whispered. "Before one of us gets hurt."

"One of us?" he said.

How she wished she could just ignore the wisdom of her elders and turn off her mind. It would be a wild relief to simply slip into his arms and let him hold her close, ignoring what it would mean for her reputation, for her heart, for her life.

"Me," she said, her voice trembling. "Before *I* get hurt."

Solomon closed his eyes and pressed his lips together. She could see the battle on his features, words he wanted to say but wouldn't. Then he took a purposeful step back.

"Okay," he said, opening his eyes again. "For you."

* * *

Solomon went back out to pull the buckets of flowers into the shade so they wouldn't wilt while Elizabeth stayed inside the shelter. A car passed, not even slowing down, followed by another.

His heart was beating hard in his chest and he moved the bucket of flowers back a foot to make sure they stayed solidly in the shade. Then he looked over at the stand again. He couldn't see Elizabeth from here, but he felt like he could feel her over there.

Was this on him? Was he toying with her feelings? Because he wasn't fooling around with her. This was sincere . . . and if she'd consent to come live an English life with him, he'd be overjoyed.

Except she wouldn't. He knew that plain as day. All the things that drew him to her were the reasons she'd stay Amish. She was an Amish woman to the core— stable, reliable, kindhearted—and she wouldn't be lured off by promises of an easier life. Amish women faced hard times with faith and dignity.

But she'd asked him to stop whatever this was between them, so he would. He wasn't like that *Englisher* bruiser who'd refused to take no for an answer. Solomon might have made mistakes, but he'd never force himself on a woman in any way—even emotionally.

A pickup truck came up the road, and his heart hammered to a stop. He straightened, staring at it hard, and it felt like his heartbeat only kicked in again when he saw that this was a middle-aged couple. They pulled to a stop and both of them got out.

"Good morning," the man said. "Glad to see you up and running."

"Yah," Solomon said. "What can we get you?"

"Do you have fresh potatoes?" the woman asked.

"Sure do—" Solomon gestured to the bin of potatoes, and for the next few minutes he helped the couple select the produce. The woman also bought two bouquets of flowers, and when the man pulled out his wallet, Solomon stood back and watched as Elizabeth accepted the cash and made change.

"Thank you," Elizabeth said. "'Bye now."

The truck rumbled off, and Elizabeth finally met Solomon's gaze. He could see the sadness there, and his heart squeezed hard. But there was nothing else to say about the matter—she'd made a good point.

Behind him, he heard the rattle of a buggy and he turned to see an Amish buggy approaching. He almost didn't recognize Elizabeth's brother Isaiah with his married beard, but Abe Yoder was immediately recognizable— looking just the same as Solomon remembered him.

"Lizzie—"

But when he turned, he saw Elizabeth had spotted them, too, and stood there, her face as pale as paper and her lips parted as she sucked in shallow breaths.

"Daet—" she whispered, and she moved toward the door, pushing outside into the sunlight. Her hands were trembling, and when the buggy arrived and Isaiah reined in the horse, Elizabeth didn't move.

She turned toward Solomon for the first time, and he could see the excess of emotion tumbling through her. Here was the father she'd resented and raged against, loved and worried about, and he was in front of her. This was her chance to get answers, to have her fears relieved, to vent all that anger that had been building up. She deserved that much.

"I'm fine," Solomon said. "I can watch the stand alone. Go see your *daet.*"

She smiled and nodded, tears glistening in her eyes, and she got up into the buggy, and her father moved over to give her room.

"I'll bring Elizabeth back this evening," Isaiah said. "If you could just tell your grandmother—"

"Yah, of course," Solomon said. "She'll understand."

But as the buggy carried on past, it wasn't Elizabeth who met his gaze but Abe. That once-revered preacher's gaze was filled with sadness and something sharper, something harder, that other people wouldn't understand, but Solomon recognized immediately. That sharp, cautious look was what was left over after time in prison.

Solomon was just about ready to close up for lunch and head to town to look for work when a silver sedan slowed to a stop. Another customer.

Solomon came out of the shelter and crossed his arms over his chest, waiting, but when the door opened, he was surprised to see a familiar face. It was Jeff Sparks, his parole officer. The man looked drab and plain outside his office, too, and he smiled mildly in Solomon's direction.

"Checking up on me?" Solomon asked.

"Yes, sort of," Jeff replied. "I might drive by from time to time and just . . . check in. It's part of the job. But I didn't have a way to reach you, so—" His gaze fell on the cell phone in Solomon's hands.

"This isn't mine," Solomon said.

"No?" Jeff squinted at him.

"It's for emergencies, and we had it here at the stall in case I needed to call the police," he said.

"Why would you need the police?" Jeff asked.

"You know . . . emergencies," he said feebly.

Jeff nodded. "Do most people around here do the same?"

"No," Solomon admitted. "There are some people I want to avoid if I'm starting over."

"Good," Jeff replied. Solomon wasn't sure if he believed him or not by the tone of his voice, but he went on. "Speaking of starting over, I have something I wanted to tell you about—a program offered by Bountiful's Church of St. Mary."

"The Catholic one?" Solomon asked uncertainly. Images of the priest from prison rose in his mind, a mild young man with a rather extensive education who'd taken a good deal of time with Solomon talking about faith, redemption, starting over . . .

"They have a program for newly released inmates," Jeff said. "Well, their diocese has the program, but they extend it to communities when necessary, and they're offering it to you."

"What program?" Solomon asked.

"It's a work placement for you as long as you're enrolled in some form of education," Jeff said. "They'd provide odd jobs that would give you a variety of work experience to help you build up a decent résumé. That's incredibly valuable these days, and there would even be a chance at getting some reference letters if you worked hard and impressed them."

"Would I get paid?" he asked.

"Yes. Five dollars an hour above minimum wage, too," Jeff replied, and he turned back to his car and opened the passenger side door and grabbed a file folder. "I've got some information about it here, but if you're interested in taking advantage of it, I'd have to get you enrolled in your GED and give them proof of that, and then we could apply for it."

It was generous, but it was also almost as far from the Amish life as just being English had been.

"I talked to a Catholic priest in jail," Solomon said. "He would come visit us. Some inmates were Catholic, and they'd do confession and whatnot, and then he'd stick around a bit longer for men like me, who just wanted to talk about Gott and if we might be able to find some for-giveness." Solomon rubbed a hand over his chin. "I liked him. He didn't see us as lower than him."

Jeff was silent.

"Thing is, if I do this, it'll take me outside the Amish life," Solomon said. "The Amish are . . . Amish. We're Anabaptist. We do things a certain way. We stick to the Ordnung—we call it the narrow path. If I go back to high school and work with a Catholic agency and find a job in computers or something that pays me something decent . . . I'm not coming back to be Amish. I can see that."

"Do you need to think about it?" Jeff asked. "There are only a couple of spots for this and I do have other people on my list. I just thought you could benefit, and I wanted to give you the chance first, before I moved on."

So this came with a time limit. Solomon looked down the drive toward the old, white house, and then up the road in the direction in which the Yoder buggy had disappeared. Elizabeth wasn't staying—and without her, would he be content living in the family home again with his mother and grandmother? He'd left the Amish life for a reason, even if things had gone disastrously wrong.

"No, I don't need to think about it," he said. "It's a generous offer and I'd be dimwitted not to take it. Do I have to do anything?"

"I'll take care of the paperwork," Jeff said. "You can sign everything at your next appointment in my office."

"Thank you," Solomon said with a nod. "I do appreciate you doing this for me."

"You bet," Jeff said, and he reached for a basket of tomatoes. "Maybe I'll get some of these gorgeous tomatoes while I'm here."

"Take them," Solomon said.

"I'll pay—" Jeff said.

"No, really," Solomon said quickly. "I insist. Take them with blessings."

Jeff smiled and gave him a nod of thanks. "I'll see you next week. I'll get started on this paperwork today. I'm glad you're taking advantage of this."

Jeff got back into his car and pulled a U-turn, then carried on down the road again, his car sending up a cloud of dust. Solomon dropped the cell phone back into the money bag and put out a little bucket with a sign that read, "Please Pay and Take Your Purchase. We Appreciate

Your Honesty." And then he started down the drive toward the house.

His grandmother would be pleased with the morning's income and intrigued by Abe Yoder's return.

For today, at least, he'd just be an Amish man, part of a family and connected to a community. For today at least, he was no longer the newest convict back in Bountiful.

Chapter Twelve

Elizabeth sat next to her brother on the couch in the small sitting room of his small farmhouse. It felt almost like a dream to be looking at her father again—his beard the same, his familiar hands resting on his knees where he sat in a rocking chair. Daet was home—except this wasn't their family home either. That had been sold along with the farm to pay off the victims who'd lost their life savings to that too-good-to-be-true scam. Abe shifted uncomfortably.

Bethany had taken the baby outside with her to do some gardening, providing for a little bit of privacy while Elizabeth and Isaiah talked with their father. Elizabeth was grateful for that, but now that they were all in the same room together, they simply stared at one another.

"Are you hungry, Daet?" Isaiah asked. "I know Bethany did some baking yesterday."

"No," Abe replied. "Not really. Maybe later, Son."

Isaiah nodded. "Lizzie, we were talking on the way to pick you up. Daet was telling me that they let him have his Bible in his cell and he read through it three times."

"That's good," Elizabeth said, and she felt her hands

shaking, so she put them on her knees to still them. She'd been wondering about that—if he'd have the comfort of his Bible or not.

"I missed all three of you more than you'll ever know," Abe said. "Have you heard from your little sister?"

Elizabeth shook her head. "No. None of us have."

"Not even Johannes?" he asked with a frown.

"No. Not even him . . ." Elizabeth sighed. "And the bishop wants Johannes to marry someone else—a widow from Edson."

"So they've given up on her coming back," Abe said, his voice low.

Elizabeth and Isaiah exchanged a look.

"Isaiah, you were the man of the family while I was gone," Abe said. "What did you do about this?"

"Me?" Isaiah shook his head. "What was I supposed to do, demand that Johannes wait for my sister after she broke up with him and left town?"

"She's young," Abe replied. "She's willful. She always was. She's tender and sweet, but underneath that is a core of steel. If I know my daughter at all, she'll come back."

"Daet, she left because of *you*," Elizabeth said, her voice tight. "She said so in the letter she left. The shame of what you did was too much for her to bear."

Abe's face paled and he sucked in an audible breath. "Was she trying to find me?"

"She was trying to escape your reputation," Isaiah replied bluntly. "Lizzie and I have had to face this ourselves. We've been treated like criminals and we've had the entire community talking behind our backs. No one trusts us because of you, Daet. This has been misery for us, and not just because we missed you. It's because we lost *everything*!"

"They hold my mistakes against you," Abe said quietly.

"Yah. We're your *kinner*. I was helping you convince them to invest, Daet!" Isaiah's voice was getting louder. "Why should they think I'm any different from my own father? I wanted to be just like you, remember?"

"But as Christians, we have to forgive," Abe replied, shaking his head. "There is no choice. There is no debate. Jesus commanded us to forgive!"

"It's the forgetting they're having trouble with," Elizabeth said bitterly.

Her father looked over at her, his gaze hurt and somewhat aghast. Daughters didn't talk to their fathers that way, and she knew better.

"Daet, at this point we get to speak our minds," Isaiah said. "That includes Lizzie. She might have lost more than I did. How is she supposed to get married and have *kinner* of her own now, Daet? I'm still amazed that I have Bethany. I didn't think I'd find anyone to trust me after what you did."

"What's done is done," Abe replied.

Elizabeth stared at her father, anger building up inside her, but it was her brother who spoke next.

"That's how you see it?" Isaiah demanded. "We're just supposed to get over it?"

"I don't mean that exactly," Abe replied slowly. "I mean that I don't think I can fix it. I want to. If I could go back and do things differently, I would."

"So why did you do it, then?" Elizabeth asked, her eyes misting with tears. "Why would you cross that line and turn to fraud to exact revenge? You're the one who just said as Christians we're supposed to forgive. What happened to that forgiveness after Mamm died?"

"I did forgive them," Abe said. "I thought I had. It was when I was going around asking them to contribute to this medical fund that would help everyone that they started remembering how it was for your *mamm*. And every last one of them told me that they didn't want to go through that with *their* loved ones—have the money run out and there be nothing left. So this would be extra insurance against that." Abe's eyes misted. "That was when I got angry."

"Because they were trying to protect themselves?" Elizabeth asked.

"Because they were finally willing to empty bank accounts, and to sell unused plots of land, and to dig up money they weren't willing to touch back when your *mamm* needed it," he said bitterly. "They'd selfishly held on to their money when your *mamm* needed help, and now they were losing it. It felt . . . like justice."

"And since when is justice more important than grace?" Isaiah asked.

"It isn't," Abe said, looking over at his son sadly. "It never was. But on a human level, it sure *felt* better."

"And now that you're back, you want grace," Elizabeth said. "You want forgiveness. You want this community to give you a home again."

"I do," Abe said quietly.

"Why should they?" Isaiah asked. "After all you did to them? Yah, they didn't give you more money for Mamm, but that was a long time ago. And they were thinking of her when they dug out their money to try to make it better for everyone. They didn't deserve that, Daet."

"I'm not so worried about the whole community as I am about my own family," Abe said. "I need to know that you two forgive me—"

Abe's words hung in the air, and Elizabeth longed to say that she did, and to take away some of her father's pain, but she couldn't.

"We're working on it, Daet," Isaiah said quietly.

"Pray for strength," Abe said earnestly. "Gott is here for us, even in these ugly times. Gott is the one who commands us to forgive, and it is only through His strength that you'll accomplish it."

That was the father Elizabeth remembered oh so well. That was the preacher who stood in front of congregations and kept them rapt with his persuasiveness. That was Abe Yoder, the respected man of this community, who everyone had looked to for guidance and as an example of right living. And he was talking with religious fervor again.

"That—" Elizabeth felt the dam suddenly splinter and crack inside her. "That, right there! You're preaching at us!"

"I'm just . . . talking," Abe replied.

She shook her head, anger swirling higher and higher inside her. "No, you were doing what you've always done, and it has to stop. It can't go on—there really is no place for your preaching anymore, Daet. We're going to move forward as a family, but things are going to be different. You no longer get to preach to us about Gott's will or the Amish way. You've given that up. You gave that up when you joined criminals in defrauding your own community!" Elizabeth's hands had stopped trembling now. "We'll love you, and we'll find a way to forgive you, but you are no longer a spiritual leader to any of us!"

"I will always be your *father*," Abe said, his voice shaking. "And just because I've made a mistake doesn't make every spiritual lesson I've ever learned untrue or useless to you."

Outside, Mo's little cry rose up, and they all suddenly fell silent, realizing how loudly they'd been talking. Bethany would have heard most of that.

"Let's not argue," Isaiah said, sounding tired. "We can fight about this for years, I'm sure, and we'll have plenty of time to do it. But our family is not whole until Lovina is home, or at the very least we know that she's safe."

"I'll find her," Abe said.

"How?" Elizabeth asked, spreading her hands. "How will you do that, Daet? We've asked around, we've contacted the police, we've gone to the library and searched for her online. There isn't anything left to do. If Lovina doesn't want to be found, she won't be."

"Lovina is *my* little girl," Abe said, his voice trembling. "She might be your sister, but she's my *child*! And if I tell you that I'm going to find her, then I will find her, or I swear before Heaven above that I will die trying. Do you understand that? Or is that too religious for you, Lizzie?"

"Daet, enough!" Isaiah cut in. "Don't fight with Elizabeth now, too. We've waited a long time to see you and you've waited a long time to see us. I don't think any of us wanted to fight with one another when we finally came together."

Isaiah shot Elizabeth a sharp look.

"I'm sorry, Daet," she said quietly. "I'm upset. But I

love you, and I'm glad you're safe. I was so worried . . ." She wiped an errant tear from her face. "We'll sort this out, but maybe not all in one sitting."

Elizabeth rose to her feet. She couldn't stay here any longer. She needed to get out somewhere big enough to cradle this ocean of emotion inside her.

"Are you ready to leave?" Isaiah asked her.

"Yah. I need to get back," she replied.

The side door opened, and Elizabeth heard Bethany come back inside. She murmured something to the baby and then the door shut.

"Can we pray before you go?" Abe asked.

They'd always prayed together. Daet had been known for his beautiful prayers. But now it felt false.

"Please, Lizzie," her father said when she hadn't answered. "Let's pray."

Would this prayer go anywhere when it was offered up by angry people who couldn't forgive? Or would it bounce off the walls and the ceiling and settle in a corner somewhere, useless? All she knew was that she could not stand there and pretend they were a united, faithful family when they were not. That kind of prayer might very well be a curse.

"No, Daet," Elizabeth said, and her voice caught in her throat. "I'll pray when I'm alone."

She started to move past her father, but then she leaned in and gave him a brief hug. Because resent him as she did, and as far away as true forgiveness seemed to be, she loved her father.

* * *

Solomon and Bridget had just finished soup and a sandwich for lunch when Elizabeth came inside, her face flushed from the heat and her forehead pink with sunburn. Solomon stood up—uncertain of why, or what he intended to do, but he wanted to help.

"Lizzie, what happened?" he asked. "Did you walk? Why didn't your brother drive you back?"

"Because I wanted the time alone," she said. "And it was one way to get it."

"That's a long walk, though," he countered.

It seemed that the time with her *daet* hadn't been any kind of happy reunion. At least Abe was home. That was something . . .

Elizabeth accepted a glass of water from Bridget, drained it, and then refilled it and drank down a second one before she sank into a kitchen chair.

"I got to talk to my *daet*," she said. "And that was what I wanted."

"And . . . he's back now?" Solomon asked. "For good, I mean?"

"I suppose," she said. "Where else will he go? Welcome or not, this is his home."

"I can understand that sentiment," Solomon replied. He was in the same position—back in a place that held his memories but didn't exactly welcome him.

"You didn't need to rush back," Bridget said softly, pushing a fresh sandwich in front of Elizabeth. "When Sol told me that you were with your *daet*, I didn't expect to see you until tomorrow, quite honestly."

"It turns out there wasn't as much to say as I thought," Elizabeth said. "Besides, there's work to do here."

"And lunch to eat," Bridget said firmly. "I know you're upset, but you still need to keep up your strength."

Elizabeth bowed her head for a silent grace, then took a bite of the sandwich. She turned her gaze toward Solomon as she chewed.

"Are you okay?" he asked quietly.

She nodded, swallowed. "Yah. I suppose so."

But she wasn't. He could see it in her dark eyes. She was rattled, upset, and unsettled. Whatever had happened with her *daet*, it had given her no peace.

"You have work to do, don't you?" his grandmother asked him pointedly.

Solomon looked up to find her gaze fixed on him, her eyebrows raised.

"Yah. Of course." He had to check on the little jar of money and the last of the produce left at the stand, to start. "I've got plenty."

"Best get to it, then," Bridget said, but she cast him a tender smile to show there was no offense intended. Maybe she wanted to talk to Elizabeth alone.

Solomon gave Elizabeth a nod, then headed for the door. If her own *daet*'s return didn't comfort her, what made him think he could?

For the next few hours Solomon dedicated himself to mucking out stalls, brushing down horses, refilling watering troughs, and hosing down the buggy. The corral fence was getting rickety, too, and Solomon thought he'd like to firm it up and replace a few slats while he was here. There were jobs his *mamm* and grandmother wouldn't get to without a man to help them, and he felt a protectiveness for this old house and the women who'd raised him.

When Solomon had finished washing the buggy, he

heard the screen door slam, and he turned to see Elizabeth heading in his direction. He turned off the hose and wound it up, and when Elizabeth got to him, he cast her a smile.

"Hi," he said.

"Hi." She sucked in a deep breath. "Your grandmother fell asleep in her chair."

He smiled at that. "She does that sometimes."

"She's earned it," Elizabeth said; then she looked out across the paddock.

They were alone—Mammi sleeping—and his first instinct was to take advantage of the solitude and pull her close, but he wouldn't do that this time. He wanted to comfort her, but he wasn't sure that his touch was going to do that. . . .

"What happened with your *daet*?" he asked instead.

"He's too much the same," she said, her voice low. "He wants to tell us what Gott wants, and to pray with us, and . . . be the preacher, I suppose. I couldn't take it. In one way I wanted my *daet* to be unchanged and just like he was . . . but he doesn't have a right to it. It's not the same anymore, you know? It's different!"

"Yah . . ." Solomon and Elizabeth slowly walked out past the buggy, glistening with water, and toward the chicken coop. The hens were outside, scratching in the dirt, and the rooster sat on top of a post, surveying his domain. They carried on past the chicken house and stopped at the fence. For a moment they both just stared out at the grassy field, at the darting dragonflies, the wind rippling over the grass. . . .

"My *daet* told me I should always speak my mind," Elizabeth went on, and she put her hands on the top rail and leaned against it. "Not how most girls are raised, but he said that Gott gave girls brains, too, and He expected us to use them. And that a wise man listened to his wife— two are always better than one. And now . . . now I question everything my *daet* told me over the years."

"I think a wise man listens to what his wife thinks," Solomon said. "She knows the house and garden. And there is more to keeping a family fed than the fields."

"But you're half English already," she said. He caught the soft jest in her voice. "When I thought my *daet* was suffering in prison, forgiving him seemed easier. But now that he's back—" Tears misted her eyes. "What does that say about me?"

Solomon slipped his hand over hers. They were in full view of the house, and this was as far as he dared to go, but he closed his fingers over hers.

"It's not so easy to do," he replied. "Even my *mamm* seems to be having trouble with forgiving me."

Was that the problem between him and his mother— Solomon trying to still be her son in the same way as before he was incarcerated?

"She'll come around," Elizabeth said softly.

"I dare say there are people telling your *daet* the same thing about you," he replied.

She didn't respond.

"Hey—" He stepped closer, but her gaze flickered back toward the house, so he stopped. "You're the best person I know right now. You're kind, and sensitive, and you have good intentions. This is hard, and I don't think a hard situation takes away from who you are, Lizzie."

Her gaze moved up to meet his, and he could see so much uncertainty and sadness swimming in her dark eyes. He longed to tug her closer, to slip his arms around her waist and feel her heartbeat through her body against his chest . . .

"I'm supposed to forgive," she whispered.

"You will," he whispered back.

"And if I don't?" she breathed. "What if the years creep by and I don't?"

What if the years crept by and his relationship with his mother stayed frayed and angry? And it very well might if he went English. He didn't have an answer for her or for himself.

"Even if that happens, I'll always think the best of you," he said.

"How would you even know about it?" she asked. "You'll be English."

"Then we'll keep in touch," he said with a small smile. "We'll write letters. I'll tell you about going to school at this ripe age, and about my *Englisher* job, and about life with electricity and television."

"And I'll write to you about starting over where no one knows me," she said. "Until I get married, at least. And then I won't be able to write."

That stung—the thought of her married. Somehow this was easier to consider when he thought of them both single, pouring their hearts out to each other on paper with no one to step between . . . but marriage was the plan for her, wasn't it? That was why she'd leave Bountiful and go strike out on her own in some distant Amish community. For a man. For a family.

He sucked in a deep breath.

"I don't want to think about years and years from now," he said softly.

"Me neither."

They both turned toward the field again, and Solomon felt the warmth of her standing next to him, smelled the soft scent of her shampoo coming to him on the breeze.

"Lizzie," he said.

"Yah?"

"Could I talk to your *daet*?" he asked.

"Solomon, I don't need you to try to fix anything between us—" she began.

"For me," he amended. "The thing is, I know you're angry with him, and I know he ruined your life and countless others . . . I know that. But he's the only one around here who's been through what I've been through, and—"

How could he explain this? He was supposed to be supporting her, telling her that everything would be okay, not seeking out his own emotional support from the man who had hurt her most.

"My *daet* has no answers," she said, and he could hear the bitterness in her tone. "If you want to be preached at and prayed with, you're welcome to go see him."

Solomon sighed. "I don't expect him to have answers."

"Then what can he offer?" she asked.

"I need to know if what I'm feeling is normal," he said. "On this side of those walls . . . I just need to know."

Her expression softened. "What are you feeling?"

"Lost . . ."

And scared. He still had that feeling like he should be watching his back, like someone might jump him at any moment. He felt like his last refuge had become this woman who wanted so much more than he could ever offer. And he felt like he was in a ditch between two lives—unable to crawl up onto either side.

It was easy enough to jump the fence and choose an

English life, but he knew now what waited for him with the *Englishers*. He'd always be different. He'd talk more slowly, with his Pennsylvania Dutch accent, and he'd think like a farmer. He'd have his Amish bones no matter what life he chose. He'd have options out there in the world, but he wouldn't ever really fit in. He knew the difficult path that was ahead of him either way.

"Oh, Sol . . ." Elizabeth's voice caught, and she leaned forward and pressed a kiss against his shoulder. "You'll find your way."

The kiss was so impulsive and sweet that he felt his eyes mist.

"Lizzie—" He slid his arms around her waist just as he heard a thump from the porch. He turned—Bridget stood there with a broom in one hand, watching them.

Solomon dropped his hand. "You have a reputation to worry about," he said with a rueful smile. "I don't think I'm much good for it."

He wasn't good for *her* and he knew it. But she was good for him right now, comforting him on a heart-deep level that he probably didn't deserve.

"So do you," she replied, and she stepped away from him.

Yah, but his didn't matter as much as hers. His was already beyond repair, and his only option was to go back to the *Englishers* and find some little spot where he could make a living and carve out a life.

Elizabeth headed off toward the house and he turned, pretending not to watch. His grandmother picked up the broom again and opened the screen door. She looked older today, a little more stooped, her hair a brighter white than he remembered. Elizabeth's skirt swished around her calves, and he realized that nothing he could imagine in his life—a proper job, a reliable income, some decent friends—compared with a few stolen moments with this woman in a community that didn't want him. And that didn't bode well for his future happiness.

He already knew what he'd be missing.

Chapter Thirteen

When Solomon finally fell asleep that night, he had fitful dreams of being a boy again and walking to school, but as long as he walked, he never seemed to arrive, and he was afraid of being late because the teacher would be upset with him. . . . Then that dream melted into a different one where he was living an English life again and he was trying to start a car in winter. The car was cold as ice, and he put the key into the ignition and turned. It kept grinding, but not turning over, and every time he turned the key, the grinding was softer and softer until nothing happened at all. It was dead, and he felt a rush of that same panic that he'd be late. He looked out the car window to see the schoolhouse in the distance, and somehow walking there wasn't an option that occurred to him.

When those dreams finally faded, another dream took their place, and this one was the old, gray, granite, cold dream of prison. He was walking to his cell, a guard behind him, a guard in front, and he felt such a wash of grief that he could have sunk to his knees and sobbed . . . but he couldn't. Not there. Not with the other inmates looking out their cells at him, glittering, angry eyes following his every move. The guard stopped—he knew this guard—and he gestured into the cell.

"Inside," he barked.

"For how long?" Solomon asked. "I thought I was released. How long do I have?"

The guard didn't answer.

"I've got someone waiting for me. I have to see her first!" Solomon felt rising panic. "She'll worry. If I could write a letter, or . . . or . . . if I could talk to her . . . somehow—"

The door slammed shut.

"Her name is Elizabeth!" he shouted. "How long am I in here?"

The dream shimmered and faded as he felt a hand shaking his shoulder. He woke up with a start, gasping for breath as his heart hammered hard in his chest. He blinked his eyes open and reached for the hand that had shaken him, clasping slim, cool fingers.

"Sol, it's me—" Elizabeth whispered. "It's okay, you were dreaming."

"Oh . . ." He reluctantly let go of her fingers and pushed himself up and swung his legs over the side of the bed. Elizabeth backed up a few feet. She was in an ankle-length nightgown, her hair pulled back in a braid.

"You were shouting," she whispered.

"What did I say?" he asked.

"My name." He could see her cheeks tinge pink in the low light. She took another step back toward the door.

"Oh, yah," he said. "I was dreaming of . . . a lot of things. Prison. I dreamed of prison."

It was fading now and he couldn't quite make sense of it anymore. The tenuous dream logic was slipping away.

"I should go back to bed," she whispered. "I just wanted to wake you up—"

"Thank you."

He was grateful for it actually. "Lizzie?"

"Yah?" She stopped at the open door.

When he was a child, his mother would wipe his hair from his forehead and tell him it was only a dream, made up of dandelion fluff and stove cinders. As a grown man, he felt that same need to reground himself into the real world again.

"Did I wake up my grandmother?" he asked, grasping for a reason to have stopped her.

"No." She smiled faintly. "This will be our secret. Now, let me get back to bed before I earn myself another lecture."

"Right. Good night."

There it was, the reality he was clutching at. Elizabeth shut the door behind her as she left, and Solomon pushed himself to his feet. He wore pajama bottoms and no shirt, and the air in the room was close and warm. He went to the window and sucked in some fresh night air.

How long was he going to dream of prison? Would his nights be plagued like this for the rest of his life?

He went to his dresser and used a match to light his kerosene lamp. Then he picked up his Bible and opened it at random. He'd read until morning. This would look hypocritical to anyone who didn't know his heart. This would look like a man faking his religion. But after jail time, and after realizing that his Amish life was lost to him, his faith was all he had left. Did it count anymore? When he'd left Bountiful, he hadn't been terribly concerned about his own soul, but now . . . now he was starting to wonder.

The next morning Seth picked up the vegetables to be sold in town, which freed up Solomon's morning so that he could go into town and check the corkboard for new jobs and, on his way back, visit Abe Yoder.

His grandmother and Elizabeth had started pickling some cucumbers, the doors and windows all flung wide open to let the air flow through the hot kitchen, by the time Solomon headed out to hitch up the horses.

Elizabeth didn't say anything about where he was going, although she knew that he was planning to see her *daet* today. She watched him leave, her dark gaze locked on him, and he wondered what she was thinking. She was angry with Abe, and for good reason. He could definitely understand her rage toward her father right now, but Abe was the only man around who'd understand Solomon's unique position—an ex-convict Amish. Still, he couldn't help but feel a wave of guilt. She'd told him how hypocritical her *daet* seemed, how much respect she'd lost for him, and here Solomon was, wondering if Abe Yoder might have some spiritual insights after all . . . insights that might be meaningless for the good people of Bountiful who'd never strayed, but might be priceless for the likes of Solomon.

There weren't any new jobs posted—none that would take a man with his experience, at least. There were some bakery workers needed at an Amish bakery, but it was run by women, and they'd never want an ex-con in their midst. There was a wanted ad for a cleaning company, but the flier stated the successful candidate had to be bonded. At least he had some guaranteed work with the Catholic agency. It might come with the requirement that he be enrolled in school, but he was starting to see how difficult it was going to be for him.

So, Solomon headed back the way he'd come and turned down the gravel road that led to Isaiah Yoder's little house. When Solomon arrived, Abe came outside and Solomon jumped down from the buggy. They shook hands, and Solomon could feel Abe's evaluation as he looked him over.

"Are you here to see my son?" Abe asked. "Isaiah's at work right now."

"I came to see you actually," Solomon replied.

"Me?" Abe's gray eyebrows went up.

"Yah . . . I . . ." Solomon swallowed. "I could use some guidance."

"I'm no longer in that position," Abe replied slowly. "You know where I've been."

"And you've likely heard that I was in prison, too, until recently," Solomon replied.

Abe moved his head in acknowledgment. "You're . . . close . . . with my daughter," he said. "I heard that as well. Isaiah doesn't like it."

Solomon smiled ruefully. "She's a friend, nothing more."

A small lie. She was more than that to him, not that it mattered. He'd never court her, and Abraham Yoder had nothing to worry about his daughter marrying an ex-con.

"Where were you incarcerated?" Abe asked.

"Forest State Correctional Institution," Solomon said. "How about you?"

"Chester," Abe replied.

They regarded each other in silence for a moment, and then Solomon took out the feed bags for his horses from the back of the buggy and attached them to the bridles.

"It might be better if we stay outside," Abe said.

Solomon looked up to see Bethany in the doorway, the baby on her hip. She looked cautious, a little worried. He wasn't sure he blamed her, and he certainly didn't want to be invading Isaiah's home in his absence. There were boundaries there, an unspoken understanding between men.

"Good morning, Bethany," Solomon called.

"Good morning." She disappeared from view again, and Solomon and Abe headed up the drive a few paces, then stopped once they were far enough from the house for some privacy.

"Welcome back," Solomon said at last.

"I could say the same to you, but I'm not sure that we're welcome," Abe replied.

"True." Solomon sighed.

"So, what can I do for you?" Abe asked.

"The thing is . . ." Solomon dug his toe into the dirt. "I've been out of jail for . . . ten days? And I don't know how to do this. I don't know how to adjust to life on the outside. It was only a year I was locked up, but it's different now. Everyone sees me differently. I see myself differently, too, and . . . I was wondering if you have any spiritual advice that might help. Something that helps you, maybe."

"You'll be the only one who cares for my spiritual insights," Abe replied.

"Maybe," Solomon agreed. "But you're the only one who will understand what I've gone through, too, so . . . it's a small club."

Abe smiled faintly. "It is."

Solomon held his breath.

"So people haven't warmed to you either?" Abe asked.

"No." Solomon shrugged. "Cold as an icebox. Except for my grandmother, of course, and Lizzie—" He felt heat hit his face. "Elizabeth. I'm sorry, I used to call her that when we were *kinner*."

Abe was silent again, and he gave Solomon an appraising look.

"I've been dreaming a lot," Solomon went on in a rush. "I dream of prison, and it's . . . it's chilling. Nightmares. I wake up in a sweat, and I can't sleep after that. I have this feeling"—he rotated his shoulders—"like between my shoulder blades. You know that feeling of someone watching you? Like the guards, or some huge, hulking bully staring at you, and you know they've got plans, and you'll have to fight, and—" He was saying too much. It all just seemed to be spilling out of him.

"I know that feeling," Abe replied. "For me, there was less fighting and more manipulation and lying, trying to set one another up to look like we were breaking rules that we weren't. They knew I wanted out early on good behavior, so . . ."

"Right," Solomon nodded eagerly. "I know what you're talking about. Violence or not, there are men against you."

"Yah," Abe agreed with a nod.

"Well, I still have that feeling. Not about the community, but . . . like I can be in the stable mucking out a stall and I get this chill like someone's watching. And logically, I know I'm alone, but tell my body that, you know?"

"I haven't been out that long," Abe said with a shake of his head. "I'm not sure what to tell you. But I feel it, too. I catch myself second-guessing anything my son tells me, as if he'd lie to me. Isaiah is honest and good—I raised him, I should know! And I react like I'm in jail still. So I think I understand."

"I wonder if that gets better," Solomon said.

"I hope so."

They met each other's gazes, and Solomon felt a wave of relief. "What's getting you through this?"

"Prayer."

"Yah . . . I've been reading my Bible more now than I ever did in my life."

Abe nodded. "Gott forgives, Solomon."

"The community might not," Solomon replied.

"But Gott does, and He's the one you'll face on the day of your death," Abe said. "Not the community. Not even your own *kinner.*"

There was sadness in the older man's voice, and Solomon dropped his gaze. He couldn't reassure him on that front either.

"What happens if the community doesn't take us back?" Solomon asked. "Spiritually speaking, I mean. If we can't get jobs here, and people don't trust us, and we're pushed out—not officially, but socially, you know? Are we supposed to just stay?"

"I'm not sure I can answer that for you," Abe replied slowly, then he eyed him closely.

"No."

The older man nodded. "I won't give you sermons

about the value of community or salvation coming from being a part of the church either. If you've made your choice already, it will fall on deaf ears anyway. Besides, I know what you've been through, and I know our community. Maybe even better than you do."

Solomon held his breath, waiting. He'd been longing for some kind of spiritual balm, something to hold on to . . . and he wouldn't get it from the bishop. The bishop just repeated what he'd always said—stay, submit, endure.

"Is there any hope for a man like me?" Solomon asked. "Or am I on my own now?"

"In the Old Testament, Gott's people disobeyed and went wrong a great deal," Abe said slowly. "They kept going astray and Gott kept calling them back . . ." His voice was going into that old preaching cadence. "When they were driven from their homeland and sent to live among the heathen, Gott was with them. He never left them. Some spent their entire lives away from their homeland and never saw it again. Generations never saw the land of Israel. But that didn't mean Gott had given up on them."

Solomon nodded. "Yah. I know the stories."

"I cannot speak for Gott, Solomon, and I cannot speak for you," Abe said. "But if you are indeed pushed out and must go forge a life for yourself away from your homeland, away from Canaan . . . away from Bountiful . . . then Gott will go with you. And while your way might be difficult, Gott will have a path for you. Gott never forgets His *kinner*, even the ones in exile."

"The bishop wouldn't say that," Solomon said quietly.

"The bishop hasn't been to prison," Abe replied.

Solomon smiled and nodded. "Thank you."

"But Solomon?" Abe caught his eye and held it.

"Yah?"

"Don't ask my daughter to go into exile with you," Abe said. "She has a chance at a good life in Gott's land. Don't ask her to give that up."

How much did Abe suspect about Solomon's feelings for Elizabeth? Had she said anything? Or was it an older man's instincts?

"Even if I wanted to ask her," Solomon said, "she knows she's worth more than me. And she wants an Amish life. She's too smart to give it up."

"Good." Abe smiled faintly. "That's my girl . . ."

And while Solomon was grateful to the man for his insights, he felt a sting of resentment, too. It was one thing for Elizabeth to know she was better than him, but for Abe Yoder, disgrace to Bountiful and ex-convict, to think that Solomon was so much lower was like a slap.

"Pray about it, Solomon," Abe said solemnly. "Pray long and hard for the Lord to reveal His will to you."

There it was—the tone that had left Elizabeth so angry. He could feel his visceral response to the words creeping up. It didn't matter, though.

He knew the direction he had to take, and it wasn't an Amish life. That was what scared him. What happened when Gott sent you away?

Elizabeth sliced cucumbers into spears and tossed them into a bowl of salted water. Her fingers knew the work, and she glanced over to where Bridget stood next to a boiling pot of water, carefully lowering Mason jars into it with a set of tongs to sanitize them.

"I'm expecting a guest today," Bridget said, replacing the lid on the pot.

"Are you? I can keep working on the pickles if you want to visit out on the porch where it's cool," Elizabeth offered.

"No, no," Bridget replied. "I wanted to have a job to do so that she could work with us. Sometimes talking is easier when we don't have to look each other in the face."

Elizabeth smiled. "That's . . . frank."

Bridget chuckled. "It's Sovilla."

Elizabeth's smile slipped. "Oh . . . I see."

"Dear, I think it would be good for you to talk to her, too," Bridget said. "If she's going to marry Johannes, she'll be around. You'll see her at quilt nights and at service Sunday. Others will be happy to welcome her, and if you're seen as being standoffish at first, it could hurt your relationship with her."

For as long as Elizabeth stayed. That was one more reason to move on to another community. Maybe she'd have Sovilla's luck and find some marriageable man elsewhere.

"So it's decided, then—" Elizabeth said.

"Not exactly," Bridget replied. "She's met Johannes, and now she wants to meet his family, his people. Marrying a man is more than marrying him . . . if you know what I mean. He comes with a whole family attached to him. And because his *mamm* passed away, he asked if she could visit with me. I was honored that he'd ask."

"I'm not sure her meeting me is a good idea," Elizabeth said. "I'm the sister of the woman he's still in love with. And I won't back down on that, Bridget. I know you don't want to hear it because Lovina broke his heart. But he does still love her, and Sovilla will discover that soon enough."

"I know he does, dear," the older woman replied. "But it's not good for him. And we're all hoping it will change— for his own happiness. Just as we're hoping for Lovina to come home. But sometimes there have to be alternative plans."

Why was Bridget so insistent that Elizabeth be here for this visit? Was it politeness? Did she really think Elizabeth would try to convince Sovilla to marry Johannes as a great many people seemed to want her to do? Or was Bridget perhaps counting on Elizabeth doing what she'd always done—speaking her mind?

When Sovilla arrived an hour later, Elizabeth opened the door to see a woman with gray eyes and a solemn expression standing there. Johannes's father, Bernard, was in the buggy outside, and he gave Elizabeth a nod.

"I'll come back in an hour or so," he called.

"Thank you," Sovilla said, and then she straightened her shoulders and gave Elizabeth a nod. "I'm Sovilla Miller."

"I'm Elizabeth Yoder," she replied, stepping back. "You're looking for Johannes's aunt, Bridget. I'm just here helping her with some pickles. Come inside."

Sovilla was slim, but she had a dominant presence. Her jaw was strong and her hands were callused—a woman who worked hard. She glanced around the kitchen. She was no young woman, shy and bashful. She carried herself with poise and a certain confidence.

"Sovilla . . ." Bridget came forward and took her hand.

"It's lovely to see you. I know this must be uncomfortable, but I hope to make it less so. I'm Johannes's aunt."

"It's good to meet you," Sovilla said, and she cleared her throat. "I see you're making pickles. I'd be happy to help."

"Yes, of course!" Bridget smiled. "Come wash up and we'll get to work."

For the next few minutes Elizabeth listened as Bridget chatted with Sovilla, asking about her daughters, giving her sympathy for the death of her husband. Elizabeth stayed silent. Sovilla spoke about her daughters—the oldest being four and the youngest barely two. She talked very easily about Rueben, too, almost as if he were simply away on a trip, and then she'd seem to remember that he was dead and her eyes would mist and her chin would tremble.

"And you're the sister of Johannes's ex-fiancée," Sovilla said, turning toward Elizabeth.

Elizabeth blinked at Sovilla's forthrightness. "Yah . . . I'm her sister."

"What's Johannes like?" Sovilla asked. "From your perspective, I mean. As someone who saw him in a relationship."

That was a good question to ask—one untainted by jealousy, by the sound of it.

"I'm not sure I could say . . ." Elizabeth said uncomfortably. Her sister had confided in her when she and Johannes had some disagreement or other, but it always blew over quickly.

"Johannes is very kind," Elizabeth said. "And he's private."

"I see." Sovilla dropped her gaze for a moment, then

reached for another cucumber to quarter. "What I mean is, does he pick fights?" Sovilla asked. "Does he get sensitive and take it out on the woman?"

The questions a woman who'd been married before asked were different apparently.

"No, he wasn't like that," Elizabeth said.

"Is he jealous?" Sovilla asked. "You see, if I'm agreeing to marry a man I hardly know, I need to be cautious. And I need to know what he is really like—not just the nice parts of him. And I think that you would be the woman who would have seen those . . . other parts."

"He never was the jealous type with my sister," Elizabeth replied.

Elizabeth glanced toward Bridget, and the older woman was watching the exchange with an intent look on her face. What did Bridget want from her?

"No one will tell me this, but does he love your sister still?" Sovilla asked, her voice low.

There it was—the right question.

"Yah," Elizabeth replied. "I think he does."

Sovilla nodded.

"They were together a long time," Elizabeth went on. "He adored her."

"And I love Rueben still," Sovilla said. "It might be fair."

Elizabeth stood silent for a moment, wondering if she should stop talking now, but then she blurted out, "Why are you doing this? Why are you willing to marry a stranger?"

Sovilla licked her lips. "I need a husband to provide for me."

"Don't we all," she said.

Sovilla smiled ever so faintly. "But I don't have your good looks, Elizabeth. You've got a beautiful face and figure, and . . . and I can treat a good man well. I can love him. I can cook for him and mend his clothes and give him more *kinner*. I can do those things for a man whose character I can trust. But I'm not sure that another man will come courting."

"Rueben did," Elizabeth replied.

"No, Rueben's uncle introduced us and told him that I was a woman he could trust and count on, and that got Rueben's attention. It wasn't seeing me in service." Sovilla sighed. "I know my strengths, and you know yours."

"Why the rush?" Elizabeth asked.

"I have some family I'm staying with, but I'm a burden to them," Sovilla said. "I'm trying to do what's right. Sometimes the best way to mend a broken heart is to move forward and love another. It might be the answer for him, too. At least your bishop seems to think so."

"Is there a connection between you and Johannes?" Bridget asked quietly.

Sovilla sucked in a breath, and for a moment her cheeks pinked. "It's hard to tell. We're both nervous. He seems kind. He's . . . gentle. I like his smile, and he has very nice eyes. We talked a little bit, and he seems very decent. But does he feel anything for me?" She shrugged. "I don't know. You'd have to ask him."

Sovilla's somber face turned almost sweet. She had gentleness, too, it seemed, that shone through when she mentioned Johannes.

"What if my sister returns?" Elizabeth asked. "What if Johannes and Lovina set eyes on each other and all those feelings come rushing back for both of them? What then?"

Sovilla picked up a jar, and for a moment she didn't move. Then she said softly, "That's the worry, isn't it?"

Elizabeth looked toward Bridget, wondering how angry the older woman would be, but Bridget was calmly adding dill weed and peppercorns to each jar, looking entirely unperturbed. If Elizabeth didn't know better, she'd think that Bridget wanted Sovilla to consider these things . . .

"*Are* you worried about it?" Elizabeth asked.

"Yah," Sovilla replied, and she met Elizabeth's gaze with a look of such open frankness that Elizabeth's heart squeezed in response. "Very."

"Have you talked to Johannes about it?" Bridget asked. "Have you asked him how he feels about Lovina?"

Elizabeth put her hands on the table to keep them from trembling. What did Johannes say about Lovina when her family wasn't there to hear it? That was a good question.

"He says that Lovina hurt him very deeply when she left," Sovilla replied. "And he's angry now. He's upset with her for having walked off like that, and he said that he doesn't want to marry and have *kinner* with a woman who could see a perfectly happy life with the *Englishers*." Sovilla's gaze flickered toward Elizabeth apologetically. "And without him."

That was what he'd said? Elizabeth caught her breath. He'd only ever told them that he missed Lovina. He'd never said he was angry. . . .

Elizabeth might be trying to freeze time for her sister, but it wasn't fair to anyone else, was it? Johannes might be feeling more complicated emotions than he'd ever admit to Lovina's family, and he had every right to them.

"Do you think she's a bad person?" Elizabeth asked suddenly.

Sovilla shook her head. "No. She just isn't *here*. And neither is Rueben. I can understand being furious with the one who went away."

At least Sovilla knew about Lovina, and she had a chance to think this through with all the information in front of her. If Johannes did marry Sovilla, there would be no guilt about withheld information. Their happiness would be entirely up to them.

Chapter Fourteen

The next morning Elizabeth walked next to Solomon up the drive toward the produce stand. All was quiet. Inside the house, Bridget was doing some needlework that she meant to sell in town that fall. Even with the long summer days and fragrant breezes, Amish minds were moving toward the harvest. The seasons didn't stop.

And perhaps that was some wisdom that needed to land in Elizabeth's heart. Time didn't halt because they wanted it to, and people moved on. Meeting Sovilla had changed Elizabeth's perspective. She'd been so intent on keeping Johannes from marrying a stranger, holding out hope that things could go back to the way they were, but she could see now that it had been selfish of her. That wasn't a possibility.

Solomon carried a bag of potatoes over one shoulder with relative ease. He walked along slowly, and when she looked over at him, he shot her a smile. He was flirting and she knew it . . . but it was nice, all the same.

The day was bright, warm sunlight filtering through the leaves overhead. The quarter horses came up to the fence, nickering for a carrot that Solomon carried in one hand. He stepped over the ditch, that bag of potatoes still balanced on one shoulder, and fed the horses one carrot each before he jumped back over. The sack of potatoes slipped and he caught it, then hoisted it back up, his muscles straining against his shirt.

"You seem happier," Elizabeth said.

"Yah. I am."

"So my *daet* was . . . helpful?" she asked, squinting at him as a ray of sunlight dazzled her eyes.

"Yah, he was." Solomon's hand brushed hers, and she found herself holding her breath.

They hadn't discussed this yesterday. She'd been afraid to ask when he came back, and then Bridget had kept them both busy—Solomon outside fixing the corral fence and Elizabeth inside finishing up those pickles. Was it intentional on the old woman's part? Very likely.

"What did my father say?" Elizabeth asked.

"He was talking about times when we might not have as many choices as we'd like. And even in those times, Gott is with us. He doesn't just abandon us because we've gone too far." His fingers brushed hers again, and this time it was more intentional. She spread her fingers and he twined his through hers. She let out a slow breath, then glanced over her shoulder toward the house.

Solomon looked back, too. "It's okay. No one's watching."

"Yah . . ." They were alone.

"It isn't that I don't believe in our way of life, Lizzie," he said quietly. "If I hadn't messed up the way I did, it would be an option for me. I could come home. But I'm not just a prodigal son anymore. This isn't just between me and my family. This involves a community."

"But you believe in the Amish faith?" she asked.

"Yah. I do."

"And you'd still leave it?" she breathed.

"I'm not leaving the faith, I'm . . . finding a life. I don't really have a choice anymore." His dark gaze met hers pleadingly. "I can't leave Bountiful and start over somewhere else—I have to report to my parole officer. And if after I'm finished with parole, I went to some other Amish community and lied, just didn't tell them I have a criminal record, I don't think I could face myself. I would live month after month and year after year wondering when they'd find out the truth."

Leaving and going to some other Amish community—that was her plan.

"You think that's what I'm doing?" she asked. "You think I'm going to be living a lie if I go find a husband in another community?"

"No." He squeezed her hand. "You're just going to where the community might have less of a personal connection to your *daet*'s crime. You're going to where people won't be thinking of your family every time they look at you. That's different. You're escaping someone else's crime. For me, it's my own. I can't run from that. No matter where I go, my prison time is going to matter."

"And that makes you feel better?" she asked, shaking her head. "You're all cheery this morning because you're more determined than ever to leave?"

"I'm not celebrating, Lizzie, if that's what you think. The *Englishers* have more options for me at this point," he replied quietly. "And after talking to your *daet*, I don't feel as guilty about accepting what they can give me. I feel like Gott could even bless it."

So her father was still at it—chasing the young people out of the community in his own unique way. Would it never end?

"Lizzie?"

They'd reached the end of the drive and stopped in the shade. The road was empty, and Solomon tugged her hand, bringing her closer so that her dress brushed his pants and she could feel the warmth of his breath against her cheek.

"Some things are inevitable," he whispered. "At least after you've made as many mistakes as I have . . ."

"Will you miss us?"

Solomon looked down at her hand in his, squeezing her fingers in a grip so tight it almost hurt, and when he lifted his gaze again, his lips were inches from hers. His soft brown gaze met hers and he licked his lips.

"I'll miss *you*, Lizzie . . . you have no idea how much."

She felt her eyes mist, and Solomon dipped his head down and brushed his lips against hers. It was a brief kiss, tender, but he pulled back just as quickly.

"You'll forget me, Solomon," she said. Right now she was in front of him, living with his grandmother, and unavoidable. But when he left again . . .

"No." He shook his head, then looked around. "I won't forget you. And I won't forget this life either. Right now I dream of prison and wake up shaking. I have a feeling that when I leave, I'll dream of this . . . of you—" He turned to look at her again, and she saw the sadness in his eyes. "I'll dream of the life I wanted but couldn't have . . ." His voice caught. "Those dreams will be worse."

Elizabeth squeezed his fingers, unsure of what to say. She'd miss him, too, more than he would know. But that was her own fault—she'd allowed herself to start down this path.

"Lizzie, do you think it's possible to keep your Amish heart out there with the *Englishers*?" he asked. "Do you think Gott will still recognize the Amish in me? Because your *daet* seems to think so."

"My *daet* might not be the best man to give spiritual guidance," she said.

"Your *daet* is the only one who can right now," he said.

She turned away. Was this her father's calling now— to convince rebels of the rightness of their cause? What had happened to their community? What had happened to all the people who had given Elizabeth roots in her Amish life?

A car stopped in front of the stand, and Elizabeth went into the stall to prepare to take money while Solomon pushed his straw hat back on his head and helped the woman bag up her purchase.

"That's twenty-two dollars," Elizabeth said.

The woman handed over two twenties and Elizabeth opened the zippered pouch to make change. The cell phone was in there, too, and she paused when her hand brushed against the cool plastic.

It was permitted for safety, but it was just another concession in this community.

She pulled out the change and handed it over with a smile.

The woman was just pulling away when Elizabeth saw a red pickup truck rumbling down the gravel road. It was moving faster than it should—definitely over the speed limit—and her heart hammered in her chest.

"Is that—" she started.

"I don't know." But Solomon's voice sounded nervous, too. "Why don't you go back to the house?"

"Are you coming?" she asked.

He didn't answer, but he also didn't move in her direction either.

"Solomon, if you do something stupid, you'll go back to prison!" she said, her voice shaking. "Come with me."

"Elizabeth, go back to the house!" He turned and shot her a glare. "Now!"

Solomon's voice boomed with authority and she reached for the money bag. The truck rumbled to a stop and the *Englishers* jumped out. Elizabeth sank to the floor out of sight and pulled the cell phone out of the bag and flipped it open. With trembling fingers, she dialed 9-1-1.

"Out here alone, are you?" one of the *Englishers* said.

"Where's the girl?" It was the big man with the grip like steel—she recognized the voice.

"9-1-1. What's the nature of your emergency?" a woman's voice said on the other end of the phone. Elizabeth pressed it against her ear.

"We need help," she whispered, keeping her voice as quiet as possible.

"I'm sorry, I can't hear you," the woman said. "Are you able to speak a little louder?"

"We need help," she whispered again, but this time her voice cracked and Elizabeth winced.

"Where are you?" the operator asked. "And do you need police, fire, or ambulance?"

"We need police," she breathed. "Please . . ." And she recited the address.

Outside the shelter, Elizabeth could hear the scuffling of boots against gravel.

"Where's the girl?" The big man's voice sent a shiver up her spine.

Elizabeth's elbow brushed against the money box, and it clanked softly. She winced, freezing.

"What's that?" one of the *Englishers* demanded. "She's here! I heard her!"

Elizabeth pressed her lips together and slowly closed the phone.

"Heard what?" Solomon demanded, his voice rising, too. "I'm a businessman here. Get lost. If you aren't buying produce, keep driving."

"A businessman," said a mocking voice. "Really? You call this hovel a business? You're more like a beggar."

The men laughed at that.

"Are you buying or what?" Solomon's voice stayed in control, but she heard him move off to the side of the stall, opposite the door. "I've got potatoes—"

"What do we want with potatoes?" one *Englisher* laughed, but they seemed to be following him. Solomon was leading them away from the stall—

Elizabeth forced her limbs forward and crept to the doorway. The voices were raised in argument on the other side, but when she stepped outside, she heard something that made her stomach drop.

"This is for getting me in trouble with the cops, Farmer," the big *Englisher* growled, and she heard the sound of flesh hitting flesh.

She didn't stop—Elizabeth lifted her skirts and ran as fast as she could go down the drive. And with every step she took and every rasping breath she dragged into her lungs, she sent up a silent prayer: *Let him win!*

Because three against one wasn't fair, but if she'd seen

one thing about Solomon Lantz, it was that he could fight like the devil himself.

And for the first time in her life, she was praying for exactly that.

Solomon's head rang from the force of the blow and he staggered backward. His first instinct was to ball his hands into fists and wait for the first chance to land a punch that would bruise a kidney. He'd learned how to do that in prison—how to aim for internal organs that would leave a grown man writhing in pain and possibly bleeding internally.

And in that second when his fingers were curling into fists, he knew which man he'd hit first, and he knew which rib he'd break, too. . . .

Except something deep inside him was holding him back. Fighting—more of it. This wasn't the Amish way, and his Amish heart, which still beat the deep rhythm of his soul, was reminding him. Amish didn't fight.

"I didn't do anything." Solomon spat bloody spittle onto the ground. "The cops sent me away and I left."

He'd go to prison again if he hit this man back. The fact that he hadn't been caught the first time he'd beaten him was a miracle, and if he took the bait this time, it would definitely be breaking parole. But he couldn't let them go after Elizabeth . . . She needed time to get out of there, and that meant they had to be focused on him.

Fighting him . . . debating him . . . or beating him.

"Fine. Then this is for breaking my nose. It was a lucky

hit. You're not going to be so lucky this time . . ." And a flood of filthy language came out of the man's mouth.

Solomon straightened, his head still buzzing, and he said, "I'm sorry about that. But it couldn't be avoided."

He was being a smart-mouth and he knew that was suicide, but he wasn't going to humbly beseech this man's forgiveness either.

Men like these who preyed on vulnerable women got beaten in prison, too.

The man swung again, and Solomon ducked this time, stepping backward.

"Grab him!" the big man barked to the other two, and Solomon's heart stuttered in his chest.

This was it—he had to choose his path now and live by the consequences. He could fight them yet—he could get away, even—but what about Elizabeth? Fighting wasn't the only way to win. The Amish had been teaching that very truth for centuries. He could still be Amish, even in exile, and that small, flickering hope was starting to surge.

"I didn't say anything to the police," Solomon said quietly. "I'm minding my own business. I'm selling vegetables. That's all. You can leave now, and I'll never say a word about this little visit."

"I'm sure." The big man shrugged exaggeratedly. "Why would you tell anyone?"

The other two men grabbed his arms, and while he twisted free a couple of times, they secured him at last, and Solomon stared into the sneering face of the *Englisher* thug who stood there cracking his knuckles with loud, liquid pops.

Oh, Gott . . . he prayed silently. That was all, nothing more. *Oh, Gott . . .*

Solomon slowly awoke to the sound of sirens. His head hurt, as did most of his body, and he turned his face to the side and coughed. As he did so, his side gave a sharp pain. He could feel gravel under his body and he moved his leg—at least that didn't hurt.

"Lie still now, sir," a female voice said.

He opened his eyes a crack and he saw two women leaning over him—one an *Englisher* police officer and the other was Elizabeth. A siren whooped again and he struggled to sit up.

"Sir, you'd best lie down until the ambulance gets here," the officer said firmly.

"No, I'm fine," he said, and he coughed again and lifted himself to his elbow. That same pain in his side stabbed again. He knew what it felt like to be seriously hurt, and while he'd been beaten, he was in one piece still.

"Solomon—" It was Elizabeth now. "No, no, lie back—"

"Lizzie, I'm fine. I feel stupid flat on my back," he murmured. "Where are those *Englishers*?"

"We've arrested three men," the officer replied. "Were there more than three who attacked you, sir?"

The red pickup truck was still there, and a couple of officers were leaning inside, doing a search by the look of it. The *Englishers* who'd attacked him were in cuffs, pushed over the hoods of two police cars, and the big thug who'd been beating him stared directly at him from where he was restrained, his face pressed against the metal hood.

Standing a few feet away with a rolling pin in one hand stood his grandmother, talking to an officer who was taking notes on a pad of paper. He squinted.

"No, just the three," he said. "Why does Mammi have a rolling pin?"

It felt like a stupid thing to ask just now, but it was so out of place.

"You should be thankful for that, sir," the officer replied. "She and this young lady were using it to fend off your attackers when we arrived."

"What?" He turned toward Elizabeth.

"What would you have us do?" Elizabeth demanded. "Bridget has some good aim with that thing, too."

He started to laugh—the humor of it all striking him all at once—and with every shake of laughter, he let out a soft moan.

"I was trying to end it peacefully," he said. "I was trying to do this the Amish way . . . and you beat on them with a blunt object?"

The police officer's lips turned up in shared mirth, then she sobered. "Do you know why they attacked you?" the officer asked.

"They came by before and were giving us trouble when they were drunk," Solomon said. "And then they were harassing me in town. I don't know them personally, if that's what you're asking."

"And your name, sir?" the officer asked.

"Solomon Lantz."

"Well, Mr. Lantz, we're going to have you looked over by the EMTs," she said. "We recommend you go to the hospital, though."

"No," he said, and he grunted as he tried to move his shoulder. "No hospital. I'll be fine."

Elizabeth leaned closer, her cool fingers lingering on his cheek.

"Oh, Sol . . . why didn't you fight back?" she breathed.

"He didn't defend himself at all?" the officer asked.

"No!" There were tears in Elizabeth's voice. "He didn't. He just . . . he just stood there, and they kept hitting him. . . ."

Her words trailed off, and she wiped at a tear on her cheek that left a streak of dirt in its place.

"I'm Amish," he growled. "We don't fight."

He hadn't been Amish for a long time, but he was today.

Another siren could be heard coming up the road, and Solomon watched as the *Englishers* were put into the police cars by the officers and an ambulance came on the scene.

"There are the EMTs now." The officer looked relieved. "And we'll have a few more questions for you, too. Do you think you can stand?"

"Yah, I can stand."

"Let us help you up."

After being checked over and patched up by two EMTs who strongly advised him to visit a hospital before they left, Solomon allowed the police officers to drive him down to the house. He answered their questions, showed them his ID, and then answered the flood of follow-up questions once they saw his criminal history. Because Elizabeth had seen what had happened, it wasn't just his word against the *Englishers* anymore, which was as close to being believed as he would get.

"So, you didn't fight back," the female officer said, still seeming stuck on that detail. "Why not? You obviously shed your Amish ideals quite a long time ago."

"Because I'm trying to come back," he said, suddenly feeling very tired. "I'm trying to be better than I was."

"Legally, self-defense is permitted, sir," she said. "Just so you know."

"Not for the Amish," he replied.

"Are you going to press charges?" the officer asked.

He shook his head. "No."

It was an automatic response. The Amish didn't press charges and they didn't sue. They forgave and they kept to themselves. They trusted Gott to protect them, to make up for their losses, and to bless them more strongly than anyone could wrong them.

"I understand that you're trying to return to your Amish faith," the officer said slowly. "I can respect that. I'm a Christian, too, so I'm even impressed by it. And if you don't press charges, we can charge them for disturbing the peace, but they'll be on the streets tomorrow."

The look in the officer's eyes was haunted, and he wondered what she was imagining happening as a result of him doing this the Amish way.

"You can't stop them?" Solomon asked.

"No. Not quite so easily as that," she replied. "The safest thing for you to do is to formally press charges so that if they come near you again, they'll face harsher penalties."

If those *Englisher* animals wanted to find Elizabeth, they'd be back. Doing this the Amish way was fine if he was sacrificing himself, if they were beating on *him*, but the thought of them getting their hands on Elizabeth or his grandmother made his blood run cold. If they tried it when he was here, he'd damn his own soul by what he did to them. If he wasn't here to protect the women . . . A shiver slid down his spine.

Solomon looked across the kitchen to where his grandmother stood with tear-filled eyes. She had one hand over her mouth and her *kapp* hung askew on her head where a pin had come loose—something she hadn't noticed yet. How deeply had he disappointed her all these years? And now to come home and bring violence and distress in his wake . . . He might not have lifted his hand in violence this time, but by holding back, he'd forced his own grandmother to do it for him.

"Mammi, I've tried to do this the Amish way," he said, his voice shaking. "You can see that, right? I tried."

Bridget nodded, tears welling, but she didn't say anything.

"I'll press charges," he said, turning back to the officer. "They were harassing Elizabeth and they wanted to find her again. Press charges."

It wasn't the Amish thing to do, but it was right.

Chapter Fifteen

That evening Elizabeth took the last of the supper dishes from the table and carried them to the sink. They'd had chicken drumsticks and mashed potatoes—Solomon's favorite when he was a child, Bridget had said. The old woman fussed over her grandson and cooked—her way of showing him how much she loved him.

And Elizabeth could only help. So she cooked alongside Bridget and cleaned up afterward, letting Bridget focus on Solomon. She scrubbed and wiped and put things away. It kept her hands busy and, for the most part, kept her mind from moving back to the memory of Solomon held helpless between those two men while the big brute pounded on him. Any time the thought rose up on her mind, tears came with it.

It had been a quiet, solemn day filled with bringing fresh ice packs to Solomon and doing the daily chores. As the day wore on, Solomon's ribs, shoulder, and face started to swell. He was resting in the sitting room, laying on the couch with one of those ice packs on his shoulder.

"I don't understand how this happened," Bridget said

quietly, joining Elizabeth at the sink. She put the plug in the sink and turned on the tap.

"It's because we couldn't call the police the first time," Elizabeth said. "If we had, they wouldn't have come back—"

But they couldn't. How many times had an Amish community been forced to forgive when something horrific happened? How many times did they turn to Gott to soften their hearts when they wanted vengeance just as badly as anyone else? Sometimes Gott didn't intervene and they were called to forgive, and to grow, and to pull together in spite of the pain. Sometimes Gott called His people to grieve.

"We're told that Gott doesn't make mistakes," Bridget said. "And I have to believe that this wasn't a mistake either. You were kept safe and we got help for Solomon in time. I'm still torn about whether or not my own violence was a sin, though—"

Elizabeth could remember Bridget, her rolling pin hoisted over her head as she walloped the men away from her grandson. She'd shouted as she ran at them, and when one of the men came at the old woman, he was met with a blinding crack upside his head.

Elizabeth cast Bridget a smile. "You were really something, Bridget. I've never seen a rolling pin wielded like a weapon before."

"Don't you act like that wasn't shameful!" Bridget shot back. "I've never beaten a human being in my life and now, with my very own rolling pin, I've pounded on the backs of human beings."

And one head, but Elizabeth didn't want to make Bridget feel worse.

"It worked," Elizabeth said.

"Yah, it worked . . ." Bridget was silent for a moment. "And yet I'm reminded of Dirk Willems, the Anabaptist man who escaped prison in the Netherlands and ran for his life. But when the soldier chasing him fell into a frozen lake, he went back to save him, and as a result, Dirk was recaptured and martyred. He sacrificed his own freedom and ultimately his life to save the life of his enemy." Bridget sucked in a breath. "He didn't beat the backs of anyone . . ."

It was a story every Amish child was raised with—the ideal they all aspired to. When life was so deeply valued— that a believer would sacrifice his own life to save the life of someone who wanted to kill him—that was truly following the Gospel.

"Dirk Willems didn't fight them, that's true," Elizabeth agreed. "But he did run for his life, Bridget. He escaped prison—he didn't just sit there and submit to his own death! His life was a gift from Gott and he didn't lay it down lightly. Those *Englishers* were in no danger of dying. You saved your grandson, and me . . . and maybe even yourself. Our lives have value, too."

"Those *Englishers* have souls that matter to Gott, my girl," Bridget said solemnly.

"And they are still in possession of them," Elizabeth replied.

"I always thought that my grandson's rashness came from his mother's side," Bridget said quietly. "My son was a sober and quiet man, but Anke was fiery and passionate.

She can't help the personality that Gott furnished her with, but I did blame her more liberal upbringing and her tendency to react emotionally before she thought things through. Her family was just . . . rash."

Elizabeth stayed silent, her hands busy with the dishes.

"But it turns out that I'm capable of some equally fiery reactions," Bridget said. "Perhaps Sol is a little bit like his grandmother after all . . ."

Elizabeth couldn't see how Solomon would make a life in their community now. When word about this attack got out, people would jump to the same conclusion—trouble followed Solomon Lantz, and so did dangerous *Englishers*. What man in his right mind would bring Solomon onto his land to work now?

Even Elizabeth was feeling shaken, and it had occurred to her that it might be wise to go back to stay with her brother, considering the circumstances. But if she left Bridget, the old woman would be alone. And Bridget couldn't be chased away from her own home because of some rebel *Englishers*. This had been the plight of the Amish for generations—the passive fight to simply live without harassment.

Besides, if Elizabeth hadn't been there, who would have called the police? If it weren't for her, Solomon might be dead.

"Elizabeth," Bridget said when they'd finished cleaning up, "I want to go upstairs and pray. Would you check on Sol and make sure he's comfortable?"

"Of course," Elizabeth replied.

"Thank you." Bridget nodded. "I'll be a little while."

When Bridget had made her way upstairs, Elizabeth

took a mug of sweetened tea into the sitting room. There were no lamps lit, and outside the window the sun was sinking low, the sky aglow in coral pink. She paused in the doorway, the mug in her hands. Was he sleeping? It was better to let him rest, heal. Sleep was Gott's gift to the injured.

"Lizzie?" Solomon adjusted himself on the couch.

"Are you awake?" Elizabeth asked. She couldn't see him very well in the low light, but she could make out the shine of his eyes now. "Here—I brought you some tea."

She crossed the room to the couch and put the cup on a side table. Then she helped Solomon sit up a little more against a pillow. He settled back against it with a soft sigh. His face was bruised, and his nose looked puffy, too. She wanted to reach out and touch that battered flesh, but she wouldn't.

"I should get a lamp—" she started, but Solomon reached out and caught her hand. His touch was gentle but firm, and while she could have pulled away, it froze her to the spot.

"No . . . it's okay," he said softly. "I don't need light. I can see you just fine."

Hardly—she could barely see him, so she knew he wasn't telling the truth. But his touch softened, and even then she couldn't bring herself to pull away.

"Your grandmother went upstairs to pray," she said.

"I heard that." He tugged on her gently, and she sank down onto the edge of the couch. Even this was too much— she should sit on the floor or, better yet, across the room. But everything seemed upside down lately, including whatever it was she was feeling for this man.

"How much did you hear us saying?" Elizabeth whispered.

"Most of it," he said. "Mammi shouldn't feel guilty. She hardly hurt them."

"She did get one of them upside the head," Elizabeth replied. "It didn't seem kind to remind her of that."

A smile tickled the corners of Solomon's lips, and Elizabeth felt laughter bubbling up inside her. Suddenly, with the danger past, she could see the humor in it all—the tiny woman, her *kapp* strings flying out behind her, beating back three large men with her rolling pin. She'd been like Gideon in the Bible—the unlikely warrior.

"This isn't funny," she said, laughing softly.

"Very serious," he replied, but he smiled ruefully.

"It is serious, though," she said, sobering. "You could have been killed, Solomon."

He lifted her fingers to his lips and pressed a warm kiss against them. "But I wasn't."

"I know, but—"

"Lizzie—" His voice held more command. "I wasn't. Okay? I'm in one piece. See?"

He moved her hand down to his chest and pressed her palm against his even, slow heartbeat. For a moment she sat motionless, feeling the rhythm beneath her fingers, feeling the warmth of his skin through his shirt and the roughness of his callused hand covering hers.

Elizabeth sucked in a wavering breath. "They were beating on you and . . . and . . . I could hear it when his fist connected with . . . with . . ." The images of his poor body at the mercy of those men was too much to carry with her. Her words choked in her throat, and Solomon pushed himself up to a seated position and before she could pull away or stand up, he wrapped his arms around her.

"Hey . . ." He breathed against her hair. "I'm okay. See? You feel me here? I'm solid and strong and just fine."

"You're not fine," she said, pulling back. "You're battered and bruised, and—"

"And in one piece." He pressed a kiss onto her forehead, then grew more serious. "Look, I know what it's like, having seen something that horrifies you. And you carry it around, and you can't let it go. But you can't do that to yourself. You have to think of me like I am right now—I might not be particularly handsome, but I'm okay." He pulled back.

She smiled mistily at his humor. "You're still rather good-looking, even battered like that."

"Yah?" He touched her cheek with the back of his finger—a gesture that was growing familiar now. "You've never admitted to that before."

"And I won't again," she said, but she felt her cheeks heat.

"I think you're beautiful," he whispered. "I really do . . ."

"Sol . . ."

"And you don't call me that very often either," he whispered. "You always call me Solomon. Or back when we were kinner, it was Solomon Lantz, like you were about to lecture me." A smile tickled his lips again. "I like it when you call me Sol."

So did she . . . She liked it when he held her, and when he kissed her. She liked it when she could feel his solid strength holding her up. She looked up and he met her gaze, his eyes burning with a low heat that made her breath catch.

"Sol . . ."

The room was growing dimmer still as the sun sank behind the hills outside, and Elizabeth knew exactly what she'd do if she was left alone with this man, even in his pained state. She'd let him kiss her, and she'd let him hold her, and she'd regret it later on up in her bedroom when she prayed for Gott to give her strength.

Elizabeth leaned over and reached for the mug of tea, then pressed it into his hand.

Taking the mug, he was forced to let go of her to get a better grip on it, and she took the opportunity to stand up.

"Solomon Lantz," she said softly, and she couldn't help the teasing smile. "Drink your tea."

Solomon shot her a boyish grin—one that reminded her of years ago, before any of them had grown up or gone wrong.

"I'll behave," he said. "Maybe you should get that lamp after all."

Yes—light. That would help to dispel whatever warmth and tenderness was lurking in the shadows. If she weren't careful, she'd let go of the last remaining fragments of her heart that still seemed to be in her own possession.

That night Solomon slept better than he had in a long time. Not that he slept terribly much, because he was in a fair amount of pain, but he didn't dream at least. When he did slip into unconsciousness upstairs, on the twin-sized bed he'd used since he was a boy, the slumber was deep and untroubled.

When he awoke the next morning, his body ached as he pulled himself out of bed, but he felt better than he had the day before. He was healing up already, and he sent up a prayer of thanks for that much.

Looking in the mirror, the blue bruises across his nose and down the side of his face looked terrible. Gott had been with him yesterday when those men attacked. It could have been much worse than it was, but Gott sped the police to their address, and the blows hadn't been as strong as they might have been either. Gott *had* protected him—not from everything, but from the worst. And somehow, even in the midst of all this, he didn't feel abandoned, or rejected. He felt . . . alive.

After he pulled on his clothes over his aching limbs, he went out into the hallway. It was early and the sky was still gray, but he paused there, listening. His grandmother's door was shut, but he could hear the soft murmur of prayer from the other side, and it occurred to him that he might have Mammi's prayers to thank for an awful lot right now.

Elizabeth's door was shut, too, and he paused at it, placing his fingertips lightly against the wood. Let her sleep . . . Elizabeth deserved some rest, and he truly hoped that her dreams were as empty as his had been, because he'd seen how upset she was yesterday.

Outside, his morning chores took significantly longer than usual. His body was bruised and his muscles ached. His side was particularly tender, but the swelling had gone down from the night before and he was left with the purple streaks of a deep bruise but nothing more. He worked one-handed as much as he could—shoveling out stalls and filling the wheelbarrow with soiled hay.

Had Gott wanted him home again for this one threat, and to protect the women? Maybe. But that didn't mean he belonged here any longer than necessary. Because when Seth learned of this, and the other men, they'd only grow more protective of their own families. And while they'd be determined to help Bridget and Elizabeth to stay safe, they'd be even more cautious of Solomon than they were already.

The Amish life was a safe and beautiful one for the people who were married with *kinner*, who had extended family who loved and supported them, and who hit those milestones the Amish appreciated. But for those who didn't get married, who didn't have children of their own, who might have made some mistakes, or whose talents lay outside the farming and handicraft structure that supported the community, it wasn't so easy. And it wasn't so blissful. You didn't have a community that stayed so uniformly the same, so safe, so predictable and quiet because they embraced change or differences. Those who were too different left . . . like he had.

He dumped one last load of soiled hay on the manure pile, then left the wheelbarrow by the door, leaning against the frame momentarily as he caught his breath. He heard the front door to the stable open and stepped back inside just as Elizabeth appeared.

"Hi," she said. She held an envelope in one hand and she looked around the stable. "You shouldn't be doing this, Solomon. You need rest."

"I need distraction," he replied. "Besides, it's not as bad as it looks."

"It looks terrible," she said, her gaze sliding over his face and down to his shoulder. She knew his injuries.

He smiled, then shrugged—the movement painful. "Yah. I don't know what to say to that."

She held out the envelope. "It's for you."

Solomon looked at it in surprise, then crossed the stable to take it from her. He recognized his *mamm*'s handwriting right away—the loops that spelled his name—and his heart pattered hard and then felt like it stopped.

"When did this come?" he asked.

"I just got the mail now," she replied.

He tore open the envelope and turned away to read it, his fingers fumbling with the single page.

Dear Solomon,

Your mammi wrote to me to say that you've returned home, repentant and ready to live a proper Amish life. I'm so glad that my prayers have been answered.

Waneta is doing well and the triplets are all thriving now, thanks to prayer and many hands holding them and loving them. Your sister doesn't need me here any longer—I'll only start getting in the way. She's got a home of her own to run, and her own kinner *to raise.*

I will be coming home shortly, just as soon as I can arrange the travel. With prayer and affection,

Your mamm

He stood there motionless, rereading the letter, waiting for his emotions to catch up.

"Is it good news?" Elizabeth asked tentatively behind him.

Solomon turned back and found Elizabeth standing there, her gaze locked on him uncertainly.

"It's good news—yah. She's coming home. My sister is doing well, as are the new babies. Mamm is glad that I'm back . . ." He paused. ". . . repentant and ready to live a proper Amish life."

Elizabeth frowned slightly. "Oh . . ."

"Mammi gave a different version of events, it seems," he said dryly.

"Or she read into it what she wanted to see," Elizabeth said. "She wants you home obviously."

"Yah." His mother had written to him at least, but her formal, emotionally distant way still shone through. Would it be so terrible to use the word "love," or was "affection" as much as she could articulate? But these were old annoyances, and his *mamm* wasn't about to change at this late date.

"When will she arrive?" Elizabeth asked.

"She doesn't know. She'll come as soon as she can arrange it." He nodded a couple of times. "She hasn't heard about the drama around here, apparently, or this letter would have had more lecture to it."

"This wasn't your fault," Elizabeth said. She came closer and tipped up her head to look him in the face. "You know that, don't you?"

"It's hard not to feel somewhat responsible when chaos seems to follow me," he said.

Elizabeth shook her head. "If you weren't here, Sol, I don't know what would have happened. You saved me—"

He caught her hand and tugged her against him. She

leaned her cheek against his shoulder and they stood there for a moment, just breathing. She was warm against him and she smelled of soap and breakfast muffins. She was so untarnished, so pure . . . and there had been a time when she knew it, too. Maybe she still did. But she was like fresh sheets on a bed, like wash fresh from the line, like a cold glass of lemonade on a hot day . . . She made everything better, whether he was deserving of it or not. She was what was good and sweet in this world and she deserved someone equally wholesome. And here he was, standing with his heart beating against hers and feeling far more than he should.

He slid his hand around her waist and tipped his cheek on to the top of her head. His stubble rasped against her crisp, white *kapp*. Outside, the sound of hooves and buggy wheels broke through the stillness. For a moment neither of them moved, and then Elizabeth took a step back and ran her hands down her apron.

It was just as well they were interrupted. He wanted more than he had a right to ask for from Elizabeth, and quiet moments in the stable didn't help that. . . .

Solomon went to the door and pushed it open to see Johannes reining in his horses. Solomon stepped outside in the morning sunlight. Johannes looked in Solomon's direction and gave him a nod and then froze.

"Sol," Johannes called, and he hopped down from the buggy. "What happened to you?"

Right, he looked as bad as he felt. Solomon rotated his shoulder slowly, trying to limber it up a little.

"Long story," he said.

"I've got time. Seriously, what happened?" Johannes came around the horses, patting the sleek side of one of the animals as he came around. "You look like someone beat you up."

"Maybe it's not so long, then," Solomon said with an uncomfortable laugh. "The *Englishers* who were hassling us before came back, and I didn't get away this time."

"What?" Johannes reached out and pulled off Solomon's hat to get a better look at his face. Then he tossed it back to him. "Are these . . . people you know?"

"No," he said tightly. "Just . . . troublemakers. We called the police. It's taken care of."

"How is Aunt Bridget and Lizzie?" Johannes demanded.

Johannes's gaze moved over his shoulder, and Solomon turned to see Elizabeth in the stable doorway behind him. He gave her a small smile, but she didn't return it. She stood there with her arms wrapped around her middle.

"We're fine," Elizabeth replied. "We called the police and they got here in time."

"Thank Gott . . ." Johannes scrubbed a hand across his jaw. "I . . . uh . . . I came because there's an *Englisher* farmer hiring day laborers to replace a fence. It's just for a day, but it's work." Johannes winced, looking at Solomon's face. "I don't imagine you're in shape for that, though."

Solomon looked back at Elizabeth. "If I went, would you feel safe here?"

Elizabeth's face pinked and she pulled the door shut as she came up beside him.

"Go," she said. "Today is washing day. Bridget and I will be busy with that. I'm not going near that produce stand, and your grandmother won't either."

"I can use some extra money right now, too," Johannes said, but his gaze flickered between Solomon and Elizabeth as if something was suddenly making sense to him.

Solomon nodded toward the house. "Let me wash up and grab a lunch. And thanks for thinking of me."

Work—the Amish man's solace. Solomon needed some money until school and work started with the Catholic mission, and Gott was providing just that. Solomon would never turn down an honest day's work.

But when he looked back at Elizabeth, his heart gave a squeeze. Her dark gaze was locked on him, the sadness in her eyes mirroring the grief deep inside him.

If only he'd been a better man soon enough . . .

Chapter Sixteen

A few minutes later, with a lunch packed in a cloth bag, Solomon and Johannes were driving down the road in the direction of the *Englisher* farm in need of workers. Solomon looked over his shoulder, out the back window of the buggy. He didn't know what he was looking for, but his heart kept tugging him back toward the house where he'd left Elizabeth carrying loads of bedding down into the basement for washing.

He didn't know why he was even letting himself do this. . . . They both had lives ahead of them that didn't include each other, and whatever was building between them wasn't going to last. And she had no idea how powerfully he felt drawn to her . . . She had no idea what it did to him when she rested her head against his shoulder. It was that thundering attraction between them that made him need to pull back. This was beyond anything he'd ever felt before.

Was Elizabeth going to leave her Amish life and join him in some apartment in town? Would she trade her Amish clothes for jeans and a T-shirt and get accustomed to internet and cable TV? Would she attend Catholic mass with him so that he could show his appreciation for the people who were helping him get his feet under him again? Of course not.

"So, what's going on with you and Elizabeth?" Johannes asked, jerking him out of his reverie.

"What?" Solomon cleared his throat. "Nothing."

A car passed them, slowing down as the occupants peered through their windows at them. Solomon looked away.

"That's a lie." Johannes fixed him with a pointed look.

"If I were courting her, you'd know," Solomon said. Johannes was family, after all. Word would get to him faster than to anyone else. But Solomon wasn't going to tarnish her reputation while he was here. Did he have feelings for her? Yah. He'd taken a beating for that woman, but he wasn't going to ruin her future, too.

"I know you aren't courting her," Johannes replied. "But I know there's something happening. I'm not blind."

"Look, I've noticed her, okay? Maybe the men in our family have a weakness for these Yoder girls. She's beautiful and kind and . . . special. But I also know that I'm not on a level to get a woman like that. I have nothing to offer her. So you don't have to remind me."

They came to a four-way stop, and Johannes reined the horses in. Two cars went ahead of them, and then Johannes flicked the reins and they plodded forward again. A pickup truck swerved past them, and Solomon's stomach leaped as the horses shied left.

Johannes's gaze snapped fire, but he didn't react to the truck as it whipped past.

"Idiots," Solomon muttered.

"It's fine," Johannes said. "The horses are getting better at not spooking."

Johannes had the proper Amish response—let it go. Be thankful for an ability to cope. Solomon's reactions weren't quite that honed.

"Look, Elizabeth is like a sister to me," Johannes said after a moment. "And she's more vulnerable right now than she lets on."

"You don't have to give me this talk," Solomon said with a sigh.

"I think I do," Johannes replied. "You can't just fool around with her. She's a good Amish girl, despite what her father did. And she deserves the respect of a good Amish girl."

"Is this why you came by, to give me a lecture?" Solomon retorted.

"Maybe. Plus, we both need work."

"You've got a job. You work your *daet*'s farm," Solomon said.

"I'm getting married."

Solomon looked at him in shock. "What? The widow from Edson?"

"Yah. I'm going to marry Sovilla," Johannes said, his voice low.

"Why?" Solomon demanded.

Johannes shot him an irritated look.

"Because, unlike some, I respect the women who dedicate themselves to a good Amish life," Johannes snapped. "And Sovilla is Amish. She's kind, hardworking, sweet, and I can see what a quality woman she is. And

I'm not the kind of man who dates around and fools around and then wanders off. She needs a husband to help her raise her little girls, and I'm willing to be that husband."

"And I'm the man who fools around and leaves women in my wake," Solomon said. "That's what you think?"

"It looks that way," Johannes said.

This was the opinion of his own kin . . . what did the rest of the community think of him?

"Hopefully you'll get to know me again better than that," Solomon retorted. "I might have been a flirt before I jumped the fence, and I'll admit to that, but I experienced a lot with the *Englishers*, and I grew up. I don't just toy with women, Johannes."

Johannes turned toward him, his cool gaze meeting Solomon's evenly. "Do you still want this ride or should I take you back?"

Solomon had never seen his cousin so direct before, and he settled back in the seat.

"I need work," Solomon said curtly. "I'll take the ride."

They were silent for a couple of minutes, the horses' hooves plodding along. They were moving past the Amish farms and onto English property. In the distance a tractor growled and a pickup truck wound over a dusty road. The *Englisher* farms weren't quite so small and peaceful as the Amish ones. They were larger, with more land to work, with a lot of streamlined machinery that appealed to Solomon. It was efficient.

"So what about Lovina?" Solomon asked.

"What about her?" Johannes asked.

"You can marry a woman you barely know?" Solomon said. "Elizabeth thinks you love her sister still."

"I do," Johannes said.

"That's not a problem?" Solomon let out a short laugh. "Really."

"She left me," Johannes replied, turning forward again. "She chose an *Englisher* life. She wrote me one letter saying that she loved me, but she couldn't live under the burden of her father's reputation, and that she was calling off our wedding. After that, nothing. No letter. No news. No reassurance that she's okay . . ."

"So you're angry," Solomon replied.

"I'm realistic."

"But you aren't over her either," Solomon countered.

"I never will be!" Johannes said shortly. "I think you get a chance with a woman who sinks into your bones once a lifetime, and she was mine. But that doesn't mean I can't love again, or have a family, or find some happiness, does it?"

"So . . . you've asked Sovilla to marry you, then?" Solomon asked.

"Last night."

"And she obviously agreed."

"The wedding will be in a week. The bishop is already getting the local women to help put something together. It'll be a small wedding, but it's worth a celebration."

"And you'll be a father—just like that," Solomon said. "Are you ready for that?"

"No," Johannes replied. "Of course not. But I don't think any man is actually ready for fatherhood. Besides, Sovilla said she'd help me with that, and she'd give me tips about getting them to behave and how to connect with them. Sovilla knows her children."

"She's a good woman, isn't she?" Solomon asked quietly.

"She's a very good woman. She has a strong reputation in Edson, and our bishop speaks very highly of her, too." Johannes looked over at Solomon, and his expression relaxed. "It might not be the family I was imagining for myself, but I'll have a wife and *kinner*, and hopefully a baby on the way soon enough. We can live with my parents for the first year or so, until I get something else lined up, and it will be good because Sovilla will have help with the girls, and it won't be just the two of us while we get used to each other. I think it will be . . . good."

A marriage with a relative stranger and children to provide for that he hadn't even met. It was risky, but Solomon thought he could understand. Sometimes a man couldn't be with the woman who sank down into his bones, as Johannes had put it, but he couldn't simply stop living either. Those years were going to pass one way or another, and a man had to keep putting one foot forward.

"You're the only one who can know what will make you happy," Solomon said.

"And I'm the one who will live with my choices," Johannes replied.

Solomon was the one who'd live with the fallout of his choices, too.

Johannes pulled a piece of paper out of his pocket and squinted at the address on the next driveway. Then he tucked it away again and turned the horses down the drive.

This was paved and, ahead, Solomon could see some buggies already parked, as well as a few pickup trucks. A farmer stood in gum boots, his arms crossed over his chest, talking to a group of men—a mixture of Amish and English—who were already in the back of a work truck. The farmer was middle-aged, with a green John Deere baseball cap. He slapped the side of the vehicle, and it rumbled off down a twisting drive.

"Good morning!" Johannes called. "I saw your post looking for workers."

"Sure thing," the farmer said, and he waited while Johannes reined in the horses. "You two want to work?"

"Yah."

"You've got fencing experience?" the farmer asked, squinting.

Johannes spread his hands and grinned. "Come on. We're Amish. If we can't build a fence, we have no right to the name."

"Right." The farmer laughed at Johannes's humor. "Okay, but I need one of you to be able to drive a truck, so unless you can do that, I'm afraid I won't be able to hire you on—"

"Oh . . ." Johannes licked his lips. "I can take the buggy, but—"

"It won't make it. Your wheels are too narrow," the farmer said with a shake of his head. "And that truck is full."

Johannes heaved a sigh, and Solomon nudged his cousin.

"I can drive," Solomon said.

Both men looked at him in surprise. The farmer pushed his hat back on his head and rubbed a hand over his chin.

"You can?" Johannes raised his eyebrows, then shrugged. "Yeah, of course you'd be able to."

"You can drive stick?" the farmer asked skeptically.

"Yah. I wasn't always Amish," Solomon replied. "I drive stick and automatic, no problem. I can drive tractors and forklifts, too, if that makes you feel any better."

"Your church lets you do that?" the farmer asked.

"I'm . . . okay with driving," Solomon said, unsure even how much to say. "My conscience is clear."

The farmer shrugged. "So what we're doing is replacing fence all along one side of my pasture. Most of the posts are okay, but a few need to be replaced, plus I want new barbed wire up . . ."

Solomon listened while Johannes unhitched, and as he mentally tallied up the instructions, he realized he was doing the right thing. Even today, if he hadn't learned to drive, they'd have come all the way out here for nothing. Jobs could be scarce, and if employers didn't want education, they certainly wanted skills that a lot of Amish workers didn't have, like driving.

"All right, I'm ready," Johannes said when he'd finished with the horses.

"Okay, well, here's the keys," the farmer said, fishing a ring of keys out of his pocket and nodding toward a rusted-out Ford pickup. It was more putty than metal, by the looks of it. "You got tools?"

"Yah, right here." Johannes lifted a canvas bag.

"Good. So, you want to follow that road down and carry on east . . ."

They'd earn some money, Solomon and Johannes, but for different goals. Johannes wanted to have some extra money in his pocket for his new life with a woman he'd barely met and *kinner* who'd need a whole lot more than Johannes was probably even anticipating. But Solomon needed some cash to help out his grandmother so that she could stop selling produce and stay safely behind her property line.

That's all he wanted—a bit of cash to hand over.

When he left the Amish life this time, he'd do so with empty pockets and a clear conscience. Johannes was getting his fresh start with an arranged marriage. Solomon would get his on the other side of the fence.

"It was a letter from Anke," Elizabeth said, shaking out a wet sheet to find the corner. "She's coming home."

"Oh?" Bridget deposited another basket of wet laundry next to the one Elizabeth was working on. "She said that?"

"I didn't see the letter, but that's what Solomon said," she replied. "He also said his *mamm* was under the impression that he'd come back penitent and ready to be Amish."

Bridget's cheeks pinked. "I may have given that impression when I wrote to her, but that was faith, Elizabeth. I do believe that Gott is working and He'll keep that boy at home. I do!"

Elizabeth smiled ruefully. "If prayers could be enough—"

"Prayers are more than enough," Bridget replied. "Prayers are more powerful than any of us imagine. They open up Gott's gates and bring us straight to the presence of the Almighty."

It was true, but Solomon seemed quite determined to go the English way, and she couldn't blame him. The Amish life was wonderful when you had a community to encourage you and need your contributions. What was an Amish life without that community but hardship and loneliness?

Elizabeth shook out the sheet and climbed up onto the stepladder, then flung it over the line. She headed down the stairs to pull it straight across the line from the ground, then accepted the stepladder that Bridget passed over the railing to her so that she could reach to add some pins to hold it in place. A gust of wind caught it and it flapped with a satisfying snap.

"I knew she'd come back for him," Bridget said. "Anke was furious with her son for leaving, but she's a mother, and a chance to see her prodigal son . . . she wouldn't give that up."

"He misses her," Elizabeth said.

"Our *mamms* are part of us," Bridget said. "They're a physical piece of us, and Gott intended it that way. You can run from a great many things in life, but you can't run from your own *mamm*."

Elizabeth nodded. "I miss mine."

"Yah. Your *mamm* loved you *kinner* dearly. And I daresay she was the one who held your *daet* up straight. Without her . . ." Bridget sighed, but she didn't finish. She didn't have to. They both knew what had become of Abe Yoder without his beloved wife.

The sound of hooves made Elizabeth turn, expecting

to see Solomon and Johannes returning, but it wasn't—
it was Isaiah. Elizabeth put the bag of clothespins on the
deck and waited for her brother to rein in the horses.

"Good morning!" she called.

Isaiah shot her a fiery look and jumped down from the
buggy. He strode across the gravel drive and didn't even
bother saying hello to Bridget.

"What's the matter?" Elizabeth asked, and she crossed
the grass, meeting her brother at the edge of the gravel.

"I heard about the *Englishers*," he said. "*Englishers*
attack you and you don't tell me a thing?"

"I meant to," she said. "I'm sorry about that, Isaiah, but
the police dealt with it, and Sol has been here with us, so
we haven't been alone."

"Lizzie—" Her brother took her by the shoulders. "This
isn't safe."

"If it isn't safe for me, it's even less safe for Bridget
alone," Elizabeth said, lowering her voice. "She needs
someone here with her for a reason. She's an old woman.
What would you have me do?"

"You can both come to our place," Isaiah said, raising
his voice.

"That would be a squeeze," Bridget called from the
deck.

Elizabeth looked over her shoulder. Bridget pulled the
clothesline with a squeak and the sheet jerked out farther,
leaving space for her to pin up a pillowcase.

"You have Daet with you," Elizabeth said quietly. "You
and Bethany are doing enough."

"Daet left this morning," Isaiah said curtly.

"What?" Elizabeth stepped closer to her brother and lowered her voice. "Where did he go?"

"He left a note saying he was leaving to find Lovina."

Elizabeth and her brother exchanged a somber look.

"What does that mean exactly?" she asked.

"That's all he said," he replied. "That he was going to find Lovina, and that he'd let us know when there was news. That's it."

Elizabeth let out a pent-up breath. "Does he know where to look?"

"He told me earlier that he heard about a few different places where runaway Amish find shelter and he wanted to check them."

"That will cost money," she said.

"I don't know. . . . He must know where to get that, too," he replied.

Elizabeth sighed. "This will be worth it if he finds her, you know."

"Yah, but what happens if Daet doesn't and he just ends up hurt, or lost, or—"

"He's no newborn kitten, Isaiah," she said curtly. "He ran a farm and raised a family. He can sort out some *Englisher* directions, I'm sure. You don't have to shoulder the responsibility for everything. At least he's doing something instead of sitting in that rocking chair, pretending nothing's changed."

Her brother eyed her for a moment. "You haven't forgiven him either, have you?"

Elizabeth sighed. "Lovina leaving was his fault, you know that. It would be . . . appropriate . . . if he brought her home."

Isaiah nodded slowly. "The last couple of days he's been talking about preaching again, too."

Elizabeth felt her face pale. "He wouldn't . . ."

"He wants to." Isaiah pressed his lips together. "I don't know what we're going to do with him. He can't be the preacher he was before all this. But we can't abandon him either."

"The bishops will never welcome him to preach in their communities," Elizabeth said.

"No," Isaiah agreed. "They won't, and it will be another embarrassment if we can't talk him out of trying."

Did their father really believe so little had changed? Or was he just needing something to think about? After preaching his entire adult life, how did a man simply . . . stop?

"Lizzie, you can't stay here," Isaiah said. "It isn't safe."

"We have Sol here," Elizabeth replied. "Trust me, we're safe."

"He was beaten very badly—"

"He didn't have to do that," she said. "He learned to fight in prison, Isaiah, and he's very competent. He wanted to let me get away, and he thought that not fighting would give me more time."

She felt strangely proud of that. Solomon was strong, fast, competent. And with him, she knew she was safe, at least physically. Her reputation, on the other hand, was hanging by a thread.

"He did that for you?" Isaiah frowned.

"Yah."

"So, he's in love with you . . ."

"No, he's—" Was he? The thought hadn't occurred to

her yet. What did love have to do with any of this? Was that what it meant when a man was willing to hand over his body for a beating to protect a woman? She caught her breath. Her brother was watching her face, and his expression fell.

"Lizzie, he's an ex-con! He comes to Bountiful and violence follows! You wanted a good Amish life. You wanted the best Amish life! What happened to that? Solomon's not going to be in good standing with the church . . . ever!"

"Isaiah," Elizabeth said quietly, "I'm not going to stay in Bountiful anyway. I want to go to another Amish community and start fresh. I do want the Amish life, but if I stay here, I'm just going to be the daughter of the man who defrauded the community and who keeps trying to preach!"

"Is Sol going with you?" her brother asked.

"No. He's going English."

Isaiah nodded slowly. "Where would *you* go?"

"Edson? Bonnyville? Newton? I don't know. But I won't get married here, Isaiah."

Her brother sighed. "I know. I've been considering that. It was a miracle that Bethany and I found each other. And you deserve a family of your own."

"I never thought there was a danger of me ending up an old maid, but now . . ." She shrugged. "It's a very real possibility."

"Then we'll find you something," Isaiah said. "A job, a family needing a nanny maybe. We'll find some way for you to meet people in another community."

"Maybe even in Indiana or Ohio," she said.

"The further the better?" Isaiah smiled when he said it, but she heard the sadness in his voice. "But we can ask around—check *The Budget* for any ads. Even if you worked at an Amish shop in another community. We'll find you something."

"You'll help me look?" she asked. "You promise?"

"I'll help you look, as long as you aren't bringing Solomon Lantz with you," he said curtly, and she knew he wasn't joking.

Elizabeth looked over her shoulder again. Bridget pushed up her glasses on her nose and bent down to pull out another heavy, wet sheet. "I need to help with the laundry, Isaiah."

"Isaiah, I have pie!" Bridget called as Elizabeth started back toward the porch. She gave the sheet another hard tug and shook it out. "Blackberry and cherry. Your choice."

"Is it any trouble?" Isaiah asked, but he was already headed toward the porch a couple of steps behind Elizabeth.

"Of course not," Bridget replied with a smile. "It's nice to have young men around the house again. It's a pleasure to feed you. Solomon already tucked into the cherry pie this morning, but I managed to save half of it."

Elizabeth took the sheet from Bridget as the older woman headed back inside the house. Isaiah followed, and Elizabeth got to work with the laundry. A couple of minutes later her brother came back onto the porch with a plate in one hand, with a generous piece of blackberry pie.

"Do you want milk, Isaiah?" Bridget called from inside.

"Thank you, Bridget, that would be nice!" Isaiah called back.

Elizabeth flung a sheet over the line, then grabbed the bag of pins and headed down to the grass to straighten it.

"I want a husband," Elizabeth said, casting her brother a serious look. "I want a houseful of *kinner*. I want a mother-in-law and a father-in-law, and new relatives to get along with. I want what you have."

"We'll find you something," he replied. "And I don't mind telling you that I'll be glad to have you away from all this."

Away from Solomon, he meant. But he was right. If she wanted a fresh start, whatever she was feeling for Solomon wasn't going to help her achieve her goal.

Solomon was a man with deep feelings and strength of body and personality. . . . His kisses could empty her brain of all logic. But it was more than that. Her feelings for him ran deeper still, because when she imagined a husband to kiss and curl up with at night, it was Solomon she saw next to her, his dark eyes, his soft lips, his strong arms pulling her close . . .

And that couldn't be.

She'd have to stop this, because Solomon Lantz was only here until he could start a new *Englisher* life, and she knew it. She'd known it from the start. Bridget might have the faith to believe that Solomon could start a new life here, but Elizabeth knew better.

Bountiful would remain a sweet Amish hub of worship and work because the ones who didn't fit into that would leave . . . and that included both Solomon and Elizabeth alike. There was a price for staying home when the space for you closed up, and Elizabeth was not willing to pay it.

Chapter Seventeen

Solomon looked around the quiet street as he headed up to his parole officer's office, the back of his neck prickling. A woman with a stroller walked down the other side of the street. The toddler pulled off a shoe and threw it onto the sidewalk, and she stopped to pick it up with a soft remonstrance and carried on. A pickup truck rumbled past, and he scanned the occupants. Just an older man with white hair and a dog.

He let out a breath.

He pulled open the door to the office building and went inside. He waited for a few minutes in one of the plastic chairs outside, and when Jeff called him in, Solomon went into the office and shut the door.

"How are you doing?" Jeff asked. "I was informed about the attack you suffered. I'm sorry to hear it."

"Yah." Solomon licked his lips. "I'm healing up. I'm okay."

"You can always come to see me in between appointments, you know," Jeff said. "If I can help—"

"No, I'm fine," Solomon said quickly.

Jeff nodded. "Okay, well, I have you enrolled in the

GED course, and I have an appointment set up for you to meet with the Catholic priest who is running the local outreach. Now, will you be staying with your family for the foreseeable future, or will you need other accommodations?"

"I'm not sure yet," Solomon replied. "I'll have to see what the bishop says, I guess."

"Let me know," Jeff replied. "I work with a social worker who can help you arrange something else if you need it."

"Thank you."

Jeff was silent for a moment, then he pursed his lips in thought. "The priest did say that they have some work you could start on early, with the understanding that you'll be enrolled in school in the next three weeks."

"Really?" Solomon straightened. "I'd like that."

"It's office work," Jeff said. "Do you have any experience with computers?"

Solomon felt his optimism wane. "No."

"I didn't think so," Jeff replied. "Well, this is a good way to get some of that experience. It's some simple data inputting. It might help to learn how to type—in fact, typing will help you in your GED studies, too. Are you willing to learn?"

Typing, computers—the very thought was intimidating, but this was his chance at a better life.

"Yah, I'm willing," Solomon replied.

"You'll get paid once a week, and this is the address of the parish," Jeff said, holding out a slip of paper. "They're expecting you."

"When?" Solomon asked.

"As soon as you're willing to start work."

He nodded. "Thank you. I need this!"

In fact, if he could be bringing some money home to his grandmother, maybe the bishop would see the benefit in letting Solomon live at home for a while. It was worth a shot. Until he had a proper job that would pay enough to let him rent an apartment of his own at least. It wasn't too likely that a roommate would want to live with an ex-convict—he wasn't too keen on living with an ex-convict himself. This had to be a proper fresh start.

"Now, I feel like I need to impress upon you that this chance you're getting to work with the church is dependent upon you sticking to the rules. They are interested in helping a convict rehabilitate if he's dedicated to bettering himself. So if there are any broken curfews, any missed appointments with me, any drinking, drugs, or trouble with the police, your chance is over and they move on to someone else. There are no extra strikes here. Do you understand?"

One chance—one very generous chance . . .

"Yes, I do."

Jeff nodded. "Good. Have a good week. And if you need to get in touch with me, please do. I'm always willing to help."

"Thank you."

Solomon rose and headed for the door. Gott was providing for him, one step at a time, and he felt a wave of gratitude. He wasn't going to be alone in this.

Outside the air-conditioned office, the day was hot already. He looked at the address on the slip of paper. He knew where the Catholic church was. It was a rather ornate building on the far end of Main Street. There wasn't any Amish parking there, though. But he had his horses settled with water and shade in the buggy parking lot, so he might as well walk.

As he headed up the street, he felt a strange sense of freedom. The last time he'd ventured away from the Amish life, he'd gone straight to the gutter. But this time he'd have guidance. Young people spurned advice, but Solomon had experienced enough that he was grateful for it now.

And he was deeply grateful for a paying job.

As he passed the farming surplus store, he slowed when he saw Johannes come out the front door, a bag in one hand. Johannes gave him a nod.

"Hi," Solomon said, stopping beside his cousin. "How are you doing?"

"Good." Johannes smiled. "Just picking up some new suspenders for my wedding."

"Right!" Solomon grinned. "Are you excited?"

"I'm terrified," Johannes replied, but he shrugged. "But I'll be terrified with new suspenders."

Solomon chuckled. A wedding in the family—an Amish excuse to celebrate. Johannes was starting a new stage of life and would be bringing everyone together to share in the joy . . . It would be a celebration where Solomon would see extended family from other communities, and that thought was an uncomfortable one.

"Fresh starts are always a little terrifying," Solomon said. "For me, too."

"Yah, I suppose," Johannes agreed. "What are you doing in town?"

"I was seeing my parole officer," Solomon replied.

"Oh . . ." Johannes nodded, and he shifted his weight uncomfortably.

"It's how it's done—leaving prison," Solomon said.

"Okay." Solomon sighed. His entire existence was going to be uncomfortable for both his family and the community. Johannes marrying a stranger was fine apparently, but a man returned from prison left everyone frozen with uncertainty.

"And I'm off to start a job," Solomon added. "I hope I'm starting today, at least. I've been promised one."

"Really?" Johannes squinted. "Where?"

"The Catholic church is getting me started with some office work," Solomon replied. "Computer stuff, they say."

"Oh!" Johannes squinted. "A Catholic church . . ."

"They're offering me help," Solomon said. "They helped me in prison, too. I can't afford to turn it down."

More than that, he didn't want to turn down the job. There was a level of kindness in the offer that had softened him. Sure, the Catholic church was the furthest from Amish possible in Christendom, but he'd found something there that he hadn't realized he'd needed until he was at his lowest—grace.

"You wouldn't rather fix a fence?" his cousin asked.

"There aren't that many day jobs available," Solomon said. "Yah, maybe I'd rather fix a fence or milk some cows or muck out some stalls—but I need steady pay, and I need to build a life. Sometimes you don't get the job you want, you work the job you're given. And you're grateful for it."

"I understand that," Johannes said. "We all have to build a life somehow. Will I see you at my wedding?"

"Is that an invitation?" Solomon asked.

"You don't need a formal invitation. You're family. Of course I want you at my wedding."

This might be the last Amish invitation he received for a long time, and that thought saddened him.

"I'll be there," Solomon said.

As he and Johannes parted ways, Solomon headed on up the road in the direction of that small but ornate Catholic church. And he was reminded of the priest who sat with him in the prison chapel—a middle-aged man with a thoughtful way of speaking that reminded Solomon just a little bit of the bishop.

God isn't surprised by anything, Solomon. He knows where you are and why. He knows what will befall you, and He knows where He is leading you, if you'll listen to His voice. And sometimes where He leads us can seem so incredibly unlikely. I never thought I'd be a priest, you know. I wanted to be a race car driver, once upon a time. . . . Yet here I am. In God's hands. Right where I'm supposed to be.

And here was Solomon, in Gott's hands, right where he was supposed to be.

If Gott was leading him away from his Amish life, what was waiting for him out there in the wilderness with the *Englishers*? And was it terrible that he was starting to feel excited about it?

Elizabeth pinched the edge of the piecrust, the dough molding to her touch. These were for the wedding that

was happening in a week's time. The community freezer—
a wagon-drawn, gas-powered freezer—had been brought
out of storage for the occasion, and the pies, once put
together and covered in plastic, would be frozen until a
couple of days before the wedding, when they'd thaw
them all out and begin baking. It was a process they all
knew by heart.

How many weddings had Elizabeth helped to bake for?
They felt countless. How many friends had she watched
take their vows? She'd stood with three friends as their
newehocker, and she'd been deeply happy to see each of
them settle down into family life, but she'd also been
praying for her own future family. She wanted a husband
of her own, and a baby in her arms. *Lord, while You bless
her, please don't forget me. . . .*

But this wedding was different. This wedding was the
community's response to Lovina's lengthy absence and it
felt wrong.

Elizabeth couldn't ask Gott to bless her as He was
blessing Sovilla and Johannes. She didn't want an arranged
marriage while her heart was elsewhere. She wanted a real
marriage—a love connection with a man who would look
at her with adoring eyes while she undid her braid in the
morning that kept her hair from tangling during the night.
She wanted the kind of marriage where she looked forward to her husband coming in after a long day of work,
where his kisses could make her feel like jelly.

She wanted all of it—a man respected in his community, a man who could give her a life of Amish goodness.
She wanted her turn at long last.

The day wore on, and Bridget and Elizabeth made pie
after pie and then moved on to baking buns. When

Solomon's buggy finally pulled into the drive, Elizabeth felt a wave of longing. He'd been gone a long time and she could only wonder what had kept him.

"Is that Sol?" Bridget asked, looking up from some rolls she was forming into balls.

"Yah, that's him," Elizabeth said, looking out the screen door.

"It's almost dinnertime . . . Oh, he'll be hungry, too. Dear, would you do me a favor?" Bridget asked. "I'm going to start dinner—something quick. Would you go get the eggs for me?"

"Yah." Elizabeth nodded. "Of course."

"Thank you—oh my, the time just flies . . ." Bridget murmured, and she flung a towel over the dough for it to rise once more and headed to the sink to wash her hands.

Elizabeth opened the side door, wire basket in hand, and headed out just as Solomon jumped down from the buggy. He shot her a smile.

"Hi," he said.

"What took so long?" she asked. "I thought you had a quick appointment."

"I started a job," he replied, and he shot her a grin. "I didn't know about it until I met with my parole officer. It's at the Catholic church. They're teaching me to . . ." He hesitated, then cast her an apologetic look. "They're teaching me to use a computer."

"Oh." She frowned. "So . . . you're starting out English, then?"

He was silent.

"Are you?" she pressed. "Are you starting an *Englisher* life, with computers and . . . and . . . other churches? If that's what you're doing, then admit it to me. Just say so."

"Yah." He licked his lips. "That's what I'm doing."

His words hit her like a blow to the gut. She'd known this was the direction he was taking, and yet it still hurt to see him doing it. Because it was still a *choice*, and it would draw a very firm line between them.

Solomon glanced down at the egg basket in her hand. "Let me unhitch. We'll talk, okay? I'll meet you at the chicken house."

So, Solomon had begun. It seemed so innocuous. Just a day away from home and he came back looking just as Amish as ever . . . but she could feel a change in him, too. He was a little stronger somehow, and a little more certain of himself . . . but that dark gaze of his was the same, pinning her down with its intensity.

"Sol, you shouldn't do this"—she started—"computers and *Englisher* jobs—there's got to be another way! You haven't looked for it!"

"Lizzie . . ." His voice was soft. "Let me unhitch."

She couldn't argue with that. The horses needed a rest, and water and silage. And she felt inside her that she was asking something of him—demanding something of him . . . she just didn't know what. She was leaving, too, wasn't she?

Without another word, Elizabeth headed off toward the coop, glancing over her shoulder as Solomon started to unhitch.

Elizabeth would leave Bountiful—that was most certain—and she'd miss Solomon deeply, she knew. She might very well find herself in Johannes's position, marrying a very good person while her heart stubbornly clung to another, less-deserving one.

Because Lovina, while her family loved her fiercely,

had let everyone down. She'd abandoned them for an *Englisher* life while they faced the unfairness of their fate head-on. Lovina had left a man who loved her so dearly that he'd grieved her leaving like a death.

And Solomon, for all his bravery, had a wild heart that wouldn't be tamed, even by prison. He was going English, even now. Computers at a Catholic church? His clothes might be familiar, and his hat might allow him to blend in with the Amish, but he was already starting out on a new path that would take him away. Straight to perdition, some would say.

The bitter irony was that this was the one time Elizabeth couldn't pray her prayer to be blessed the same as others and it would be answered. Who was she to judge Johannes and Sovilla for their arranged marriage? She'd be little better when her turn came. What divine cruelty. Or perhaps it was just the rain falling on everyone—a broken heart being the great equalizer.

Elizabeth nudged a hen aside and pulled out a warm egg. The chicken coop was hot and dry. The hens squawked irritably as Elizabeth collected the eggs, gently placing them in the wire basket. Her nose tickled and she rubbed it with the back of one wrist. When she'd collected all the eggs, she went back out into the fresh air.

Solomon had finished with the horses, and she watched as he patted the flank of one large quarter horse, sending it out into the field. He looked up as if he'd felt her gaze on him, then he headed in her direction.

"So?" she said as he reached her.

"What do you want me to say?" he asked.

"I want an explanation," she said. "You came home, Sol! You came back, and your mother is on her way. . . .

Your grandmother has been praying for you so fervently—did you know that?"

"Yah, I know," Solomon replied.

"I thought Johannes found you at least a day of work—"

"Which we wouldn't have had if I didn't know how to drive a truck," he said, cutting her off. "If I'd been sticking to all the Amish ways, we wouldn't have had that day of work."

"Oh . . ." She felt tears of frustration rising up inside her.

"Lizzie, I can't be an Amish farmer! Or a carpenter, or . . . or . . . a businessman. I can't! They won't accept me—"

"You haven't waited long enough," she said. "It takes time for people to forgive. You have to wait—"

"Accept my punishment from the community, you mean," he interrupted.

"Maybe." She straightened her shoulders.

"Prison wasn't punishment enough?" he demanded. "I have to accept more? I have to bow under their derision for a few more years until they think they can let it go?"

Elizabeth felt her eyes mist. "Maybe I was hoping your grandmother was right."

"About what?" he asked.

"That Gott was still working and that a miracle was possible, and that you'd find your place and settle back in, and . . ."

"And watch you leave?" he asked gruffly. "What a beautiful homecoming, where I settle in for *what*, Lizzie? To be alone here? To keep my grandmother company while you head off to Indiana or Ohio or wherever you decide to find that ideal Amish man of yours?"

Elizabeth looked toward the house and Solomon caught her hand and tugged her behind the chicken coop and out of sight of the kitchen windows. She tugged her hand free of his grip and glared up at him.

"Since when did you come home for *me*?" she demanded.

"I didn't!" he retorted. "I came home to see my mother, and to find some redemption of some sort. . . . I didn't come for you! But that doesn't change that we've developed something—"

"Developed what?" she demanded. "When your grandmother saw us in the kitchen and she lectured me afterward, she thought you'd been making *promises* to me . . . that you'd been talking marriage and *kinner*. I told her you hadn't been, and do you know what she said to me? She said, then what are you doing?" Elizabeth shook her head. "There are no promises between us, Sol!"

Solomon caught her hand again and pulled her against him. His lips came down over hers in a hard, heartbroken kiss. He slipped his fingers behind her neck, and when he pulled back, she saw tears glistening in his eyes.

"Are you saying that what we feel is nothing?" he breathed.

"It has no future and you know it!" she shot back. "There are no agreements, no promises, no—"

"Come with me," he said hoarsely.

"What?"

"Come with me," he said, and he pulled her closer. "I promised your father I wouldn't do this, but not every life is meant to be lived Amish. There are good people out there, Lizzie. I've made too many mistakes to give you any kind of Amish life here . . . but I can get an education. I'm starting in a few weeks! I've got a job that will pay me enough to get a tiny apartment, and you could come with me . . ."

"And do what?" she breathed, her heart suspended in her chest.

"We didn't make promises yet," he whispered. "I know that . . . We both tried to stop feeling this, and to be reasonable. But it didn't work, did it? So let's *make* a few promises!"

"I can't promise to leave Bountiful and run off with my *Englisher* boyfriend!" she said. "No!"

"I'm not asking you to run off with your boyfriend," he whispered. "I'm asking you to marry me."

Her heart thudded to a stop.

Chapter Eighteen

Solomon stared down at her, the words hanging between them. He hadn't realized he'd even said them out loud before the words came out of his mouth, and now that he was looking down into those shocked eyes, his breath was stuck in his chest, waiting. . . . She didn't move, though, and he licked his lips.

"Lizzie, I tried so hard not to feel this," he whispered. "I tried! But I love you."

"You love me?" She shook her head. "Don't say things like that, Sol. You only make it harder for us—"

"I think about you constantly," he said. "I worry about you, I pray for you, I think ahead, wondering how I can take care of you—" He swallowed. "Without a second thought, I throw myself between you and men who would hurt you . . . and the thought of walking away from Bountiful tears my heart and lungs right out of me, not because of the community, or my family, or the Amish life I wish I could have, but because it means walking away from *you*. So yah, I love you, Lizzie. I can't help it."

He ran a finger down her cheek, feeling the softness of her skin. With the words out, he knew he meant them.

There was no getting around it now. It was like getting the words out had left a void inside him that was slowly filling with pent-up emotion. Telling her how he felt wasn't going to make anything easier, but he had to say it.

"You're asking me to leave the Amish life," she said.

"First, I want to know if you love me, too," he said.

"And if I did love you back, you're asking—" she started.

He lowered his lips over hers once more and kissed her long and slow. She melted into his arms, and he could feel her pulse trembling through her entire body. He wanted to know if he was alone in this . . . if when she stripped away the logic and reasonable response, she was just as helpless as he was. When he pulled back, she blinked her eyes open and stared up at him.

"Do you love me?" he whispered.

Her eyes welled with tears. "Yah . . ."

He laughed shakily. "That's very good news, Lizzie."

"No, it isn't!" She pulled back and wiped her cheeks with her fingers. "I love you, and what does that do for me? You're leaving, and you're asking me to walk away from everything I believe in!"

"I'm asking you to *marry* me," he said.

"And walk away from my Amish life!" she insisted.

"I have no future here," he said helplessly. "I can't support you here, or any *kinner* we have. I can't be a proper Amish man following the Ordnung and make enough to provide, Lizzie! Don't you see that? Don't you see that if I stay Amish, if I don't get more education, if I don't accept the help that's being offered to me, I won't have any other option but to slide back into a lawless life of crime just to survive!" He pulled off his hat and shoved his fingers through his hair. "This is the problem! Bountiful won't accept me. If I'm going to have an honest, law-abiding life, it's going to be an *Englisher* one!"

"You don't know that—"

"Do you know the percentage of convicts that end up back in prison again after they've done their time and are released?" he asked. She didn't answer, so he continued. "Almost eighty percent. And do you know why? Some of them are addicts. Some of them were part of gangs and can't get away from it. And some of them are poor. It doesn't take much to get tossed back into prison, and theft will do it. What does a man do when he can't get a job, when no one will trust him and he has *kinner* to feed? How far will he go to make sure they're fed, Lizzie?"

She stood there, her chest rising and falling with her quick breaths. "So you go English?"

"Yah . . . I go English," he replied. "I have people willing to give me work experience, a good reference if I earn it, and almost twice the pay I'd get working as farm labor. I'll get schooling, which means I can get better jobs still when I'm done. I'll be able to earn back some trust and find a place where I can contribute and live in a decent part of town, away from the type of people I got into trouble with before. I can step up, Lizzie. I can do better!"

"Better doesn't come with more money," she countered.

"It comes with less desperation!" he said.

"We lean on Gott!"

"And a community!" Solomon shook his head. "Being poor and Amish isn't the same as being poor and English, Lizzie! I know you don't understand that—you haven't seen it. But I've lived it! And I have a chance to take a step up, to live an honest life, to accept the help that's being offered to me. I want to be one of the convicts who stays out of prison and lives a good life once he's out. I have to accept every hand that's offered."

Did she understand this? Could she comprehend the kind of downfall he was trying to avoid? He'd gone with the flow before and ended up in jail. He'd never make that mistake again. He searched her face, looking for some comprehension of what he was trying to explain, but all he saw in her eyes was deep sadness.

"I'm not going English," she whispered.

His heart sank. He'd known this was coming, but he'd let himself start to hope . . .

"It isn't even fair of you to ask me!" she went on, and her voice trembled. "Or to tell me that you love me, or to . . . kiss me like you love me!"

"I'm supposed to pretend I don't?" he said miserably.

"Yah! Exactly that. You should have pretended you didn't, because then I would have been able to be angry with you, and feel used by you, and tell my daughters stories about wicked men who try to take advantage! That would have been easier!"

"I'm no wicked man trying to use you," he growled.

"Would you stay Amish for me?" she asked.

But this was his very freedom at stake. If he messed up, he'd be back in prison . . . He'd already started down a very dangerous path and if he wasn't incredibly careful, he'd lose every helping hand he was currently counting on.

"Lizzie, I don't dare," he breathed.

She turned away from him, and he stood there helplessly watching her. When she turned back, he saw anger flashing in her eyes.

"I pitied Johannes," she said. "I pitied him!"

Solomon stared at her, mute.

"I felt sorry for Sovilla, too, and do you know why?" she went on. "They're getting married to each other in a matter of days and they don't love each other. Johannes loves my sister and Sovilla loves her dead husband. But they're getting married . . ."

"It's their choice," he said.

"Oh, I know that," she said. "But I still pitied them. I thought they should think it through, and remember that they had hearts to consider. I thought that if I was in a similar situation, I would do better than they are—"

"You can," he said, shaking his head. "You can choose the man you love—"

"No, I can't!" Elizabeth pushed a loose tendril of hair away from her cheek. "I can't do better! Do you know why? Because I'm in love with a man who's going English, and no amount of pleading from me is going to change it! So I'm going to do the smart thing, and I'm going to restart my life in another state, and when I do that, I'm going to find a good man and marry him."

Her words were like a slap. "I'm a good man, Lizzie—"

"Good or bad, you'll be *English*!" Her chin trembled. "And when I marry that good man, my heart is going to belong to another, and I'll be no better than Johannes or Sovilla!"

He caught her hand and tugged her close to him again. "Your heart will be *mine*!"

She pulled her hand free. "But my body and my life and my *kinner* . . . they'll be *his*."

"You have a choice!" he said.

"I do *not* have a choice!" she said, her voice rising. She

dashed a tear from her cheek. "I have no choice left! I'm Amish, Sol! And I will have my Amish life!"

"You love me," he said softly.

"I know . . ." Her tears fell freely now. "But I can't be your wife."

Elizabeth sniffled and wiped her face. They loved each other, but it wasn't going to be enough. He couldn't stay Amish and she couldn't follow him into his new, *Englisher* life. . . .

He was going to keep on loving her—that was the problem. He'd known he was in trouble when he'd taken a beating to give her a few extra seconds to get to safety. That kind of love wasn't going to stop, but she was right—they were still the same people headed in different directions. Love wasn't going to be enough to overpower that.

Elizabeth started back toward the house just as Bridget opened the door. His grandmother looked between them, concern etched in the lines on her face.

"Elizabeth?" he heard his grandmother say. "Are you all right? Are you crying?" She raised her eyes toward Solomon. Elizabeth went up the steps, handed the eggs to Bridget, and disappeared inside.

"Sol?" his grandmother called.

Solomon pushed his hat back onto his head. "I'm going for a walk, Mammi."

He headed in the opposite direction, toward the fields. He couldn't face his grandmother right now and he couldn't face Elizabeth. They'd said all they could.

The irony was, he had nowhere to go. No friends who would take him in, no place to bide his time . . . All he could do was walk alone until he was tired, and then go home when it was late enough that his grandmother and Elizabeth would both be in bed.

He couldn't live here and push forward in an *Englisher* life. It would never work. If he was committed to this new chance, he'd have to jump in with both feet.

Earlier that day when he'd sat in that office, typing lists of names and baptismal dates from decades past for historical preservation, an elderly nun had put a wrinkled hand on his shoulder. She wore a knee-length black skirt with a matching vest and a black veil over her white hair.

"Solomon?" she'd said. "That is a very powerful name, young man."

"Yah," he'd said. "My parents thought so."

"King Solomon started out strong, but he lost his footing," she said softly. "He forgot his way and went from the wisest man on earth to a very sad old man indeed. . . ."

He'd stopped his one-fingered typing then and looked up at her.

"You don't need to be like him," the nun said. "You're still young. You have time. You can choose a better path and stick to it."

And the bitterly ironic part was that the better path that Gott seemed to be guiding him toward wasn't the Amish life he'd been raised for—it was this confusing new *Englisher* life, with opportunities that stretched him beyond his abilities, and a way to stay honest.

That very wise King Solomon had also said, "Give me neither poverty nor riches . . . Lest I be full, and deny thee, and say, Who is the Lord? or lest I be poor, and steal, and take the name of my God in vain."

And that was the middle road that Solomon was trying

to achieve—just enough that he'd never be tempted to slide back down into crime.

Let him learn from his biblical namesake and stay on the righteous path, because if he stayed Amish, he'd tumble right back into prison.

Elizabeth hardly slept that night. She heard Solomon come back in late and the creak of his footsteps on the stairs, and then she lay there awake. It had been stupid to fall in love with Solomon Lantz, especially when she'd known from the start the kind of man he was. He was dangerous to a woman like her—he made her imagine what it would be like to be with him out there with the *Englishers* . . . For just a moment, she'd been deeply tempted.

But she'd never be happy away from her culture, her family, her Amish faith. *Englishers* might have faith of their own, but it wasn't the same. Spiritual salvation came from within the Amish church, not out there with the relative heathen . . . and yet it was the "heathen" who were helping Solomon, showing more Christian acceptance and love than he was getting from his own Amish community.

And they were taking him . . .

Even if he stayed, Solomon couldn't give her a solid Amish life of respect and simplicity. She'd be the daughter of a criminal married to an ex-convict . . . That wasn't the life she'd worked for! She deserved better than that. Wasn't that what her *daet* had told her and Lovina when they were but girls? *You are more than my daughters, you are Gott's and you cannot accept less than what you*

*deserve. Too many girls make that mistake, and they live
to regret it. Do you understand?*

Tell that to her aching heart, because she'd seen a different side to Solomon. She'd seen his bravery and his
determination to do the right thing. She'd seen him sacrifice himself for her safety. She'd seen that traumatized
heart and she'd wanted to protect him just as fervently as
he'd wanted to protect her. . . .

But he wouldn't stay Amish. He'd asked her to leave
with him, to marry him, but how could she when it meant
giving up the very core of her being?

And so she lay in bed that night, listening to the sound
of his footsteps in his bedroom, then to the sound of his
bed's springs squeaking when he turned . . . then she
drifted off, her whole body seeming to be emptied out
from crying.

The next morning Solomon ate his breakfast in silence.
Elizabeth sat in front of her bowl of oatmeal and couldn't
bring herself to even take a bite. Bridget eyed both of
them but didn't say anything. Bridget had seen that
something had happened between them—there weren't
any secrets that well-kept in a home.

"Sovilla needs some help in adjusting her wedding
dress to her figure," Bridget said as she sat down at the
table. "I suggested we help her, although really, with my
arthritis, I was hoping you would, Elizabeth."

"Of course," Elizabeth replied.

"I know it's hard because she's marrying Johannes,
but—" Bridget began.

"No, it's fine," Elizabeth said. She might have more

in common with Johannes and Sovilla than she'd like after all.

"I'm going to be working today," Solomon said, and he pushed back his chair.

"With the Catholics?" Bridget asked uncertainly. "Really, Sol—"

"It'll be fine." He bent down and kissed his grandmother's cheek. "I know you don't agree, but this is right. You might see it eventually."

Solomon caught Elizabeth's gaze, but he didn't say anything. She could see the grief in his eyes, too, and it made her want to fall into his arms and sob out their mutual sadness together, except they couldn't. It wouldn't help. This kind of grief could only be gotten over by forcing oneself to take a step forward, and by hoping that time would indeed heal a few wounds.

"Wait—" Bridget said. "You'll need a lunch!"

"No, they said they'd provide one actually," he replied.

"That's kind," Bridget admitted.

"Yah." He nodded, and his gaze moved back to Elizabeth again. He looked tired—his eyes were a little red and his face was pale. Had he slept as poorly as she had? Had he lain awake last night, fighting tears and feeling his chest might split open from the effort? Because she had.

"See you later," Solomon said, and that dark gaze enveloped her with a look of such sad longing that it made tears spring to her eyes.

Elizabeth didn't trust herself to answer, and Solomon headed out the door. She sat in silence for a moment, trying to rein her emotions in once more so that she could pretend she was fine.

"Elizabeth?" Bridget said.

She looked toward Bridget. "Yah?"

"Are you all right?" the older woman asked gently.

"Yah." Elizabeth sucked in a breath. "I will be."

"Did you two make any promises to each other that you can't keep?" Bridget asked.

Was that the way her generation described this? Elizabeth rubbed her hands over her face. "There were no promises, Bridget," she said. "It's okay."

Elizabeth was here to help Bridget and be a support to her, not to fall in love with her grandson.

"But you two love each other, don't you?" Bridget pressed. "No one looks this miserable if they aren't in love with each other."

Elizabeth smiled faintly at the old woman's dry wisdom.

"He's easy to love, Bridget," she admitted. "But not so easy to marry."

Bridget nodded. "Sovilla and Johannes aren't so crazy as you thought, are they?"

"Maybe not . . ." Elizabeth rose to her feet and picked up her bowl, still full of oatmeal.

"Sometimes it's easier on the heart to marry the one who's easier to marry instead of giving up everything for the one who's easier to love," Bridget said.

"Is that your advice?" Elizabeth asked.

"For Johannes, yes," Bridget said thoughtfully. "Only you can choose your future."

After they'd finished cleaning up, Sovilla arrived with her dress in a bag and her two little girls in tow. They were sweet *kinner*, with big blue eyes and rosebud lips. They stared up at the adults solemnly. They'd just lost their *daet* after all, and Elizabeth squatted down to their level.

"Hello," Elizabeth said softly.

"Hello," the older girl whispered.

"I'm Elizabeth. What's your name?"

"I'm Becca. And that's Iris," the girl said, pointing at her toddler sister.

Becca was only five—Elizabeth had heard that already—but she seemed mature for her age.

"Shall we make your *mamm*'s dress pretty for the wedding?" Elizabeth asked.

"I'm going to have another *daet*," Becca replied.

"He's very nice," Elizabeth said. "I know him well. He's a kind man, and he can be really funny, too. I think you'll like him."

"I have a *daet* already," the girl said, and tears welled in her eyes. "I don't want another one!"

Iris looked up at her big sister uncomprehendingly, then toddled toward Bridget, who held out a cookie. Sovilla bent down and scooped Becca up in her arms. She held her for a moment, then kissed her tear-wet cheek and looked into the small, mournful face.

"I miss him, too," Sovilla whispered.

Elizabeth watched the mother and daughter for a moment, then dropped her gaze. What would it be like to be mourning the loss of a husband and to be getting married again this quickly? It wouldn't be easy on the *kinner* . . . and it wouldn't be easy on Sovilla either.

"I have more cookies," Bridget said, and she held up a plate of chocolate chip cookies for Sovilla's older daughter to see.

"Go on," Sovilla said, and she put Becca back on the ground. "You love cookies."

Sovilla watched her daughters silently for a moment

while they munched on cookies with Bridget, then she glanced over at Elizabeth.

"They do like Johannes," Sovilla said. "He's very sweet with them."

"I'm sure they'll grow to love him," Elizabeth replied, and she felt an unexpected lump rise in her throat. This should have been her sister's wedding. She swallowed and forced a smile. "Why don't you put on the dress and I'll see what I can do to make it fit better."

Sovilla left the room, her toddler following her with a cookie in hand. A couple of minutes later Sovilla came back into the room wearing a new blue dress. Iris trailed after her, munching on the cookie contentedly. Elizabeth could see right away what the problem was—the hem was two inches too long and it needed to be taken in at the sides. But it could be done, and it wouldn't take long. She reached for a pincushion and beckoned Sovilla closer.

"I can fix this up for you in no time," Elizabeth said. "Here. I'll pin up the hem and show you where I'm taking it in and you'll see what I mean—"

Elizabeth turned the hem under, leaned back to get a better look, and then readjusted it before she pinned it in place and continued around the dress.

"This is very kind of you to help me," Sovilla said. "I appreciate it."

"It's nothing," Elizabeth replied. "I'm happy to help. Everyone enjoys a wedding."

It wasn't entirely true, but Elizabeth was determined to make it true with the force of her will.

"I remember helping a woman who was new to Edson get ready for her wedding before Rueben and I fell in love," Sovilla said. "I was helping her make the gifts she'd

give to the guests—tying ribbons, I believe. I spent hours
with her in her happiness. I hated her."

"I don't believe that!" Elizabeth said, looking up.

"I didn't truly hate her, but I was jealous," Sovilla said.
"I'm not accusing you of such base emotion. I'm just saying
that I really do appreciate your kindness right now."

"I like you," Elizabeth said quietly. "I honestly do. And
I didn't want to, because of the situation with my sister,
but you're very nice, and I'm glad you're here. If someone had to marry Johannes, I'm glad it's you."

Sovilla smiled. "You mean that, don't you?"

"I do." Elizabeth nudged Sovilla to make her turn so
that she could pin the back of the dress. A faint ringing
sound came from the kitchen, and Elizabeth straightened.
What was that?

It rang again, and Elizabeth put the last pin in place,
then stood up.

"Bridget, what is that?" Elizabeth asked.

Bridget opened some drawers, then pulled out the cell
phone the bishop had given them for safety. Elizabeth
looked down at it, then flipped it open. She put it up to
her ear.

"Yah. Hello?" she said awkwardly.

"Lizzie? That you?"

"Daet?" She pulled the phone away from her face and
looked down at it. The battery sign showed almost empty.
"Daet, is that you?"

"Yah, it's me."

"Where are you?" she asked. "And how did you get
this number? What's going on?"

"I stopped to see the bishop on the way out of town,"

her father replied. "He gave me this number so I could reach you if it was an emergency, and . . . it is."

"What's wrong?" she asked. "Where are you, Daet?"

"At the Erindale Hospital," he replied. "I'm fine—but I found your sister."

"You . . . you found her?" Elizabeth nearly dropped the phone, and she pressed her other hand against her ear to hear better. "What's going on? Is she okay?"

"She was in an accident. She's been in the hospital for a week," her father replied. "I found a mission where she was staying for a few weeks last year, and they said she left. I didn't know what to do, so I asked the police if they could help me, and they had her in their system—well, a woman of her description, at least. She was at a hospital, and the hospital was looking for her family. I don't even know why I thought to ask at that police station—Gott must have nudged me. But I found her, and she's ready to be discharged, and . . ." There was a fuzzing sound.

"Hello?" Elizabeth said, spinning in a circle. She walked closer to the door. "Hello?"

"Lizzie?" Her father's voice came back. "It's bad reception. Just come! Erindale Hospital. Give them Lovina's name and they'll tell you what room. Bring her some clothes to wear—she can't wear what she's got. Get Isaiah and come!"

Her father's voice went fuzzy again, and after trying repeatedly to get the reception back, she hung up, her mind spinning. Lovina was there—did she want to come home? Or was this just a chance to see her before she left for her *Englisher* life? Elizabeth wished she knew, but regardless, she'd take the chance to see her sister at least one more time. . . .

Bridget and Sovilla were both staring at her.

"That was Daet," Elizabeth said feebly. "He found Lovina . . ."

Bridget's eyes widened. "Where?"

"She's at Erindale Hospital. I don't know what happened. But they're ready to send her home, and Daet wants me and Isaiah to come."

Sovilla stood where Elizabeth had left her, her dress pinned up, and her arms limp at her sides. She licked her lips, then nodded.

"I think the wedding might be off, then," Sovilla said softly.

"Oh, Sovilla—" Elizabeth only then realized what this would mean to her. "I don't know what's happening. I don't know if she's coming home, or if this is just my chance to see my sister. I have no idea—"

Sovilla nodded. "Will you bring Johannes with you?"

Would she? Elizabeth felt the weight of the moment sink down around her. This was the chance she'd been waiting for—to make it all right, to turn back the clock. But looking into Sovilla's pale face, she realized that nothing would go back to the way it was. There was no way it could.

"No," Elizabeth said at last. "I think this is a family affair." She looked helplessly toward Bridget. "Do you think your neighbor would drive me to my brother's work?"

"I think he would," Bridget said. "You go on . . . I'll see what I can do with the dress. I'm sure Sovilla and I can manage something between the two of us."

Elizabeth stepped into her shoes and pushed out the door, but when she looked over her shoulder, she saw tears in Sovilla's eyes. Lovina had left and everything changed. Now Lovina was found . . .

Elizabeth angled her steps in the direction of the *Englisher* neighbor next door.

She'd worry about the fallout after she saw her sister.

Chapter Nineteen

The Livingstons were very understanding about the emergency. The older man offered to bring her to her brother's home and then drive them both to the Erindale Hospital twenty miles away.

"It's no problem," he said earnestly. "Really. Bridget does more for us than we ever do for her. I don't think we've had to buy a single piece of produce over the summer in five years—she just brings it over in baskets. I'm glad to drive you there. It lets us feel like we're giving back a bit."

Isaiah sat in the front seat, Elizabeth in the back. She'd packed up some clothes for her sister to wear: a dress, socks, shoes, some underthings, and a fresh *kapp* all together in a plastic bag. What had happened to her *Englisher* clothes? Had they been ruined in the accident? Or did her *daet* just want her back in some proper Amish clothing to make her look like his daughter again? Elizabeth sat in the back seat, that plastic bag on her lap, her heart in her throat.

They'd get a taxi back to where Isaiah had his buggy parked that evening, and Isaiah's father-in-law would give the horses some extra feed and water before he left. They had plans in place.

Daet had found Lovina . . . It was a miracle, really. Elizabeth and Isaiah had looked for their sister—asked the police for help, written letters to some places they'd heard runaway Amish went—but they'd heard nothing back. And what were they supposed to do—pick a city and wander the streets? And yet she'd been relatively close by all this time—Erindale was hardly even a city by *Englisher* standards.

Elizabeth fought back some tears. She'd missed her little sister over the last year. She'd prayed for her safety, worried over what might be happening to her, and waited for a break like this one. But now that they were on their way, she had to wonder . . . Lovina hadn't written or sent any kind of message to let them know that she was all right. Would she even want to see them? Had she cut off Elizabeth and Isaiah at the same time as their father?

Lovina *could* have written. She'd chosen not to . . .

The scenery swept past and her stomach quivered with nausea. How *Englishers* traveled like this on a regular basis, she had no idea. The speed itself always upset her stomach, and the musty smell of a car's interior didn't help.

When they arrived at the sprawling hospital, Isaiah thanked Bridget's neighbor sincerely, and when he offered to drive them back again, Isaiah turned him down.

"Thank you," he said, "but we don't know how long we'll be. We'll get a taxi back. I have some money to pay for it. But thank you for this kindness. Gott bless you."

When the car pulled away, Elizabeth stood there with

the plastic bag of clothes in one hand and anxiety mounting in her chest.

"Come on," Isaiah said. "Daet said to ask for her by name, right?"

"That's what he said."

"Then we do that."

The building was painted white, and various signs pointed people in different directions, for a Windo Wing, or the Geraldine Cardio Ward. So many signs with medical terminology that just melted together into an anxiety-inducing puddle. An ambulance arrived—no sirens or particular hurry—and stopped and unloaded an older gentleman from the back. He climbed down with some help and they got a wheelchair and sat him in it. Elizabeth stepped out of their way and scanned the signs until her brother nudged her shoulder and marched off toward wide glass doors.

She followed him and, once inside, there was a small desk area. There was a gift shop to one side with flowers, balloons, some little teddy bears, and a magazine stand. A coffee shop that seemed to attract most of the people there, many of whom were wearing hospital scrubs and looked tired, accepting their lidded, cardboard cups with a grateful smile.

"Excuse me," Isaiah said at the desk. "I'm looking for my sister, Lovina Yoder. My *daet* said that she's here?"

"Let me check," the woman said with a brisk smile. She nodded. "Yep. She's upstairs on the third floor, room number 3511. If you take that elevator up and follow the signs to the Windo Wing, you'll find her room."

"Thank you."

Isaiah seemed more confident than Elizabeth felt, and

they headed to the elevator. They were crammed in with several other people, two of whom were patients in wheelchairs, and they got off on the third floor as directed. Elizabeth had lost track of where they were—everything looked the same—white- and tan-colored, metal doors all looking the same unless you looked at the numbers on them. Some people were in wheelchairs, and they scooted themselves down the hallway in hospital robes and sock feet. There were a few different reception desks that Isaiah strode past, but he stopped when they spotted Daet.

He stood by a window, his hands clasped behind his back, his straw hat on his head, and standing out from the rest of the hospital as starkly as possible.

"Daet?" Isaiah called.

Their father turned and smiled and headed toward them.

"Where is she?" Elizabeth asked.

Daet gave them each a hug and then put up a hand to stop them when Isaiah moved toward the nurse's desk.

"Wait, Isaiah—" Abe caught his arm. "It's not so simple. She's been in a bad accident and she was hurt."

"How bad?" Elizabeth breathed.

"Bad enough. She hit her head," Abe said. "And she got bruised up and some scrapes. So physically, she's not too bad. But the hit on the head, it—" He swallowed. "They called it post-traumatic amnesia. She doesn't remember us."

Elizabeth stared at her father, stunned. "What?"

"It's a temporary condition, the doctor says," Abe said. "But physically she's fine, so they need to send her home. And someone needs to pay her bill. Every day she's here it only costs more. They say her memory should come back soon enough."

"She didn't know you?" Isaiah asked, and he looked past their father toward the room numbered 3511.

Abe shook his head. "She doesn't remember anything—her name, her life, her friends . . . her family."

Nothing . . . Elizabeth felt her heart hammer hard in the center of her chest. Her sister remembered nothing . . . Nothing good, and nothing bad either. Their father's incarceration would be gone, too, then. Her mind was spinning.

"What do we tell her?" Isaiah asked. "Do we explain who we are and—"

"I've been thinking about that," Abe said, cutting him off. "I think we should tell her that we're her family. That's all. Nothing more. Did you bring her clothes?"

"Yah." Elizabeth lifted the bag. "Right here."

"Good." Abe sucked in a breath.

"We don't tell her that she's had an English life?" Elizabeth asked. "What if there's someone worried about her?"

"It's been a week," Abe replied. "If they haven't tracked her down yet, how much do they care?" He sighed. "Look, she left because of me, right? Well, what if she gets a chance to come home without any of those painful memories? What if she could just come back and we could help her remember her Amish life?"

Elizabeth exchanged a look with her brother. It wasn't a bad idea.

"Do we know anything about her *Englisher* life?" Elizabeth asked. "Are there any clues with her belongings?"

"No. That's why they couldn't find anyone to come get

her," Abe replied. "She had some cash on her, and that's about it."

"Can we see her?" Isaiah asked.

"Yah, but let's be careful what we tell her," Abe replied. "Do you agree?"

Elizabeth and Isaiah exchanged a look.

"Do we?" Abe asked.

Elizabeth was silent for a moment, her mind sorting through these strange facts. Her sister had a chance to start over without the burden of their father's guilt. Was it a lie simply not to tell her?

"What about Johannes?" Elizabeth asked. "Not everything is the same back in Bountiful. He's marrying Sovilla—"

"Then we don't tell her about him," Isaiah said.

"And if he sparks a memory?" Elizabeth asked.

"Her memory will come back eventually," Abe interjected. "We do want her to heal, don't we? This is just temporary."

They were silent again.

"Do we agree, then?" Abe asked again.

"Yah," Elizabeth said. "We agree. Where is she now?"

"She's in the room. She was resting," Abe replied.

"Let me go in first," Elizabeth said. "If she doesn't know us, I think a woman would be less alarming for her."

Isaiah nodded, and Elizabeth brushed past her brother and headed for the room. She knocked softly on the door and then pushed it open. There were two beds in the room, but only one was occupied. Lovina seemed to have woken up, because she was sitting up in the bed, her blond hair hanging loose around her shoulders. Lovina always had been petite, and she looked smaller still in that blue hospital gown. She looked up when Elizabeth came inside.

"Lovina . . ." Elizabeth said, and she couldn't help the tears that sprang to her eyes.

"Who are you?" Lovina asked in English.

"You don't remember me?" Elizabeth said in Dutch. She wanted to see if Lovina would notice the switch in language, and she went to the bed and was about to sink onto the side of it when she was stopped by the look on Lovina's face. So she stood instead. "Think . . . really think . . . Am I familiar at all?"

Lovina frowned, then shook her head. "I don't remember anything. Everyone keeps telling me to think really hard, but I don't remember any of it, okay? So just tell me—who are you?"

Lovina had answered in Dutch, and Elizabeth felt a rush of relief.

"I'm your sister," Elizabeth said and she swallowed. "You always called me Lizzie."

"Oh." Lovina looked over Elizabeth's shoulder, and Elizabeth turned to see her brother and father come into the room, too.

"That's Isaiah, our brother," Elizabeth said. "And Daet, of course."

"So he says," Lovina said woodenly.

"We're your family," Elizabeth said softly. "We've been worried sick about you! We've come to bring you home."

"Where's home?" Lovina asked.

"Bountiful," Elizabeth said. "Well, just outside of Bountiful. We—" She looked over at her brother, thinking fast. "You live with Isaiah right now. I'm staying with an older woman who needs some extra help, but I'll be moving back with Isaiah soon, too. Daet is there, but just temporarily."

"It's a tight squeeze," Isaiah said.

Well, where else were they supposed to bring Lovina— to Uncle Mel and Aunt Rose? Their uncle had already made it clear that he didn't like having them all staying there.

"It is a tight squeeze," Elizabeth said, forcing a smile. "But it's home . . ."

Lovina shrugged weakly. "At least I have a family. There was a nurse who suspected I might be Amish."

"Oh?" Elizabeth said hopefully.

"Something about the way I talk," Lovina said.

"Of course." Elizabeth reached for her sister's hand, and this time Lovina let her take it. "Well, you do have a family, and a home, and a community. I brought you a dress—it isn't yours, it's mine. So it isn't going to fit as well as it could, but—I'm sure it will feel good to get back into some proper clothes again."

Lovina nodded. "Maybe I'll remember."

Elizabeth looked back to see her father's expression strain. "There's time for that, Lovina," he said gently. "Let's just get you home. I should go call for a cab."

"Yah, that would be good," Isaiah said. "I'll step out-side so Lovina can get dressed."

"Good idea," Elizabeth said, and once the men left the room, Elizabeth passed the bag to her sister. "Do you know what happened?"

"There was a car accident," Lovina said. "I was riding a bike, apparently, and the driver was drunk. I got thrown over the car and landed on the road really hard. My head was hit the hardest, they said, and I was unconscious for a couple of days."

"How do you feel now?" Elizabeth asked.

"I feel—" Lovina shrugged. "Confused. I know my name is Lovina Yoder, but only because that man showed up and told them so. I don't remember *being* Lovina Yoder."

"Who do you remember being?" Elizabeth whispered.

"I don't know." Lovina shook her head. "I have no idea. I don't remember anything before waking up in the hospital."

"And nobody came to find you?" Elizabeth asked. Lovina had no one in her life who'd missed her, cared to search for her?

"Well, you did," Lovina replied.

Elizabeth nodded. Right—they weren't going to complicate this.

"We didn't even know where to look!" Elizabeth said. "Next time, Lovina, please"—her voice caught, but she pushed on—"*please* stick closer to home."

"Okay," Lovina said. "Sorry."

And it was like the last year had evaporated and her younger sister was back. Except Lovina didn't remember any of them, or the Amish life they were about to bring her back to.

"Get dressed," Elizabeth said, turning toward the door. "It's going to feel so good to get you home again. You have no idea."

When she stepped out into the hallway, rejoining her brother, she sucked in a deep breath.

"I can't believe we found her," Isaiah said softly.

"I know." Elizabeth looked up at him. "But there isn't

going to be a lot of space in your place, Isaiah. There is one extra bedroom, but with Daet back, and now Lovina—"

"Don't worry about that," Isaiah said curtly. "We'll figure something out. Maybe Daet can stay with Uncle Mel."

"Mel would hate that," she said.

"So would Daet," he replied. "But they're brothers, and I don't really care how much they dislike each other right now. We have to let Lovina remember her Amish life. She's the one who needs us most."

Abe came back around the corner. "There's a cab arriving in twenty minutes. Is Lovina dressed yet? We need to talk to whoever can discharge her and get home."

Lovina came out of the room just then. She was in the Amish dress—she'd remembered how to put it on, it seemed—but she held the *kapp* in one hand.

"I think I need help with putting up my hair. I don't have a tie. Or pins."

"Here," Elizabeth said. "Let me help . . ."

As her fingers worked through the familiar job of twisting her sister's hair into a bun, she wondered how alike she and Lovina were after all. Elizabeth was planning to do what Lovina had done . . . but the proper way. She wasn't cutting off her family, but she *would* venture out on her own . . . But it wouldn't change anything, would it? It wouldn't change who her father was, or where her heart belonged. It wouldn't change who would come to find her if she lost everything, and who would bring her home again. There was no erasing her family, just getting some space from them.

The only thing her leaving might change was her ability

to start over . . . beginning with letting her heart heal from Solomon Lantz.

Solomon washed his hands in the mudroom sink, watching the dirty water curl down the drain. He scrubbed his hands again until the suds stayed white, then rinsed them and dried them on a folded towel his grandmother had waiting.

She was fastidious that way—there was always a fresh towel waiting every evening, never a dirty one.

"In the hamper, dear," Bridget called without even turning.

He tossed the towel into the hamper by the basement stairs and then came into the kitchen and froze. Bridget wasn't alone at the stove; his *mamm* stood at the counter, a tin of muffins in front of her that she seemed to be in the middle of removing from the pan, but she was equally frozen, her gaze locked on him.

"Son . . ." Anke said.

She was plump and she pressed her hands against her stomach in the same pose he remembered from all those years of lectures. She'd stand there with her hands against her stomach as if she were holding herself physically together.

Her hair was grayer than when he'd seen her last, or maybe that was his imagination. Her face was a little more lined.

"Mamm—" He felt heat rush to his face, and he took a step toward her, then stopped.

"Oh, come here, you," she said, and she half ran across the kitchen and pulled him down into a strong hug. She clung to him for a moment, and when she released him and stood back, he saw tears in her eyes. "Your *mammi* told me you'd come home and I knew Gott would answer my prayers."

Solomon looked toward his grandmother, who immediately dropped her gaze.

"Mamm, you should know something," he said quietly.

"I made muffins," she said brightly. "Blueberry—your favorite."

She went back to the counter and plucked one from the pan.

"Mamm—" he said.

"And we'll finally have a family dinner," she went on. "Your sister is doing well. I told her that you were back and she can't come yet, but she wants to see you, too. The babies—your new nephews—are just adorable. And Waneta is such a doting mother to those triplets—"

"Mamm!" He raised his voice.

"I don't want to hear that you aren't staying!" His mother dropped her hands to her sides and the tears that had been trembling on her lids finally fell, sliding slowly down her cheeks. "I *can't* hear that, Solomon! You belong here with us. I don't care what the *Englishers* are offering you. I don't care!"

She came back with the muffin and handed it to him. He stared down at it, his throat tight.

"Eat a muffin," she said, lowering her voice. "And sit down."

Solomon sank into a kitchen chair, then took a bite. It was as good as he remembered, but his mouth was dry, and he swallowed with effort. She sat down in the chair next to him, watching him eat.

"You turned your back on me," he said, and his voice shook. "I sat there, waiting for a visit from my mother while I was at the very lowest point of my entire life. . . . I *needed* you!"

His mother was silent, and she wiped at the tears on her cheeks.

"You turned your back and you walked out," he went on. "You said I was no son of yours—"

"I'm sorry—"

"And you didn't come back!" His hands had started to shake. "You gave up on me, Mamm, and now you want to tell me what to do? I'm suddenly your son again? You think you can tell me where I belong *now*?"

"I had to be tough on you," she said. "I obviously wasn't tough enough over the years! What would you have me do? You came home, didn't you? Would you have come if I'd been easy on you? Would you?"

"I'm not home," he said hollowly. "I'm here for a few weeks while I sort out something else. That's it."

"Something else . . ." Her voice was weak. "Like what?"

"I have a job in a church office," he said. "And they'll get me jobs in other places, too, so I can get some experience. And I'm finishing up high school. I might even go on after that to some more training. I'm going to make a life for myself, Mamm."

"Why not here?" she asked.

"Why not here?" He almost laughed. "Because I'm an ex-con! I'm a criminal, Mamm! My own mother turned her back on me. No one trusts me. No one will give me a job!"

"Then *make* your own job," she said. "Start a business."

He shook his head. "No one trusts me—"

"The *Englishers* don't know you!" she shot back. "We have all this land, and your grandmother and I can only do so much alone! Why not dig more gardens this fall and plant more in the spring to sell at the farmers market? Why not buy some calves and rear them for the meat market? You could breed them and sell them—you don't need a whole ranch to make a living!"

"This isn't my land, I didn't think—"

"You didn't ask!" his mother shot back.

"I need a life, Mamm, not odd jobs."

"You need to stick with something long enough to grow it," she retorted. "Do you think you'll start at the top with the *Englishers*? You're willing to start small and prove yourself with them. Why not here?"

"Because they were willing to give me a second chance," he said. "They were willing to show me a bit of compassion. Funny how alluring that is when you've lost everything."

"And because we tell you the truth, you walk away?" she said, shaking her head. "They're willing to give you a chance, Son, but only one, I'll warrant you. You mess that up and their charity will be at an end."

He was silent. She was right.

"If you want respect, *earn it*," she said. "If you want a community, learn to give them something they value! And if you want your mother's love"—she reached out and put a hand over his—"you already have it, Solomon."

Tears welled in his eyes and he clamped his hand over hers. How many months had he waited to hear that?

"I missed you, Mamm," he whispered.

She had made a good point, but it wasn't growing

vegetables or buying calves that had stuck in his heart. Elizabeth was leaving Bountiful for some other community, and she was starting over . . . Did he have anything he could offer her that would entice her to stay . . . to choose him?

In order to offer Elizabeth a life with him, he had to be able to offer something to the community, too. Being Amish was about everyone, not just one man, or one couple.

What did he have that could be of use to Bountiful *now*? All he had was a life filled with regrets for all the mistakes he'd made. It had started small and then it had snowballed. If he knew back in his youth, before that fateful Rumspringa, what he knew now . . .

There was a knock at the door, and they both turned toward it. They hadn't heard a buggy approach, but when Bridget bustled over and opened the door, Johannes came inside.

"Aunt Anke!" Johannes said. "Oh, I didn't know you were back. I—" Johannes pulled off his hat and bent the rim between his finger and thumb.

"Come in, come in," Bridget said. "You look—Johannes, are you all right?"

"She's back," Johannes said, sinking into a kitchen chair. "Lovina's back. They found her at Erindale Hospital and brought her home."

"I know . . ." Bridget said, putting a hand on Johannes's shoulder. "I already told Anke about it."

"What do I do?" Johannes turned toward the woman, his gaze moving between them. "I'm supposed to get married on Tuesday!"

"Lovina's back?" Solomon demanded. "What's going on?"

"Abe went to find her," Johannes said. "He ended up talking to the police in an attempt to locate his daughter, and the hospital had put a call into the police station a few days earlier, needing help in locating Lovina's family. She was in an accident and her head was hit rather hard. She's okay, now, and they released her to come home, but she doesn't remember anything. It was the hit on the head, and they think her memory will come back, but—"

"Have you seen her?" Solomon asked.

"Yah. I just left Isaiah's place. . . ." Johannes rubbed his hands over his face. "She looks the same, Sol. Just the same! Except she doesn't know me. She looks at me like I'm a perfect stranger. It's the same for everyone. She doesn't know Elizabeth or Isaiah either. She's very polite and really confused, but I might as well be a man on the street."

"And your wedding is in a matter of days," Bridget said quietly.

"Yah . . ."

"Bridget filled me in about Sovilla," Anke said, her voice low. "And she is a good young woman. She'd be a good wife to you, Johannes."

"I know."

"What does your father think?" Anke asked.

"My *daet* says he doesn't envy my position." Johannes shrugged. "He isn't pushing me either way. It's my choice."

Johannes turned to Solomon. "If you were me, Sol, what would you do? I have a good woman counting on me to marry her and provide for her and her daughters. I was willing to do it. I was happy to do it! But that was when Lovina was gone and I had no hope of even seeing her again. . . ."

"I don't know," Solomon admitted. "Who do you love?"

"Lovina," Johannes said without missing a beat. "But not only does she not know me, she seems to have lost any interest she ever had in me. It's like without our history, I'm nothing—I spark absolutely nothing inside her!"

"She's been gone for a year," Bridget added quietly. "A lot can change in a year's time."

Anke nodded at that but didn't say anything.

"Maybe her memory will come back," Solomon said. "And she'll remember you, and—"

"Would she stay?" Anke asked. "If she remembers you, she'll remember why she left, too. Would that change?"

Johannes shook his head. "Sovilla is counting on me. Her family, Bountiful, Edson . . . everyone is counting on me."

It was an impossible situation, Solomon could see that much, but there was something to be said for a man everyone was counting on. It might be painful and impossible and require all his physical and emotional strength, but he had a community.

Solomon pushed himself to his feet.

"I have something I have to do," Solomon said. "My *mamm* and grandmother will have more to offer advice-wise anyway."

"Where are you going?" Anke asked with a frown.

"I'll be back," he replied.

A man could offer nothing to a woman unless he could offer something to the community, and Solomon had finally realized what he had to give that no one else could—experience.

He'd made every bad choice and ended up in prison as a result. The only one who could match his experience was Abe Yoder. But Solomon wasn't going to ask the community to forgive him. He was going to ask the bishop to let him share his story with the young people. Instead of trying to hide his scars, he could show them.

He might not be much of a role model right now, but he certainly was a morality tale. He could show the young people what happened when rebelliousness went too far, and he could tell them exactly what was beyond the fence.

Maybe Solomon could find a way to belong again, in a different way than he ever had before. And maybe then he could sell produce, raise calves, and help provide for his *mamm* and grandmother, too. At least they'd be safer with him here. . . . He'd never be a man of high position in the Amish sense—a man deeply respected or looked to for his wisdom. No, he'd never be that, but there might be a place for him all the same, somewhere near the bottom, off in a corner. It could be enough.

If Bountiful could find its way to forgive him. If he could follow his mother's advice and give them something they could value.

And if he could offer Bountiful his bare, remorseful self, maybe Lizzie could see her way to accepting him, too. This tattered, beaten, sorrowful heart was all he had left.

Chapter Twenty

Elizabeth finished the alterations on Sovilla's dress from her brother's home. She'd gone back to Bridget's house when they came back from the hospital and discovered that Anke had returned. All was back to normal . . . Solomon could make his peace with his mother as he'd hoped to all along and Elizabeth needn't stay any longer. It was good timing because Elizabeth wanted to be with her sister. Lovina still didn't remember people or places, but she seemed to recall some basics about Amish living—how to start a fire in the belly of the stove, how to pin her dress, how to wear a *kapp*, how to cook. . . .

The survival skills were there, just not the memories.

Elizabeth snipped a thread and glanced up at her sister, who sat across the table from her, watching her work.

"This is for a wedding?" Lovina asked.

"Yah. The bride's name is Sovilla. She's a widow—she just lost her husband a couple of months ago. It was a terrible accident." Elizabeth shook out the dress and held it up. It looked good, but it still brought a lump to Elizabeth's throat when she looked at it. This should be

Lovina's wedding dress. Elizabeth should be helping her sister get ready to marry Johannes, and Lovina should be excited and flustered and anxious all at the same time. . . . Instead Lovina sat there in mild confusion, watching Elizabeth work.

"Is she happy?" Lovina asked after a moment of silence.

"Yah, I think so," Elizabeth replied. "She doesn't know the man well, but he's kind and a hard worker."

Should she tell her who the groom was? Would that spark anything? Or was that cruel? Johannes had made his choice, and the wedding was going forward. It wasn't like there was anything they could do anyway.

Johannes had been here to see Lovina, and he'd sat with her, asked her questions, tried to hold her hand . . . Lovina had pulled back and then left the room. Maybe it was Lovina's detached disinterest in him, or just the passage of time, but Elizabeth couldn't blame him. He'd made a promise to Sovilla, her family, and the bishop, and Johannes was the kind of man who would keep it.

"Do you remember Johannes at all?" Elizabeth asked hesitantly.

Lovina sighed. "Everyone is asking me that. No! I don't remember him. I don't remember *you*. I don't remember this house—" She looked around herself.

"This house is different," Elizabeth replied. "So you wouldn't remember it. But Johannes was close to you. Very close."

"Oh . . ." Lovina sighed.

"You loved him, Lovina." Elizabeth leaned closer. "You really loved him. And I think he loves you—"

"I don't remember him!" Lovina rubbed a hand over her face. "This is just a story to me. I believe you that this is my life, but I don't remember any of it. If I loved him, why wouldn't any of that remain? If we meant so much to each other, why didn't I feel anything when I looked at him?"

And she had a point there. She had been a year away from Johannes . . . a year of her own choosing. Maybe there was less left between the two than Elizabeth liked to think.

"I don't know . . ." she said softly.

"What do you want me to do?" Lovina demanded. "Do you want me to throw myself into his arms to make all of you feel better? I don't remember him!"

Bethany came down the stairs, Mo in her arms. He'd just woken up from a nap and had needed to be changed and fed.

"Lovina, do you want to hold your nephew?" Bethany asked. "I'm going to do some baking and Mo insists on being held these days or he just howls."

Lovina smiled and held out her arms for the baby. "Yah," she said. "I'd love to hold him. Come here, you."

Mo consented to be shifted into Lovina's arms, and Elizabeth stood up.

"I have to deliver this dress," she said. "If Lovina is helping out here, I can just run down to the Miller farm and be back in a few minutes."

"Yah, good idea," Bethany agreed, and they exchanged a somber look. It wouldn't be fair to bring Lovina to Johannes's home, where his bride-to-be was staying with his family. Elizabeth had already said too much.

They'd asked Johannes before he left the day before if he was going through with the wedding, and he'd said he was. When Lovina's memories came back and Johannes was married to Sovilla, would Lovina resent Elizabeth for not having done more?

Though when Lovina's memories returned, she'd also know that she'd been gone for a year, and she'd understand why lives had moved on. . . . But hopefully by that point she'd have rediscovered what made her Amish life special, and she'd be rooted back in the home where she belonged.

That was the prayer at least.

The Miller farm was a twenty-minute walk from Isaiah's house, but Elizabeth opted to walk instead of hitching up the buggy. It was a chance to be alone for a few minutes, and to talk to Gott.

Her mind was in a knot. Lovina was home, and they'd all agreed to let her slowly adjust, let her memories return, but not everything would be the same as before, would it? Their *daet* was back, and the community had no respect or warm feelings for him. Johannes was marrying another woman, and Isaiah had gotten married in her absence as well. The only one who hadn't changed was Elizabeth, and she was doing her best to maintain some calm around here for Lovina's sake. . . .

Gott, will she hate me for not stopping this wedding? Elizabeth prayed silently. *She doesn't remember how much she loved him . . . but I do! I remember what they were like together. I remember how happy she was planning her wedding.*

Until she disappeared and shocked them all, that

was. Obviously there had been more going on under the surface that Lovina had never shared.

What do I do, Gott?

There seemed to be silence from Heaven, and as Elizabeth walked on, her heart was heavy. Lovina had left Johannes, and it was her choice. Elizabeth shouldn't be grieving her sister's relationship, especially when her sister wasn't grieving it herself! And Lovina had a point—if Johannes had truly been the man Gott wanted for her, why did she feel nothing when meeting him again? Even without her memory, there should be some attraction at least, shouldn't there?

But it wasn't Lovina's lost love that weighed so heavily on Elizabeth this morning—it was her own. She'd fallen in love with a man who was all wrong for her, and she was attempting to let those feelings go. . . .

Solomon isn't mine, she prayed. *I know that! He's not meant for me. I'm not for him either. So why can't I stop loving him? Why can't I put whatever that was behind me and move forward? I'm trying!*

So far she'd avoided seeing Solomon. When she went to check on Bridget, he hadn't been there, and she'd thought that was a gift from above—a respite from being faced with these overwhelming feelings. But now all she wanted was to see him again, to slide back into his arms and listen to the slow, solid beating of his heart.

"Is that a sin?" she whispered aloud.

Was it terrible that her emotions didn't care one bit whether or not there was a future for them? She missed him *now* . . .

When Elizabeth arrived at the Millers' driveway, she

headed down toward the farmhouse. The barn loomed close by, and another barn, farther away, glowed red in the late morning sunlight. The men were nowhere to be seen, and that was just as well. Elizabeth didn't think she could handle another polite back-and-forth with Johannes right now. She headed up to the side of the house just as little girls' laugher pealed from indoors.

"That's silly," Sovilla's voice said. "Take that off your head, Becca."

Elizabeth knocked, and it was Sovilla who pulled open the door.

"I came with your dress," Elizabeth said, and she held out the bag.

"That's very kind. Come in," Sovilla said.

Elizabeth stepped inside. The kitchen was spotless, some fresh bread on the counter. There was a hamper of dry, folded laundry sitting on the tabletop, and Elizabeth had to appreciate what Sovilla had done to this kitchen at least in the short time she was here. The Miller house hadn't been this welcoming since before Johannes's mother passed away.

Becca stood with a funnel balanced on the top of her head, and Iris, not to be outdone by her sister, had a pot on hers that covered her face and made her little laugh echo from the depths of it.

"Girls, you go on upstairs and play in our bedroom," Sovilla said, scooping both pot and funnel from her daughters. "Go on, now."

The girls did as they were told, Becca leading her little sister. When their footsteps could be heard overhead, Sovilla turned to Elizabeth.

"I'm not marrying him," Sovilla said softly.

"What?" Elizabeth put the bag on the table next to the hamper and her heart stuttered. "Did he call it off?"

"No, I did." Sovilla gestured for Elizabeth to sit.

"I'm fine," Elizabeth said. "You called it off? Why?"

"Because she's back." Sovilla caught Elizabeth's gaze and held it. "Your sister is back, and even if she never remembers him, and even if she doesn't want to be with Johannes, he loves *her*. Deeply. He's not over her. And while I was willing to be the wife of a man who was grieving his own losses, I'm not willing to be the wife of a man in love with a woman in the community."

"Did you tell him?" Elizabeth breathed.

"Yah. He'll tell the bishop and everyone else . . . I'll pack and go home. Or something. . . . Maybe I can find a job here in the community and somewhere to stay in the meantime. I have to figure it out still."

"Was he upset when you told him?" Elizabeth asked.

Sovilla shook her head. "Johannes was relieved. So am I. I'll find another way to keep myself, but I realized something I should have remembered earlier."

"Which is?" Elizabeth asked.

"Loving a man deeply—adoring him, sinking into his arms and feeling like the world disappears around you— that's worth waiting for. It's worth grieving a little while longer, too."

"Rueben was like that?" Elizabeth asked softly.

"Yah . . ." A wistful smile came to Sovilla's lips. "He was a good man, but it was more than that. He only had eyes for me. He'd hurry home because he missed me, and he'd wink at me during Sunday service." She brushed a tear from her cheek. "I felt like I was whole when I was in his arms. I don't know how to explain it. I may never feel that way again, but I did feel it with him. . . ."

Elizabeth did know that feeling, and she'd been running from it. Even now, she longed to feel Solomon's fingers closing around hers, to lean her cheek against his strong shoulder, to smell the musky scent of him . . .

"If Lovina hadn't come back, would it have been enough?" Elizabeth asked earnestly.

Sovilla looked a little surprised at the intensity coming from Elizabeth, but she couldn't seem to stop it. She needed to know this.

"If my sister stayed away, and you married Johannes, and she never came back," Elizabeth pressed. "Would you have been able to live happily with him?"

Sovilla was silent for a moment. "I saw his face when he heard the news that your sister had returned. . . . I might have married him, but I do think I would have lived to regret it. When you've loved someone as passionately as Johannes loves your sister, it doesn't just go away. Another woman can't just claim his heart. Like it or not, Lovina has his. And she very likely always will."

Sovilla was being offered a man with a good reputation, with a solid character and a tender heart. And she was turning him down because she knew what happened when someone loved that deeply. And now Elizabeth would never be blind to what a love like that felt like ever again either.

"Johannes is a good man, though," Elizabeth said. "Is that enough? If my sister had never come back, would a good man without the distraction of the woman he'd once loved—he would make a good husband, wouldn't he?"

Sovilla sighed. "I wanted to believe so. It would have been good for me if that were so—I'd have a man to provide. But I'm not so sure. They say marriage is long, and that can be both a blessing and a curse. A good reputation is a start, but long, cold nights aren't filled with a good reputation, if you understand me."

Elizabeth blushed at that. Could she really go marry a man who was very kind, very good and respectable, knowing that neither of them loved each other half enough? Could she do it for a chance at marriage and *kinner*? Long, cold nights weren't filled by the good words spoken around the community. And neither was her heart, it turned out.

"Elizabeth?" Sovilla said, and Elizabeth pulled herself out of her thoughts.

"Sorry," she said. "I was just thinking . . ."

"Who is he?" Sovilla asked softly.

Elizabeth felt warmth in her cheeks and she looked down. Was she that obvious?

"He's the one who makes me feel whole when I lean my head against his shoulder," she whispered, tears welling in her eyes. "And he's all wrong for me, in every logical way."

"What will you do?" Sovilla asked.

"I don't know," Elizabeth replied. "But I have a feeling I'm going to be a whole lot like Johannes—not much use to anyone else while my heart is tied up this way."

"Is he Amish?" Sovilla asked.

"Yah." Because Solomon was Amish, even if he was pushed out.

"Well," Sovilla said with a faint shrug, "you might not be much use to anyone else, but possibly just everything for one man."

Elizabeth smiled wistfully. "You're a very wise person, Sovilla."

"It comes with the heartbreak," Sovilla said. "I hope you avoid it."

If only Elizabeth had known what she was toying with when she and Solomon started pulling together, but then, it wouldn't have stopped her. There was something about Solomon Lantz that sank deep into her heart, and she wasn't going to be able to marry another man quite so easily as she thought.

She loved Solomon . . . but that didn't mean he'd stay. And love him as she did, Elizabeth wouldn't jump the fence for any man, even if she mourned him for the rest of her life.

Solomon stood in the center of Bishop David Lapp's barn. It was a large one, newly built in the spring, when his small barn was badly damaged in a storm. The community had pulled together, and this was the result. The bishop leaned against his shovel and eyed Solomon thoughtfully.

"It's an interesting idea," the bishop said quietly. "I can see the wisdom in it."

"People don't trust a man who's trying to prove he's not that bad," Solomon said. "But they can learn to trust a man who knows exactly where he went wrong and he's doing his best to teach the young people to avoid his mistakes."

"And you think you can do that," Bishop Lapp said quietly.

"I want to tell my story," Solomon said. "Maybe in an evening service after church. Let the adults be there to supervise and make sure I'm not leading anyone astray. But I want to tell how easy it is to slide downward, and exactly how horrible prison was. I want the young people to know that when their parents give them limits, it's for their protection."

The older man nodded thoughtfully. "It's a good idea, Solomon."

"And I want to be baptized." The words nearly caught in his throat. Baptism was about more than faith; it was about community. It was about joining his neighbors as they all tried to live for Gott together.

A smile tickled the bishop's lips. "You're ready for that commitment?"

"Yah, I am," Solomon replied. "I know the life I want to live with Gott and my community, and I'm ready to join the church."

"There will be baptismal classes," the bishop said. "And it will take time to regain trust in the community. I won't lie."

Solomon nodded. "I understand."

The bishop pursed his lips. "You've been fighting, though."

"Once," Solomon replied. "The second time I received a beating, but I didn't fight."

"Why not?"

"Because I wanted to protect a woman," he replied. "And there was this part of me, deep inside, that kept thinking that the Amish way might work. . . ."

"Did it?" the bishop asked.

"I was beaten rather badly," Solomon said wryly. "So it would look like it didn't. But considering that one of us was going to end up battered, I suppose it was just as well that it was me. I won't end up back in prison, and my principles could remain intact."

"And if the *Englishers* come back?" the bishop asked.

"You provided a cell phone." Solomon smiled faintly. "We'll use that again."

The bishop nodded slowly. "You need a job. An Amish one."

"That might be harder to come by," Solomon admitted.

"Old Aaron Stoltzfuz who was picking up the milk and carrying it to the cheese factory is retiring," the bishop said quietly. "It's an honorable job. It's solitary, mostly, and you've got to be on time. Milk can't just sit out getting warm in the sun. We all pay a bit for the pickup service, and the cheese factory pays some, too, for a carting fee."

Solomon's heart sped up. "Yah? What about Aaron's son? He won't take over?"

"He's busy with the farm. That was just an extra job Aaron took on," the bishop replied. "If I let the others know that I've hired you to pick up my milk, they'll likely do the same."

"And you'd do that?" Solomon asked.

"So long as you keep to the narrow path and don't

disappoint me," the bishop replied. "Yah, I would do that."

"Thank you!" Solomon grinned, then nodded.

"And you'll be telling the young people about your mistakes," the bishop said. "Honestly and fully. And you'll not glamorize it or make it sound exciting, or appealing—"

"There's *nothing* appealing about prison," Solomon replied, his voice low. "I have nightmares, Bishop. If I can stop them from messing up like I did, I'll feel like I'm giving something back."

The bishop nodded slowly.

"I'm going to be bringing my family's produce to market," Solomon added. "And my *mamm* wants me to buy a couple of weaned calves to raise, too. A bit here and a bit there, and I can cobble together an income."

The bishop smiled. "A bit here and a bit there, and you might cobble together a reputation, too. Now . . . if you wanted to earn a few hours' wages, I could use some help around here today."

"Yah." Solomon looked down at his hands. "Yah. Let me just unhitch my horses and then I'll be back."

As Solomon headed back toward the barn door, he felt a wave of gratitude. He'd give back . . . what little he had; he'd find a way to make himself useful.

And when he'd finished work today, with a little money in his pocket and a plan already knitting itself together in the back of his mind, he was going to stop by Isaiah's house and ask to talk to Elizabeth.

She might still leave Bountiful and find a man more worthy than he was, but before she left, he had to tell her his new plans. He wouldn't be a deeply respected man in these parts, and it would be a long while before he built himself up, but he could offer a few things—this strong, bruised body in her protection, his loyalty for life, and a promise that he'd work every day making sure she was happier than the last.

It might not be enough—he had to be realistic and accept that—but if she'd take it, all he had, heart and soul, would be hers.

Chapter Twenty-One

The sun had set, slipping behind the hills, and the moon climbed slowly up into the dusky sky. A few stars appeared, and Elizabeth stood by the window, looking out.

Lovina had gone to bed early. She was tired—her body was still healing from that accident, and she wasn't used to the workload of an Amish day anymore, it seemed. She did her best to keep up, but when she started yawning after dinner, Elizabeth and Bethany had both told her that they'd finish the cleaning and she could go on up to bed. The baby was already in his crib for the night, too.

Johannes had arrived just a few minutes ago, and Johannes and Isaiah sat at the table, mugs of coffee in front of them, and when Elizabeth and Bethany had wiped down the last counter, they went to the table to join the men. Everyone knew that the wedding was off now, and Johannes seemed to be fine with that arrangement.

"I'm sorry about Sovilla," Elizabeth said.

Johannes shook his head. "I didn't come to talk about

that. I wanted to know what we're going to do about Lovina."

"What do you mean?" Elizabeth asked. "It will take time. She has to heal. The memories will come back when they come back—"

"Does she know that she spent a year living English?" Johannes asked.

Elizabeth glanced around the table. They were all silent.

"No," Elizabeth said. "We didn't tell her that. We were hoping that she'd . . . remember *us* first, and not that year."

"Is it possible to keep that secret?" Johannes asked.

"We don't know, but if she can at least remember her Amish life first, it might give her what she needs to stay home with us," Isaiah replied.

"Here's an idea . . ." Bethany said, speaking up for the first time. "Of all of us, I think she'll remember Johannes first. She loved him—yah, she left, but that was because of Abe."

"She broke it off with me," Johannes said.

"But she doesn't remember that," Bethany replied. "What if . . . now, just for argument's sake, what if we tell her that Johannes is her fiancé still, and we let her remember the good times first?"

"Lie to her?" Isaiah said, frowning.

"Yah," Elizabeth said. "Isaiah, you and I have both said that she's lucky she can forget some of this. . . . If Lovina could experience those sweet times again, we can fill her in on what really happened later. But this is our chance to give our sister what she needs to stay."

"I'm not taking advantage of her," Johannes said curtly.

"Of course not," Bethany replied. "You be the perfect gentleman. You take her for walks, talk to her, remind her of the good times. But I really do think she'll remember you first, Johannes. Just speaking as a woman. We can tell her that considering her accident, the wedding is off, so there would be no pressure on her in that respect . . ."

"I agree with Bethany," Elizabeth said. "This is for Lovina. She's frustrated. She's confused, and too much has changed around here to be a comfort to her. The one who hasn't changed"—Elizabeth looked up at Johannes hopefully—"is you."

They were all silent, and Johannes looked around the table.

"If she loved you again," Isaiah said slowly, "if she remembered you and fell back in love . . . would you want to be with her?"

Johannes swallowed. "Yah. I don't think I can just stop loving her anyway."

They were silent, watching him, waiting for him to come to a decision.

"You all want this?" Johannes asked.

One by one, they nodded.

"Okay . . ." Johannes sucked in a breath. "For Lovina. But you have my word that I won't take any advantage. And if her feelings for me don't come back within a few weeks, we end this—and we tell her the truth. Is that a deal? I don't think my heart could take any longer than that."

"I think that's fair," Isaiah replied. "Let's try it at least."

The conversation turned to other things—Abe's return, Lovina's old friends and how they'd react to her return—and then Mo started to cry upstairs and Bethany went to check on him. Her sibling would have the ones they loved at their sides, and she was happy for them, but she was also grieving her own loss.

Elizabeth brought the men a plate of muffins to the table, and then she went toward the door.

"Where are you going?" Isaiah asked, looking up.

"Just getting some fresh air," she replied.

The men turned back to their conversation, and Elizabeth headed out onto the porch, letting the cool night air embrace her. She was tired from the day, from the exhaustion of other people's heartbreak, and she needed a few minutes with her own.

She'd hardly had a chance to process her own emotions, and she'd been working so hard at trying to keep her feelings for Solomon under control that when the pressure of people around her lifted, she felt a yearning for him so powerful that it nearly rocked her.

I love him, she prayed. *And I don't care if he's considered noble and good by anyone else, I love him . . . and I know what's inside him . . .*

She headed down the steps, away from the soft glow of the windows and let out a slow breath. Tonight was too late to go find him—it was dark out, and dangerous for a woman alone—but tomorrow morning she could try. At least Bridget might be able to send her in the right direction.

Was he missing her, too?

Horses' hooves clopped through the night air, and she

saw the bounce of lanterns as a buggy turned into their drive. She froze—who would come out here this late? And then she heard a voice she knew . . .

"Whoa," Solomon said, reining the horses in.

He hadn't seen her, and she watched as he hopped down from the buggy, paused at the horses' heads, and then started toward the house. He walked with the easy gait of a strong man, and she felt her heart speed up in her chest. Was he here for her?

"Sol?" she said softly.

His boots scraped as he stopped and turned. "Lizzie?"

He spotted her then in the darkness, and he crossed the few yards between them and pulled her into his arms. She lifted her face, and when his lips came down over hers, she slipped her arms around his neck. He smelled like hay and sunshine and hard work. He felt so warm and solid and strong, and when he pulled back from the kiss, she looked up at him, her breath bated.

"Did you come to see my brother?" she whispered.

"What?" Solomon laughed softly. "No, I didn't come to see your brother. . . ." He shook his head. "I missed you."

"Me too," she whispered. "So much."

"Look—" Solomon stepped back, catching her hand. "I need to talk to you about something. The last time we talked, I asked you to go *Englisher* with me, and that was wrong. It was stupid. So I have to tell you that I'm not leaving. I figured out what I need to stay here, and it's to contribute something. And I do have something this community needs desperately—experience beyond the fence. I can tell people exactly how easy it is to get into trouble, and how hard it is to get back out—"

"You'll stay?" she breathed.

"Yah." He smiled down at her. "I'm staying. The bishop gave me some work today, and he's going to hire me to drive the milk from his farm to the cheese factory. I think it's a good job—it'll keep me away from people enough that they can't worry about me too much, but I could build up a bit of a business that way. That and selling produce in town, and slowly buying a few cows, and—" His voiced faded away. "I'm going to have a life here, Lizzie."

"That's wonderful," she whispered.

"Thing is," he went on, "I don't want to do this without you. And I know I don't have much to offer. I don't have a great reputation, or much to give you material comfort, or . . ." He swallowed. "Lizzie, I love you. I'll work to provide the best I can. I'll be faithful and true. I'd just be so grateful to come home to you . . . I mean—" He stopped again. "Lizzie, please don't go."

She shook her head. "I'm not leaving."

"No?" He laughed in relief. "Really?"

"I was talking to Sovilla today, and she made a very good point about what keeps a woman warm at night, and it isn't a soaring reputation, although it might be nice," she said, and she put her hand against his warm chest, feeling the solid beat of his heart. "It's love. And I don't think I'll ever love another man like I love you. If you're staying—"

Solomon pulled her back into his arms and kissed her again. This time his kiss was strong and insistent, and she leaned into it. Then he pulled back and rested his forehead against hers.

"Then marry me," he whispered. "Please . . . Let's get married, and have *kinner*, and I'll work my fingers to the bone to provide for all of you. I'll prove that you made the right choice—I promise you that. We'll have that good reputation. We'll build it together, and it'll be worth the work. But marry me."

Those were the words she'd been waiting for, and she nodded. Solomon froze, his gaze locked on hers. "Yah?"

"Yah!"

He picked her up in his strong arms and swung her around, and then he kissed her again, just as the side door opened and the light from inside spilled out onto the porch, revealing her brother standing there.

"Lizzie?" he called.

Elizabeth looked up at Solomon, laughing breathlessly. "Are you willing to face my brother?"

"I've faced worse," Solomon replied with a grin.

"Don't count on it," she murmured, but she laughed and, hand in hand, they went up toward the house where Isaiah was waiting.

Elizabeth would marry Solomon Lantz, and she might not have quite the life she'd imagined for herself all those years—she'd have something deeper, and sweeter, and so much better. She'd have her Amish husband, and she'd have a man whose strength and tenderness could make her heart stop altogether in her chest. . . .

Would the Amish community of Bountiful look at him with respect in their eyes? Would they defer to his opinions? Maybe not for a very long time. But she would gaze at her husband with respect, because she knew the man Solomon Lantz was, the strength he had, and the love he bore for her. He was worthy of all their respect, but if he could be happy with just hers for a little while, he'd have it and more.

They'd have a proper Amish wedding where they'd be joined before Gott, and Solomon Lantz would have her heart for life. And somehow, looking up into his adoring eyes, she knew that whatever they faced would be easier together.

There was nowhere safer, nowhere warmer or more satisfying, than in Solomon Lantz's arms.

Romantic Suspense from
Lisa Jackson